Accidents Happen

By Kassie Ward

Columbia, South Carolina

Acknowledgements

A big thank you to my fantastic editor, Fiona Skye, for not only being a great editor, but also a great friend.

Special thanks goes to Renee Goen for all her help in making this happen.

Accidents Happen

CHAPTER ONE

Driving from North Myrtle Beach to Columbia usually made Julian Fursey smile. She loved taking as many back road short cuts as possible before eventually ending up on the interstate, but the drizzling gray morning dampened her spirits. She shivered and turned up the heat. The morning was unseasonably chilly for late October in South Carolina. Frustrated at her inability to roll the windows down and crank her stereo, Julian ran a hand through her shoulder-length, chocolate-brown hair and decided to twig it back in a clip when she stopped for gas, which would be soon.

She grinned remembering the events of the weekend at the writer's conference. She had enjoyed meeting some of the writers face-to-face she normally only chatted with through social media. Getting the funds together for the trip had crunched her savings account, but blowing through the money had made her feel like Queen Latifah in Last Holiday. "Totally worth it," she whispered to the empty car with a grin.

Julian pulled her mini-SUV into a gas station and up to the

pump. First things first, she twisted her hair and clamped a large barrette through it to hold it in place. Then she swathed some lip gloss on her dry lips. After pumping gas, she moved her car to a space in front of the convenience store and hustled inside. Distracted by a car alarm going off, Julian bumped into a man exiting the store, knocking the items from his hands. Bags of potato chips, a couple of candy bars, and a soda bottle sprawled on the floor. "I'm so sorry!" she said, mortified. The man had to catch his balance. He stood a good deal taller than her, maybe five inches, with dark hair and eyes and a smile that could stop any woman in her tracks.

"No, I'm sorry," he said. "Guess we were both trying to figure out whose car that is."

They both stooped to pick up the items, Julian holding the door open with her foot to keep the chips from being crushed. She thought the man could be a movie star with those good looks and grinned. With her imagination piqued, she envisioned him as an actor she had never heard of and would see in a movie in the future. "Sometimes I really hate car alarms," he said with a good-natured laugh.

She handed him the soda with a grin. "Um, you might want to wait to open that."

He chuckled. "Thanks for the helpful advice."

A man standing behind the ridiculously handsome man spoke. "Yeah, I would prefer not to have that all over the interior of my car." Julian noted the close resemblance between the men, deciding they were brothers. This man had a few years on the other and towered over her, a couple of inches taller even than the younger man.

She had to tilt her head back to look at the second man, handsome in a rugged, weather-beaten way with the same dark hair and eyes, but stronger. "I guess not," she murmured.

He carried a bottle of water without the same smile as his traveling companion. Weariness lined his features. He politely inclined his head toward Julian as she moved out of his way. Instead of walking past her, he stepped back and held the door for her to enter as the younger man thanked Julian. Together, the men walked out to an SUV with a Semper Fi bumper sticker. The older man stood ramrod straight as he walked, and Julian decided he must be the Marine. She turned back into the store and shrugged. Men like those two rarely gave her a second glance. Julian took care of herself, exercising and eating a fairly balanced diet, but she had more curves than what Hollywood deemed appropriate, and she liked it that way. Of course, the particular outfit she had chosen on this morning could have been more flattering—jeans with a plain, shapeless black sweater and lace-up black boots all covered with a nondescript jacket. After purchasing bottled water and some almonds, Julian headed back down the road. She turned the radio on and hummed along with the music, tapping one boot-clad foot in rhythm with the song.

A few miles down the road, she saw the SUV with the Semper Fi sticker. Julian hated this type of weather. Just enough rain to make the decision of using wipers difficult and just enough rain to make the road slick. But she smiled remembering the good-looking men. One didn't come across guys like those every day. Her overactive brain worked out different scenarios as a new story idea bloomed.

As Julian silently plotted, a deer darted from between a clump of trees and directly into the path of the SUV. The vehicle swerved to miss the animal and caught the railing of the bridge ahead, causing the rear of the SUV to swing toward the slope of the embankment. Julian stood on the brake pedal, her car skidding for what felt like an eternity before stopping. She watched the black vehicle roll down the embankment with terrible screeching of metal and breaking glass. Her heart slammed in her ribcage as the SUV finally stopped, partially in the river water, propped upside down on a boulder. Julian snatched her cell phone from the charger, dialing 911 to breathlessly detail the accident to the operator while throwing her door open and leaping from her car. She raced down the hill toward to SUV on shaky legs.

Julian's breath caught in her throat at the realization that both men had to still be in the flooded vehicle. She dropped the cell phone and finished running down the hill. The passenger side of the vehicle sat beneath the rushing water. She crawled onto the rock to the driver's side door. Inside the cabin, Julian saw both men hanging upside down, trapped by their seat belts. The younger man's head hung in the water, but the other man's entire torso had been submerged. He struggled to free the seatbelt. The first man's arms dangled limply into the water.

"Oh, God," Julian gasped, paralyzed for a moment. Shaking off her hysteria, she wrestled with the door, but the mangled metal refused to give with her efforts. Julian placed one booted foot against the side of the SUV and pulled with her entire weight. The vehicle shifted on the boulder, but stayed afloat as the door shrieked open. The seat belt gave easily for the first man. He dropped into her arms like a rag doll. Julian grunted at his weight, struggling to drag him through water to the muddy riverbank. He sputtered, but his eyes did not open.

She raced back to climb into the vehicle again, grabbing the other man's fumbling hand so he would know she was there. With her free hand, Julian found the seat belt release. The man fell from the seat and barely poked his head from the water to gasp air when the SUV moved with the force of his fall, sliding from the boulder into the rushing water. Julian yelped as the rolling vehicle caused her side to slam into the gearshift. Her head hit the steering wheel with a crack. Then they found themselves trapped in a sinking vehicle. She and the man tangled with each other trying to escape. Then the man shoved her through the window then slid past her underwater, catching her around the waist. He brought them to the surface where they both gulped deep breaths.

"Can you swim?" he asked. He seemed no worse for wear other than coughing out water, but pain shot through Julian's side and throbbed at her temple. Dazed, she nodded in answer, and he released her waist. They headed toward the shore. Relief washed over Julian at the sounds of sirens and flashing red lights.

Julian prided herself on her strong swimming skills, but her arms and legs fought against her, and each move caused more pain in her side. To her horror, she felt herself sinking. Her face slipped below the water. She kicked her legs harder despite the pain it caused and broke through the surface again, struggling to suck in air before she sank again. She wanted to call for help, but spent all her energy trying to get air. When the water covered her face, she felt an arm slide around her waist once more. The man pulled her above water. "I gotcha," he said.

Embarrassment washed over her. "I'm normally a good swimmer," she croaked.

"It's okay," was all he said as he towed her toward the nearby shore. As soon as their feet touched the riverbed, he grabbed one of her hands and placed it on her temple at the place where she hit the steering wheel.

"Keep pressure here." His voice held so much authority that Julian obeyed without question. She realized the warm liquid running through her fingers had to be blood, and her knees went weaker than before.

The man swung her into his arms as soon as the water became shallow enough. Julian wanted to protest, but his set jaw and her own dizziness convinced her to keep quiet. Before Julian could digest the scene, her rescuee-turned-rescuer deposited her on the ground next to the younger man as paramedics tended him. She barely registered his mangled leg as they lifted him onto a stretcher and wheeled it toward a waiting ambulance, the older of the two men following close behind. Then another paramedic wafted into her line of vision. He removed her hand and asked her questions, but she just looked at him in confusion. "My side hurts." Her feeble voice melted away as the world turned into black dots and then a black curtain.

* * *

Drake Salvatore watched the paramedics load his brother into the ambulance and hurried through the doors behind him. He glanced back at the woman who had saved both their lives. She had shown up none too soon and likely paid a dear price. The cut at her temple looked to be almost to her skull. He wondered what damage had been done to her side as she had held it in obvious pain. He felt foolish not to have noticed her struggling in the water sooner, but everything had happened so fast. One moment, he had been sleeping while his brother drove. The next thing he had known, the car had rolled and crunched around them. Then he had been breathing in water before he realized he dangled in the river.

He shoved his panic down deep as he tried to assess the severity of his brother's injuries. Drake kicked himself for letting Amerigo drive, but he had been so sleepy. His anger with Amerigo for putting them all in this predicament competed with his overwhelming worry. The young man's leg looked awful, with bone visible through the skin. He had seen injuries like it during his tours in Iraq and Afghanistan. Not every man had been able to keep the use of the leg or even keep the leg. But some recovered completely, he reminded himself. Although it had been a long time, Drake silently prayed as the ambulance raced through traffic. Please God. Let Amerigo and the woman be all right. He held Amerigo's hand as the paramedics bandaged a cut on his upper left arm and stabilized him.

Amerigo remained unconscious through the entire trip to the hospital, but Drake encouraged him, hoping he could hear. "Hang in there, Amerigo. It won't be long till we get there. Hang on." One of the paramedics looked Drake over, checking his eyes and asking questions. Drake assured him that other than coughing up a ton of water, he had escaped unscathed. He shivered, and the man gave him a blanket as soon as they had done all they could for Amerigo. An alarm went off on a machine, and the paramedics sprung back into action.

"He's going into shock."

"Sir, let go of his hand."

Drake watched in horror as they used paddles on his brother. All remnants of Drake's annoyance vanished. "Amerigo, don't you dare die! Mom will come after you." As if responding to Drake's command, the younger man's vitals stabilized again.

One of the paramedics gave a soft chuckle. "Mom must have some real sway in your family."

"You have no idea."

Once they reached the hospital, all motion turned into a blur of scrubs and white coats. Drake saw the woman wheeled in right behind Amerigo. The staff stopped him from following into the surgery center. "You'll have to wait out here. We'll come get you as soon as you can see him."

Drake took a moment to call his parents from a phone the nurses offered him since his had been lost in the water. His mother descended into hysterics before his father took the phone. Drake relayed everything he knew to them. They promised to leave as soon as they ended the call. He heaved a sigh of relief. At a time like this, even a Marine could use his parents.

Drake settled into a seat of the vacant surgical waiting area, still wrapped in the blanket. A young woman in scrubs strolled to him with a rolling computer to take all the registration information he could give her without Amerigo's wallet.

"What about the woman that came in with my brother? Is she okay?" he asked her.

She shook her head. "I can't share anything about another patient, Mr. Salvatore. Federal privacy laws." The woman finished the registration process and left him alone again.

Drake leaned back in the chair in frustration but said nothing else. A career in the Marines had taught him about bureaucracy. He pushed away every worst case scenario that crowded his mind, stretching out on the waiting room couch with the blanket, planning to close his eyes for just a minute or two. When he opened them again, his parents sat on the couch across from him. He cursed silently. He must have slept for a couple of hours, since they would have had to drive that long from Columbia. Drake sat up, and his mother lunged the distance to throw her arms around her son. He hugged her tightly.

His father stood and crossed to them, his hands on each of their shoulders. "Thank God. Thank God." Drake saw tears welling in the older man's eyes and, to his embarrassment, felt his own eyes burn.

"Has the doctor been out?" Drake asked.

His father shook his head. Drake pulled his mother away to meet her eyes. Tall and slender, her auburn hair and fair skin stood in sharp contrast to the dark-haired men. How Mary, his Scotch-Irish American mother, had ever ended up with Anthony, his brooding Italian father, still boggled his mind. And yet, he doubted he would ever find the kind of happiness his parents shared. "I'm okay, Ma, and Amerigo's gonna be okay." She gave him a thin, watery smile and nodded. His parents sat on either side of him, and he noticed a gym bag on the floor then.

"Your father packed you some dry clothes," Mary said.

Drake sighed gratefully. He kissed his mother's cheek and patted his father's arm as he grabbed the bag and headed for the restroom. Once there, he chuckled. His father's version of packing his bag had consisted of clean underwear to go with his already packed gym clothes. Still, a dry, clean pair of sweats, socks, sneakers, and a t-shirt beat the wet jeans and button down shirt. He changed quickly and swiped a hand through his short, tousled hair, wishing he could find a shower.

Drake returned to find the doctor speaking to his parents. He hurried to hear the doctor explain they had operated and stabilized Amerigo, but he would need more surgery with a specialist. "I don't think he'll lose the leg, but the damage is extensive," the man said. "I wish I could give you a more positive prognosis, but sometimes, it's a wait-and-see game. Doctor Miller will have to give you more information once he gets here and assesses the leg."

"What about the woman who came in with Amerigo?"

The doctor eyed him carefully. "You know I can't give you information about another patient."

"She saved our lives. I'd just like to know if she's okay."

The scrub-clad man tilted his head before answering. "I can't release any information about another patient. For example, I couldn't tell you if she had a torn spleen that was repaired or if her head required twenty-three stitches. I also couldn't tell you if she's already in a room and doing fine. Privacy laws prevent that." With that, he narrowed his eyes. "I couldn't tell you that kind of information, right?"

"You couldn't. I understand."

"Good. A nurse will let you know when Amerigo is in a room. It shouldn't be too long."

They thanked the doctor, and he departed back through the double doors. Drake ran his hand through his hair again. "They're okay."

Anthony nodded. "But his leg…" He sat down heavily. Mary sat next to her husband and slid an arm around his shoulders. He turned and embraced her, waving for Drake to sit with them. "Let's pray for Amerigo together." They clasped hands as his father prayed for healing and wisdom for the doctors and strength for their family. Then he prayed for the mystery woman who had been injured helping them. After praying, they sat together in silence until a nurse found them and led them to the room in which Amerigo had been ensconced. Amerigo opened his eyes when they entered.

"Sorry about your car, Drake."

Drake crossed the room and grabbed his brother's hand. "Just buy me a new one when you're rich and famous."

Amerigo looked away. "That won't happen now."

"Stop that now." Mary's order made both younger men jerk their heads toward her. "We don't know enough to draw any conclusions so we won't yet." Drake moved to allow his parents to hug and reassure Amerigo, his emotions roiling as he sat.

Drake felt responsible. Amerigo's latest irresponsible stunt had been to quit his serving job at a restaurant, empty his checking account, and fly to New York for a reality show audition. When the casting director had rejected Amerigo, Anthony had called Drake to retrieve his stranded brother. Needing to be back at the fort for work Monday, Drake had driven all day to get to him then turned the car back around to head straight back to South Carolina without so much as a fifteen minute nap. The trip had reminded him that he was no longer the young grunt he had once been, and sleep deprivation had caught up with him. When Amerigo had offered to drive, he had relented, but if Drake had stopped at a motel for a couple hours of sleep, neither Amerigo nor the woman would be here.

He stood. "I'm gonna go find the woman to thank her."

Amerigo looked confused. "What woman?"

Lost in thought, Drake failed to respond and left the room as his father recounted the events. Drake noticed a police officer carrying a clear bag with a purse and a cell phone entering a room down the hall. Drake stood outside the door to listen as the officer asked questions about the wreck. He heard a soft female voice answering. When the officer finished, she thanked him for her belongings. Once the man left, Drake stepped into the room with a gentle knock on the open door.

* * *

Julian sucked in a surprised breath and instantly regretted it. She placed a hand over her side and bit her lip. The man from the wreck showed concern. "Do I need to get a nurse?"

He started to turn, but she stopped him. "I'll be okay. I have a morphine pump for the pain, and I just had a dose. I should warn you; I'll probably get pretty dopey soon."

He smiled at her, and Julian revised her opinion of his looks. The younger man might be movie-star handsome, but she preferred this man's rugged looks.

"May I join you?" he asked.

Julian raised a hand to offer the recliner off to the side. "Knock yourself out."

Before sitting, the man offered his hand to her. "I'm Drake Salvatore. My younger brother's name is Amerigo." Rolling his eyes, he offered, "My mom has a thing for history and famous sailors."

She giggled as she shook his hand. "Julian Fursey."

He frowned. "I wish we were meeting under different circumstances."

She grinned in reply. "We did, remember? At the gas station where I tried to knock your brother down." Her grin turned into a chuckle. "I'm just a tad bit clumsy." Julian swatted some hair from her eyes and gently touched the bandage at her temple. "See? You don't even seem to have a scratch, and I managed to get a torn spleen and a gazillion stitches." Julian smiled at him again. "Thank you coming back for me. I didn't realize how hurt I was. I might have drowned."

Drake shook his head in disbelief. "Ms. Fursey, you saved our lives. We're the ones who should say thank you. In fact, it's why I came."

"Call me Julian, and I'll call you Drake whether you like it or not." She giggled a little again. Uh-oh, she thought. The medicine must be taking effect. "How is your brother?"

She watched him struggle to hide his worry. "He's got a long recovery ahead of him and at least one more surgery," he said evenly.

"Poor kid. What does he do for a living?"

Drake snorted. "He fancies himself an actor, but right now he does whatever menial job he can get."

"And you're a Marine?"

He nodded. "I cross-train different skills to soldiers at Fort Jackson."

"You look like you're going to go work out." She saw him glance down at his gym clothes. She let out another giggle. "You probably work out a lot. You're very muscular but not like an iron man or something. That's good." She felt her words slurring a little and noticed his amusement. "Oh, I'm talking gibberish, aren't I? Sorry." Julian felt her face flame in embarrassment. "I always rattle when I'm nervous."

"I make you nervous?" He grinned in obvious enjoyment of her doped state.

She grimaced. "This isn't fair. The medicine is destroying my filter, and now I'm making an idiot of myself in front of a really good-looking guy. Ugh. No wonder I'm single. I'm creepy."

He laughed at her then. "You're not creepy. You're drugged. You should try to go to sleep."

She rubbed her face absently. "I don't like hospitals." Julian pulled a lock of hair in front of her face and groaned. "My hair is full of muddy river water."

Drake stood and pulled the recliner to the side of the bed and sat back down. "Do you need me to call anyone for you?"

"I called my mom a few minutes ago. She's on her way here from Columbia."

He leaned the chair back. "My family and I live in Columbia. Do you live there too?" She nodded. "It's a pretty nice city," he said.

Julian murmured, "Burned once and still hot." She remembered the saying from a t-shirt she had from high school which referred to when Sherman's troops burned the capitol city during the Civil War.

Drake laughed. "You're pretty amusing while doped up. I'll stay with you until your mom gets here."

"No! You don't have to do that. I'll stop being a baby." She patted his arm then looked at it. "See? Muscles." Then she reclined her head and let sleep overtake her.

CHAPTER TWO

Julian's eyes opened to her mother's worried face in her own. She jumped. Gale Fursey gasped, "Sorry!" The older woman wiped the tears from her blue eyes and gave Julian a small smile. "I didn't mean to startle you." Julian reached up and wrapped her arms around her mother's neck. Gale hugged her tightly, patting her daughter's hair.

Julian swallowed around the lump in her throat. "I'm so glad you're here."

Gale leaned back to look at her then sat in the recliner next to the bed. "I'm glad you're here. Drake told me everything that happened. You left a few things out."

Julian pinched the bridge of her nose. "Some of it's kinda fuzzy to me still. The doctor said that would get better. I can go home tomorrow, I think." She frowned. "His brother, Amerigo, won't be as lucky. I guess his leg is pretty bad."

"That's what Drake said. He also said he didn't know how to thank you. I told him dinner would be nice and gave him your number."

"Mom! You have got to stop giving out my information!"

Gale folded her arms across her chest. "I'm an excellent judge of character. That is a fine young man, and I didn't want you to miss a chance at a date."

"Excellent judge of character, huh?" Julian narrowed her eyes. "What about that guy from the online chat room in your internet poker game? He turned out to be married with kids my age. I still get emails from him sometimes."

Gale turned her head away indignantly. "Make a mistake once…"

"Once?"

"All right, but I'm telling you this one is a good one."

Julian scrubbed her hand over her face. "Mom, he only came in here to say thank you. I'll never hear from him again, which is fine with me."

Gale grunted. "You're not as smart as you think you are. Now go to sleep."

"I don't want to go to sleep. I just woke up."

"Too bad. I already pushed the button on your morphine pump. See how you're not as smart as you think you are?"

Julian groaned, annoyance etched on her face. "Mom—"

"You need to sleep. I didn't want you to wait until the pain was out of control. I know you. You would."

Julian thought about that statement. Her mother had a point. "All right, Ma. I'm going to sleep."

"Good."

Julian argued when the doctor told her he wanted to keep her another day. She watched her mother preparing to sleep in the small makeshift bed built into the wall under the window. "Mom, go get a hotel room or go home. I'm okay. I don't like hospitals, but I can't stand for you to sleep like that another night. It'll bother me more than being here alone."

Gale rubbed her eyes sleepily but perked up as a couple her age stood in the doorway with Drake. He introduced his mother and father, Mary and Anthony, then excused himself. Gale gestured to the two empty chairs. "Come in and have a seat. Julian was just trying to convince me to go get a hotel room."

Mary nodded. "We've been trying to convince Drake to do the same thing. We offered to pay for it, but he's stubborn."

Anthony clucked in frustration and spoke with his heavy Italian accent. "He is hardheaded, that one. We'd like to pay for your room too, to say thank you to your family."

Gale shook her head. "That's not necessary, but thanks for offering. It's generous of you."

Mary and Anthony exchanged glances. Mary explained, "Well, we already paid for two rooms, and now Drake won't use his. Why don't you use it instead?"

Julian gave her mother a pleading look. "Use the room. I'll pay them back."

Anthony's jaw tightened. "Absolutely not. We owe you the lives of both our sons. I won't take no for an answer."

Julian pointed to the door. "Mom, go. Get some sleep in a real bed. I just can't look at you over there like that."

Mary smiled at Gale and said, "Anthony and Drake are bullying me to use the other room. If you go with me, I won't feel so guilty." She grinned mischievously. "And then we can have some girl talk." Gale's eyebrows shot up, and her eyes sparkled. Mary continued, "Drake'll stay with Julian, and Anthony'll stay with Amerigo."

Panic bubbled up in Julian. She felt gross with dirty hair and no makeup. She inwardly cringed at the thought of an incredibly good-looking Marine watching her sleep, and she'd probably snore. "I don't need anyone to stay with me. I'm fine. I'm going to sleep. Really."

Gale tilted her head at Julian. "Are you sure you'll be okay?"

"Yes, Mom. Go."

The two women left, chatting like old friends while Anthony stayed behind. He pulled his chair next to the bed with a fatherly expression. "You are a very brave woman, Julian Fursey. You will be one of our family from now on."

Julian opened her mouth to protest.

"Don't bother arguing. You'll lose," Drake said from the doorway. He turned to Anthony. "Amerigo is asking for you."

Anthony took Julian's hand and patted it. "Get some sleep."

Drake headed for the reclining chair Anthony vacated, but Julian stopped him. "I'm fine. You don't need to stay with me."

* * *

Drake inwardly sighed. Lord, but she was stubborn. Beautiful, but stubborn. "Just humor me."

Her shoulders relaxed slightly. "All right, but when you get tired and want to go, you shouldn't feel guilty about it."

He wanted to roll his eyes. Stubborn. Still, he liked her and her mother, even if her mother's readiness to volunteer Julian's information disturbed him. With a smirk, he glanced at the morphine pump. "So have you had any of that recently?"

She turned pink. "No. And after last night's debacle, I'm not gonna have any more."

He grinned at her. "It would help you sleep."

"I've slept all day. My mom keeps doping me up, pushing the button when I'm not looking and then the nurses make me get up and walk, and I'm stumbling around like a drunk." She shook her head. "I'll pass while she's not here. If I start to feel bad, I'll use it, but until then…" Julian heaved a sigh loaded with frustration. "I just want to go home."

Drake nodded. "I understand. I'm hoping we can get Amerigo moved to a hospital in Columbia. This is so far away for my parents."

"My mom too." Julian frowned. "How is your brother doing?"

Drake shrugged. "He's still in a lot of pain. He's depressed.

It's going to be a long, uphill battle, and frankly, that kid has never had to persevere at anything." Drake looked away from Julian. Why was he telling her that? He normally kept things pretty close to the vest. "He's a good kid, though."

She laughed a little. "I don't think he's a kid. Your brother is a grown man."

"He'll always be a kid to me."

"There's a big age difference?"

"Yeah. Thirteen years."

"Egads," Julian gasped. "You were an only child for thirteen years and then suddenly became a big brother?" She grinned at him. "That had to be some kind of adjustment in your family."

Drake chuckled. "That's an understatement." Silence fell between them. Drake looked around the room and leaned the chair back.

Julian cleared her throat. "Wanna watch TV?"

"Sure."

She used the remote to flip through the limited channels. She passed the news, but Drake stopped her. "Wait. Go back to the news for a second, please." Julian turned the channel, and they both gawked at the screen. The news anchor described their wreck as a shaky video of Julian scrambling through the water to the SUV played. They looked at each other with mouths agape. "Did you see anyone else when you stopped to help us?"

Julian shook her head, her face pale. They watched as the SUV rolled from the boulder into the water then saw themselves emerge gasping for air. Julian grimaced at the gaping wound on her own head and put a hand over her lips in horror. "Don't they have to have our permission or something to show that?" she asked.

"I have no idea." His blood boiled. He valued his privacy and his family's privacy, particularly after what he'd gone through with Mariella. He imagined what his friends and family would have to say to this. What would his commanding officer say? Drake groaned aloud when he imagined the soldiers he trained watching the video. He turned to Julian, and his gut twisted when he saw tears welling up in her eyes. Drake reached out and awkwardly gave her hand a squeeze. "Hey, now. It'll be all right." He gave her hand another quick squeeze before releasing it.

After a deep shuddering breath, Julian swiped her hand over her eyes and forced a smile. "Well, at least you really can't see our faces." They looked back up at the screen and saw a close up of Drake carrying Julian from the water as she held her hand against the cut on her head. They paused the video there and used it as a backdrop for the news anchor. "Oh, my word," Julian murmured.

Drake closed his eyes and let his head drop into his hands until he heard Julian giggling. He raised his eyebrows at her. She shook her head, but the giggling continued. "What?" he demanded but smiled, unable to resist her infectious amusement.

Julian breathed deeply to pull herself together. "Well, it's just… It looks like a parody of a romance novel cover. I mean, you look like you belong, but me… That and the blood. If you had just been shirtless and if my sweater was half torn off, it would just be a perfect romance novel cover." She dissolved into giggles again.

He had to admit she had a point about the picture captured from the video of him carrying her to the riverbank, but they looked disheveled and dirty from the mud, and there was blood covering the side of Julian's face. He subtly assessed her—not tall, not waif thin, not sporting hair to her waist, not giving a sultry, pouty look. No, the woman before him stood average height, maybe a little shorter. Her thick, chocolate hair reached a little past her shoulders, and though not overweight, she had curves. He seriously doubted she had ever even attempted a sultry, pouty look, but he liked her open smile and her big, round eyes lined with long, dark lashes. And he had dated those waifs and eventually realized he preferred sexy curves. He liked Julian Fursey. He teased, "Did you take a hit of morphine when I wasn't looking?"

She continued to giggle as she shook her head. She took a deep, calming breath. "Ouch." She clutched her side, a smile still gracing her lips. "That hurt, but I needed to laugh."

"Me too," he admitted.

Julian's cell phone played the theme from a popular offbeat television show, and she grimaced. "Uh-oh. I figured." She held the phone up and looked at the name. "I can't talk to her right now."

"Is it your mom?"

"No, it's my best friend, Hannah, but she'll have a hundred questions I'm just too horrified to answer now. I'm sure she saw the news." The phone stopped ringing only to start again. Julian frowned at the contact name. "Coworker." Though she ignored the steady onslaught of calls, she gave a description of each caller. "Writer's group buddy." "Another friend." "Someone from church." "Hannah again."

His nerves frazzled, Drake finally took the phone. Ignoring her protests, he turned the phone off and glared at her as she glared at him.

"If you're not going to answer, it may as well be turned off. Besides, I'm sure you still need sleep. I definitely do."

Her anger dissolved. "I'm keeping you up, and you've got to be tired. You should go—"

Drake gritted his teeth and gave her the same look he used to quell rebellious trainees. "I'm not leaving."

Her response took him back. "Look here, buddy. I'm not one of your soldiers, and I'm not afraid to tell your mom."

He roared with laughter at that, his mood changing with her threat. "Whoa, whoa, whoa! We can work this out. No need to bring Mom into it." She smirked in response, and he shook his head at her. "Didn't Pop tell you you're part of the family? Did you notice the accent? Once you're in, you can't get out." He winked at her. "I'm trying to help. I promise."

Julian handed him the remote as he handed her the phone. She looked at it and set it down still turned off. He realized he might have overstepped his bounds, but it was his nature to be protective of friends and family. For good or for ill, Julian and her mother fell under that umbrella now.

She shifted on the bed, struggling to find a comfortable position. "Pick out whatever you want to watch as long as it doesn't pertain to us again." She gingerly touched her side once more.

"Why don't you use the morphine?"

"I don't want to look stupid in front of you again."

"You couldn't," he told her.

Julian acquiesced and pushed the button. Within five minutes, her eyes closed in blissful sleep. Drake watched her with interest. He wondered how long her temple would need to stay bandaged and how long she would be out of work. Guilt roiled in his belly again. He rubbed his forehead. After a few minutes, he found an extra blanket in the room and returned to the reclining seat next to the bed. He leaned back and closed his eyes. The television and lights off, the only light came in from the hallway and the only sound from the nurses' station.

He tried to sleep, but worries continued to crowd his mind. He wondered about Amerigo's leg and his spirits. He worried about his parents practically living between the hospital and a hotel for who knew how long. Turning his eyes in the darkened room toward Julian, he wondered how missing work would affect her. It struck him then that he had no idea what she did for a living. He had no idea where she had been coming from or why. He felt like a heel. She shivered and burrowed further under the covers. Drake stood and went to the drawer with the linens and found another blanket. He carefully unfolded it and placed it over the woman's sleeping form. Gingerly, he tucked it around her and returned to his recliner. He closed his eyes again and sleep finally found him.

* * *

Julian tried to figure out the time but remembered Drake had turned her phone off. She scanned the room for a clock but only saw the light from the hall. Drake slept in the recliner next to her bed. Julian felt odd having this man she barely knew sleeping in the room with her, but at the same time, she felt comforted. He looked gruffer than his younger brother but when he talked about Amerigo, she'd seen genuine love and worry in his eyes.

Julian slipped her legs from the bed, her feet touching the cold hospital floor. She hissed and pulled the rolling IV pole with her as she slowly walked to the small bathroom across from her bed. After using the bathroom, she glanced down the hall and saw Anthony leaving Amerigo's room, his shoulders slumped in exhaustion. The older man walked to the elevators and pushed the button. Julian waited until the elevator doors closed on him before she gripped her IV pole and teetered down the hall. The medicine made her groggy, but she pushed through it, shuffling toward the door to Amerigo's room. She cinched the belt of her robe tighter and tucked a stray lock of hair behind her ear. Julian tapped softly on the door and heard a man's voice telling her to enter.

Amerigo met her eyes in surprise. She stopped with the door only partially open. "Feel up to some company? I saw your dad leave."

He waved her in with a tired smile. "Sure. You must be Ms. Fursey. I heard you're stuck here another day."

"Yeah, but it's okay. I hope you don't mind me coming to

say hello."

"Of course not. I owe you my life."

She made a sound of disgust. "So I keep being told. You don't owe me anything. Just get better."

He looked around, the tightness around his eyes revealing his pain. "Where is everyone?"

"Your mom and my mom went to a hotel. I think your dad probably went to the cafeteria to get something from the machines, and Drake is asleep in a chair in my room." Amerigo's eyebrows shot up. Julian shrugged. "Your family thinks it's their duty to make sure neither you nor I are alone for more than five or ten minutes."

He rolled his eyes with a grin. "Yeah. That's my family, alright. Especially duty-driven Drake." They looked at each other and then giggled over his alliteration.

Julian repeated, "Duty-Driven Drake." They giggled again. "You should call him Triple D for short." Giggles turned into real laughter, and Julian clutched her side. "Ow," she said between laughs.

Amerigo waved his hand at her as he wiped away tears of humor. "Stop laughing if it hurts! It's not even that funny. We're just being stupid."

She pressed her lips together in an effort to compose herself, but a snort escaped her. They started laughing again. "Think it's our pain medicine?"

"Maybe." He eyed her carefully through his amusement. "Ms. Fursey, I really am grateful. Drake and I don't always see eye to eye, but he's my brother. I can't imagine if he…" He looked at the wall for a long second. "We worried about him when he was overseas. I couldn't imagine him coming home and being killed because I'm a bad driver."

Julian sat in the chair next to his bed and squeezed his hand. "Accidents happen, Amerigo. And my name is Julian." He met her eyes again, and Julian felt her chest constrict for him. "It was raining. There was a deer. Life happens. But you're alive, and Drake's alive, and I'm alive."

Amerigo looked at his leg with a frown. Julian wondered if what he said next came out because he felt comfortable with her or if it felt safer to tell someone he didn't know well instead of worrying his family. "I'm scared I'll never walk right again." Julian's throat tightened at his admission. "The doctor says I won't lose the leg, but…" Julian could see him struggle to keep his face blank, but his eyes were bright with unshed tears. "I'm sorry. You don't want to hear this. I…" He stopped short as emotion made his voice warble.

Julian stood, still clutching his hand. She had no idea what to say. Instead, she squeezed his hand again and gently pushed a lock of dark hair from his forehead. "You can say whatever you want to me." She gave him an encouraging smile.

Amerigo looked away but held her hand tightly. "Thanks."

"Your dad will be back any minute, I'm sure. I better get back to my room."

Anthony returned then carrying a cup of coffee and a sticky bun from a vending machine. "Are you all right?"

Julian felt her face flush as if she had been caught doing something wrong. "I'm fine. I was just leaving."

"Do you need help back to your room?" Anthony asked, sincere concern in his voice.

Drake spoke before she could respond. "I'll help her, Pop."

They turned to see Drake standing in the door. He leaned against the door frame. When Julian gave him a quizzical look, he said, "I saw you were gone and just wanted to make sure you were okay. Figured you might have ended up here."

Julian quickly squeezed Amerigo's hand. "I'm glad we had a chance to talk. Get some rest." After bidding both Amerigo and Anthony a good night, she swallowed her pride and allowed Drake to help support her by holding her elbow as she stepped out of the room. "Thanks," she whispered once they reached her room.

"No, Julian. Thank you."

CHAPTER THREE

When the doctor finally said Julian could go home, it felt as if time sped up. Suddenly, Julian and Gale were saying goodbye to the Salvatore family and on the road back to Columbia. Julian slept most of the trip as Gale silently drove. As they pulled into Julian's driveway, Gale called her name to wake her. Julian opened her eyes to see her best friend waiting in the driveway.

Tall, leggy, perfectly-groomed with dark blond hair and blue eyes, Hannah Cameron opened Julian's car door with care. "I'm so glad you're home!" She gingerly hugged Julian and took her purse. "Where's your car?"

"The Salvatores are getting it home for me. They're so sweet, but I feel bad. They don't owe me anything."

Hannah helped Gale get Julian's luggage from the trunk as Gale explained, "Anthony, that's the boys' father, is taking care of everything, and for once, Julian's going to let someone help her."

They made their way to the front door of Julian's tiny house, which was situated in a quiet part of northeast Columbia in a recently-built subdivision. Hannah used the spare key Julian had given her for emergencies. The three women stopped in the foyer to set down the luggage. Tears welled in Julian's eyes. Flowers lined the foyer from people she knew—friends, extended family, church members, coworkers.

She looked at Hannah, who shrugged. "Everyone wanted their flowers to be here for you when you got home so I brought them all in." After a pause, Gale left them to place one of the bags in Julian's bedroom. Hannah whispered, "I told your mom I'd stay here with you this afternoon while you get settled in so she can go home and get some rest."

Julian allowed herself a sigh of relief. "Thank you, Hannah. I'd be okay by myself, but I'm pretty sure Mom wouldn't go home if I was by myself, and she needs some rest too." Julian called, "Why don't you go on, Mom? I'm going to bed."

Gale returned and threw her arms around her daughter, squeezing her tightly. "Call me if you need anything, Julian. I mean it." She looked at Hannah. "Make her call me."

Hannah nodded. "Yes, ma'am, Miss Gale."

After her mother left, Julian looked with despair at Hannah. "I lied. I'm not going to bed until I've had a shower. I have to wash my hair."

Hannah laughed. "Okay. Where are your discharge care instructions?"

They read through them together and determined she could remove the dressing on her head, take a shower, dry the area with the stitches, and reapply the bandage. Exhausted, Julian took a shower while Hannah made her a sandwich. After Julian showered and dressed in pajamas, she sat on her bed exhausted and brushed through her wet hair. Hannah knocked on her bedroom door with the sandwich. Julian thanked her and smiled weakly. "I'm just so tired."

"Eat and then go to sleep."

Julian took a bite of the sandwich and breathed deeply through her nose. Hannah gave her a mischievous grin. "So what are they like?"

"Who?"

"The hunky brothers you saved. What are they like?"

Julian rolled her eyes. "You're so boy-crazy!"

Hannah sat next to her on the bed and leaned back on the pillows. "I saw that picture on the news. That is a fine specimen of a man who carried you out of the water. And a Marine too? Wow…"

Julian laughed at her friend. "He's pushy, but he means well. His family is incredible. They were so nice to us. Wait until you meet the younger brother, Amerigo. He's a looker, too." Julian took another bite of her sandwich and sighed. Through her food, she grimaced. "The whole time, I had mud in my hair and probably smelled bad."

Hannah snorted at her. "I doubt they were paying attention to any of that."

Julian frowned. "Hannah, I don't remember seeing anyone else when I got out of the car, so who took that video? It's creepy to know someone was recording. And it was horrifying to see it on TV. Drake was watching with me. I wanted to crawl under a rock." She put the remainder of her sandwich on the plate and closed her eyes as she leaned against the headboard next to Hannah. Julian admitted, "I can't finish it. I'm sorry."

Hannah chuckled and took the plate from her. "Now I know I need to be worried. We've been friends since ninth grade, and I've rarely seen you not finish your food." They giggled together.

"I'm just so tired." Julian felt like a broken record. Hannah took the plate to the kitchen while Julian slumped down under the covers, asleep almost immediately.

Julian's goofy ringtone woke her, and she rubbed her eyes.

Grabbing the phone, she looked at the caller ID. Blocked. She answered, "Hello?" No one spoke. "Hello?" Still nothing. "Who's calling, please?"

A muted male voice hesitantly responded, "I'm the one who took the video. I saw you help them."

"Do I know you? I didn't see anyone—"

The call ended. Julian glared at her phone and called Hannah's name. She swung her legs from the bed.

Hannah hurried into the room. "What's wrong? Do you need medicine? Are you in pain?"

They walked into the living room, Julian's knees shaking. "This guy called and said he videoed the wreck, but he wouldn't tell me who he was or anything. It was creepy." She shuddered.

Hannah made a face. "Maybe it's just a prank. People saw you on the news, and they're stupid."

"Maybe." Julian forced a smile at Hannah despite her skepticism. "You're probably right."

By the evening, Julian assured Hannah she felt fine to be alone. Hannah left with the stern instruction to call if she needed anything. "I'm only five minutes down the road." Julian hugged and thanked her friend.

After Hannah left, Julian sat at the desk in her home office and opened her laptop. Once the screen appeared, she pulled open each social media site on which she had a profile and checked her security settings, being sure no contact information was available. Even though she thought her settings fairly strict, she tightened them all. None of her profiles remained public except the author profiles she used to promote her writing. Julian checked all the doors and windows to make sure they remained locked as she normally kept them. Satisfied, she curled up on the couch with a throw blanket, a book, and a cup of tea.

Julian called her mother preemptively before she launched

into her book. It never failed that once she started reading, her mother would call to tell her something trivial. Julian smiled as she waited for her mom to pick up. Gale might call too often, but the conversations usually contained laughter.

When Gale answered the phone, Julian told her, "I just wanted to check in with you."

She heard her mother's sigh of relief. "I was trying to make myself not call so you could sleep. Has Hannah left?"

"Just a few minutes ago." Julian decided against telling her mother about the strange call. Probably nothing, she reminded herself.

They chatted about Julian's status. Was she in pain? Did she need something to eat? Had she been able to take a shower? Once Julian had given her mother a total update, she ended the call and sank back into the cushions, opening the book.

When her cellphone rang again, she realized she had been sleeping with the book in her hands. She put the bookmark in its place and snatched the phone up. She didn't recognize the number, but it wasn't blocked, at least. "Hello?"

"Julian?" She recognized Drake's deep voice. Relief flooded her.

"Oh! Hi."

"Are you settled in at home? How are you feeling?"

"I'm home. I'm good. Thanks for asking. How is Amerigo?"

"He's actually doing better. He's going to be transported to Columbia and see another surgeon there."

"That's a relief. I'm glad you guys can come home."

"Me, too. How long did the doctor tell you to stay home from work?"

Julian heaved a dramatic sigh. "Three weeks. I think that's longer than I need to stay home, but—"

"I'm sure it feels like too long, but it's probably for the best."

She sighed again. "I guess."

He chuckled at her. "You sound pitiful."

"If only you could see my pout."

More laughter. "You'll survive it."

"When are you going back to work?"

"Wednesday."

A moment of silence passed finally broken by Julian. "I had a call from a man claiming to be the one who took the video." Julian could almost feel Drake tense over the phone.

"What did he say?"

Julian gave him the blow-by-blow description of the call, including the fact that it came from a blocked number, then bit her lip as she waited for his reaction.

"Tell me if it happens again."

Julian frowned. "Maybe he's just embarrassed because he didn't help." It sounded hollow to her own ears, but she wanted to believe that.

"He should be," Drake growled. As if sensing Julian's worry, Drake changed the subject. "Anyway, my family always has lunch after church together on Sundays. You and Gale are invited. And by invited, I mean my parents will come looking for you two if you're not there."

She grinned. "Hard to say no to that," Julian drawled.

"If you don't think you'll be feeling up to it, I understand, but it would be nice if you can make it." He sounded sincere, and Julian felt an unexpected lump in her throat.

"I'll try. Thanks for the invitation."

"Have a good night, Julian."

"You too, Drake."

* * *

Drake clenched his jaw. He had only left the soldiers in someone else's care for a few days. How could they have regressed some much in such a short time? He had barked orders and had required the soldiers to do more than normal all day in an effort to get them back in line. Drake glared at his second in command. The man seemed unfazed when Drake muttered, "I hold you responsible."

"What do you care? You're separating out in a week."

He glared at the younger man. "I care because these men are headed for battle. I'll be pushing them just as hard on my last day here." The younger man straightened and nodded. By the end of the day, Drake's nerves felt stretched and frayed. He had answered countless questions about Amerigo and fielded good-natured ribbing about the video on the news, particularly regarding the screengrab of him carrying Julian out of the river. As he prepared to dismiss the soldiers, Drake saw Master Gunnery Sergeant Martin Patterson approach.

Drake nodded to him. "Master Gunny."

"Master Gunny," Patterson replied with reference to their same rank as they watched the soldiers. Drake dismissed them and scowled at each in turn as they left. His friend reserved his chuckle for when the men outdistanced earshot. "I miss training Marines."

"Me too. Let's go get a drink."

They ended up at the local hangout on base, shooting pool and chatting. Martin Patterson reminded Drake of a bulldog. He stood shorter than Drake but was broader and bulkier with dark brown skin and black hair. The man loved his weights. Even though not required, he kept his hair cut in the typical military high-and-tight style. He planned to retire from the Marine Corps and had three more years to go. "So. One week, eh?"

Drake nodded and took his shot. He made it easily and prepared for his next. "One week."

"Still gonna help your parents with the family business, huh?"

"Yeah. Why do you ask like that?" Another ball went in the

hole.

Martin said, "Seems weird to think of you working at a vineyard."

Drake shrugged. After the combat he had seen and the years of military structure, the lifestyle of the vineyard appealed to him. Being near his family appealed to him. Settling in one spot appealed to him. It was why he had requested to be transferred to this base and to work with Army soldiers instead of Marines as he prepared for the transition to civilian life.

"How's Amerigo?" Martin asked.

"Better. More surgery this week, though. Steel rods, pins, the works."

"That's rough for the kid, but he comes from a tough family."

Drake snorted. "Doesn't mean he's tough, but he's in better spirits now that we're back in Columbia. His little fan club of women can flock to him again."

Martin laughed at that. Then he grinned. "So what about the woman I saw you carrying around on TV? You got your own fan club now?"

Drake shook his head in disgust. "Really? Et tu, Brutus? Any idea how many times I've been asked that?" He missed his shot, and Martin smiled.

"About time. I was startin' to wonder if I was gonna get a turn."

Drake took a deep breath and glanced around the room. Some of the men and women watched him with interest. He rarely watched the local news and could not have anticipated how many people did. One woman met his gaze and winked. Young, slender, and dressed in a short skirt. Drake kept his face impassive. He grabbed the eight ball and shoved it in a pocket. "You win," he told Martin. "Let's get out of here."

In the parking lot, Martin laughed openly at his friend. "Since when aren't you interested in a woman like that?"

He looked away, frowning. "I just have a lot on my mind."

Martin's laughter died. He walked over to Drake and put a hand on his shoulder. "Seriously, Drake. If your family needs anything, you let me know. Jill and I want to help." Drake tilted his head in acknowledgment. Martin looked at his watch and turned to leave. "It's just as well you 'lost.' Jill's probably already home from her book club, and I want to talk to her about the new house."

"I still say she's too good for you," Drake tossed as he opened his car door and slid inside.

Martin chortled as unlocked his own car. "I'll tell her you said so."

As Drake left the base, he called Julian.

She sounded nervous. "Hello?"

"Am I catching you at a bad time?"

"No. Just reading."

"Good. I thought I'd call and be nosy. How ya doing?"

She took a deep breath, and he could hear her smile. "I'm okay. Just getting stir crazy already. Today was your first day back to work, right? How was it?"

He grinned. "Well, you know. I'm gone for a couple of days, and things fall apart. I'm sure you can relate."

Julian laughed. "I can. I'm afraid to see what my desk will look like when I get back to the office." Drake laughed with her.

"You never actually told me what it is you do."

"I work for Johnson Electric. I process invoices and receipts."

"That's... uh..."

"Boring? I know. I work in a cube farm, but I don't mind. I listen to audiobooks while I'm working, and I love my manager. I have nice coworkers. Plus the company has good benefits and a retirement plan."

"A cube farm is a room full of office cubicles?" She

confirmed it. Drake tried to imagine Julian in a "cube farm." He cleared his throat. "Well, I'm sure it's very nice."

She laughed at him. "You're a bad liar. It's my day job, and I like it just fine. It pays the bills so I can come home and write novels."

Drake blinked. "What kinds of novels do you write?" The line went quiet. "Still there, Julian?"

"I write romance novels."

Drake felt his mouth drop open. Then he guffawed. "No wonder your mind immediately went to a romance novel cover when we saw the news the other night." He heard Julian giggle through the phone. "Have you eaten?" he asked as pulled into a restaurant parking lot.

"Not yet, but—"

"I'll be there in about thirty minutes."

"How do you know where I live?"

"I arranged for your car to be returned."

"I thought your dad did that."

"Sometimes I help the old man with stuff. Anyway, I'm on my way with food."

"No, Drake, you don't need to—"

"See you soon."

* * *

Julian struggled off the couch and to her feet, dumping the phone on the coffee table. She straightened the cushions on the couch then plucked dishes and napkins off the table. She put the dishes in the dishwasher and wiped off the kitchen counters. Satisfied with the quick cleaning job, Julian staggered to her bedroom and glared at the clothes in her closet before rejecting the idea of changing though she decided to don a bra under her soft sweatshirt. She brushed her clean hair and pulled it back into a ponytail. She swept a little mascara over her eyelashes and rubbed a rose-tinted lip gloss over her mouth. Exhaustion hit her accompanied by a wave of frustration at tiring so easily.

True to his word, Drake rang the doorbell within thirty minutes. She padded in her socks to the door. Her breath caught in her throat as she looked through the peephole. He wore a camouflage uniform and cap. What woman couldn't appreciate a man in a Marine uniform? Julian unlocked the deadbolt and swung the door open.

Drake smiled at her as he removed his cap. "Hope you like Italian food." He carried a large bag from a local Italian restaurant.

She stepped aside to allow him to pass her. "It's a sin not to like Italian food," she responded. Julian always felt awkward entering someone's house for the first time—as if she needed to ask permission to touch anything.

Not Drake. He strode confidently into the house and placed the food on the dining room table, taking in the open concept floor. "I like your house."

"Thanks."

She pulled two plates from the cabinet in the kitchen along with silverware and napkins. Julian placed them on the table and filled two glasses with ice and water. "What are we having?"

"A little bit of everything," he said and pulled the carryout plates free of the bag. He put together a sampling of different dishes including manicotti, ravioli, and tortellini and handed the plate to Julian with a flourish. "For you."

Julian accepted the plate and grabbed a fork. She waited as he prepared his own plate then motioned for them to sit on the couch. "I know, I know. It's better to eat at a table, but I just don't feel like sitting in those hard chairs right now."

They spoke little as they ate, both too hungry to talk. As they neared the end of their plates, Julian narrowed her eyes at

Drake. "So. Why are you really here?"

Drake stopped eating and gave her an innocent look. "I'm here to eat with the woman who saved my life." Then he smirked. "And to spend time with a romance novelist."

Julian chuckled. "You're incorrigible. My novels would probably disappoint you. They're really tame."

Drake reached over and grabbed the romance novel from the coffee table. "Is this one of yours?"

Horrified, she reached to take it back. "No! It's an advance copy I'm reading for a friend." He held it just out of her grasp. "She's giving me feedback on my latest manuscript in exchange for me reading hers." She continued to try to reclaim the book, but Drake put a hand on her shoulder and easily stopped her.

He opened the book with the other hand and looked at the print. After a few lines, his eyes widened. "Whoa," he muttered.

Julian felt her face burning. "I know. Her stuff is much racier than my normal reading, but I promised." She stopped struggling and covered her flaming cheeks with her hands. He kept reading and dropped his hand from her shoulder to flip to the next page.

"Wow." He glanced at her and back to the pages. "I knew romance novels had a reputation for being more like porn than literature, but I've never actually read one before."

"It's not porn," Julian protested then cleared her throat. "It is kinda racy compared to mine…" Taking advantage of his distracted reading, she plucked the book from his hands. "You're welcome to borrow this when I finish reading it. I promised Janet I'd finish it before the weekend. After that, it's all yours."

He snickered. "I might. It certainly held my attention."

Julian tossed the book back on the coffee table, shaking her head and grinning. "Well, it's inventive." They laughed together as her phone rang. Her smile fled. "Blocked."

Drake sobered instantly. Julian answered the phone on speaker. "Hello?" Silence was the response. "Hello?"

"I was on the bridge when I took the video. I wanted everyone to see what a wonderful person you are."

Julian and Drake exchanged glances. "Thanks, I guess. Do I know you?"

The line went dead. Julian's met Drake's eyes. He scowled at the phone as she dropped it back onto the coffee table. She shuddered. "Wonder how they even got my phone number."

Drake suggested, "Maybe your mom gave it to them. She gave me your information pretty easily."

Julian rolled her eyes. "I've told her to stop doing that, but she does at least normally tell me when she's done it. You're the only one she's mentioned in a while."

He looked thoughtful. "This guy's probably just a harmless weirdo, but don't take any chances. Keep your doors and windows locked. Always keep your car doors locked. Be careful when you're out."

She waved a hand. "I appreciate your concern, but I already do all of that." She took their plates and put them in the sink, her hands shaking just the tiniest bit. "He's not making threats or anything. It's just creepy," she said, more for her benefit than Drake's. She returned to the couch and picked at her nails, frowning at the time on the wall clock. Julian noted Drake looked at the clock as well. Did he feel obligated to hang around? She didn't want to admit that the call made her nervous to be alone. She knew he needed to be getting home since he most likely had to be at the base early in the morning. She yawned and stretched her arms. "Wow. I'm exhausted." Julian leaned back on the couch and sighed.

"You're not very subtle." He grinned at her. "You could just ask me to leave."

"That would be rude! I'm a Southerner, sir. I'm not allowed

to be rude."

He tilted his head at her and tapped his lips with one finger. "I think you're just giving me an out so I won't feel obligated to stay after that weird phone call."

Her mouth gaped slightly at his insight. "You don't need to stay with me. I'm okay."

Drake rolled his eyes the way he had at the hospital that said he struggled for patience. "Tell me you're not weirded out by that call, and I'll be gone."

Julian bit her lip. She wanted to sound brave, but said nothing. Even though they had only known each other for a short period of time, she already knew the set to his jaw. Arguing with him was pointless.

"That's what I thought," Drake said then put a hand on her arm. "It's okay to let someone help you." He gave her a charming grin. "Just give that book back to me."

When he reached for it, Julian snatched it up and giggled. "No! I'll find a movie." She put the book back on her bookshelf and then knelt in front of the entertainment center to read movie names.

* * *

Over halfway through the movie, Drake glanced over at Julian and saw her sleeping, curled under a warm throw blanket with her head on the arm of the couch and her cold feet pressed against the side of his thigh. He grinned and turned his attention back to the movie. Julian had freshened their drinks and microwaved popcorn before she drifted into dreamland. Drake's grin spread to a smile as he let his eyes slide closed. He jerked awake when Julian's silly ringtone blared. She drowsily rubbed her eyes while he picked up the phone and looked at the caller ID. Blocked.

Without waiting for her permission, Drake answered the

phone. At the sound of his voice, the caller disconnected.

Julian's expression betrayed her worry before she could hide it, but she forced a half-hearted laugh. "I think I'll look into having my number changed." She hugged her knees as Drake placed the phone back on the coffee table.

Anger bubbled up in Drake. Julian had saved their lives, and her reward was to be harassed by some unknown coward? He gritted his teeth and looked at his watch. The TV had turned itself off long ago. Embarrassed, he told her, "I'm supposed to be at work in five hours."

She gasped. "Oh no! How far away do you live? Do you want to just stay here?"

Unwilling to leave her alone after the phone call, he told her, "That would be great, actually. I have some clothes and stuff at work. I'll just leave from here."

He saw a flash of relief on her face before she adopted a nonchalant expression. "I have a set of travel toiletries I haven't used yet if you need them—toothbrush, toothpaste, soap, shampoo."

He said, "I appreciate it. I'll replace all of it."

She gave a snort. "That's all right. I'm not rich, but I think I can handle the eight dollars' worth of travel-size stuff. Let me show you the spare room."

The room was sparse, but the bed was made and ready for company. She disappeared and reappeared with a clear plastic bag containing the toiletries. Julian pointed out the bathroom. "Help yourself to whatever's in the kitchen." As she turned to leave him, she stopped and looked back. "I know you're staying to be nice to me. Thank you." She gave him a thin smile and left him in the room alone.

* * *

Julian shuffled into the hall and saw the guest room door

standing open. The bed had been made, and a note rested on the comforter. She picked up the note written on a piece of paper from the tablet on her kitchen counter she used for keeping lists. "Thanks for the hospitality. See you soon. Drake." She looked at his neat print and then at the pristine room. In the guest bathroom, she saw the used towel hanging to dry and leaned against the door frame, aware she'd only been able to sleep because she had known a big, bad Marine slept in the room across the hall.

Slowly, Julian dragged into the kitchen area and made a cup of coffee. Sipping the coffee slowly, she shuffled into the living room and made her way to the bookshelf for her friend's book. Might as well try to finish it while she had nothing else to do. As she lifted the book, she noticed a hole in her neatly organized novels and immediately recognized what was missing. He had taken one of her books. Her nerves stretched a little tighter at the thought of him reading one of her works. She nearly jumped out of her skin when her phone rang in her pocket. She answered as calmly as possible. "Hello?"

"I'm on a break. I wanted to let you know I borrowed one of your books." Drake sounded vibrant and alert, his deep voice cheerful.

"I just saw that."

"I would have asked, but I didn't want to wake you. I hope you don't mind."

Julian made a strangled noise before composing herself enough to say, "Of course not, but you don't really need to—"

"Gunny, get over here now!" another male voice barked in the background.

Drake grumbled back before telling Julian, "Gotta go. I'll check on you later. Get that number changed then text me the new one." The line went dead.

Julian stared at her phone, her mouth gaping slightly. "Bossy," she muttered. "I'll do what I want," she said and tilted her chin up. Then she called Hannah.

"I need to get my phone number changed. Any idea how to do that?"

She could almost hear Hannah's frown. "Unfortunately, yes. Most cell phone companies let you do it from the company's website. Did you get another call from that blocked number?"

"Two. Drake answered the second one, and the guy hung up." Julian regretted the words as soon as they left her mouth.

"Drake was at your house?" Hannah asked breathlessly.

"He stopped by unexpectedly and brought take out."

"How did it go?"

Julian shrugged as if Hannah could see her. "Okay. He watched a movie with me after we ate."

"Y'all had a date!" Hannah squealed. "That's fantastic. I'll be your maid of honor."

"Hannah!"

Her friend chortled. "Your babies will be so beautiful."

Julian's face flame even alone. "Stop it! You're as bad as Mom."

"I know!" Hannah's gleeful tone made Julian chuckle in spite of herself.

Julian sighed. "Look, he's only being nice because of the accident. He's one of those overly protective people. Has to take care of everyone."

Hannah said, "Sounds familiar."

Julian rolled her eyes. "I'm hanging up now."

Hannah laughed. "Oh, don't be like that. Feel up to lunch tomorrow? My treat."

"I guess," Julian drawled with mock exhaustion.

"Pull yourself together, woman," Hannah ordered and disconnected.

"Boy. Everyone's bossing me around today," Julian mumbled.

The next few days seemed to go by in a blur of novel reading and writing and phone calls between Julian and her mom, Julian and Hannah, Julian and church members, Julian and coworkers, and Julian and Drake. She had passed out her new phone number to anyone in her contacts she trusted and continued to be vigilant. Some of her friends from church brought her food and visited with her, and though she spoke to Drake on the phone, he did not return that week. His mother called her to check on her and when Julian asked about Amerigo, Mary told her his second surgery had gone well and that he would get to come home soon. Julian felt relief for the family. She remembered how hard it had been when her father had been in the hospital for an extended amount of time before he passed away.

On Sunday, when she would have gone to church and then to the Salvatore's house for lunch with her mother, she woke up sore and weak from overdoing things on Saturday. Stir crazy and unsettled, Julian had attempted to resume her daily walk through the neighborhood. By the time Julian had returned to her house, she had been exhausted. She called Mary early. "I'm so sorry. I hope you haven't gone to too much trouble, but I don't think I'm up to leaving the house today. I was too ambitious yesterday, and now I'm paying for it."

Mary cooed, "Oh no, dear. Do you need anything? I can bring some food to you."

"Oh, no, thank you. I'm fine. I'm just gonna go back to bed. I already talked to Mom, and she's gonna bring something for lunch. I'm really sorry. I was looking forward to seeing y'all again," Julian told her with a frown, annoyed with herself for overdoing it the day before. She had wanted to see them, particularly Amerigo since he had come home. And don't forget getting to see Drake, she admitted to herself. Their phone calls consisted mainly of small talk as he checked up on her, but she still looked forward to the calls.

"Well, I'm calling your mother to make sure you're telling the truth about lunch, young lady."

Julian laughed at Mary. "I promise I'm fine. Just tired."

"I'm still calling her."

After the conversation with Mary, Julian took a shower and changed into a pair of sweatpants, thick socks, and a worn, soft t-shirt. She crawled back into bed with some over-the-counter pain medicine and drifted back to sleep.

The doorbell woke her later. Julian sat up and rubbed her eyes blearily then looked at the time on her phone. "Must be Mom," she muttered to no one and dragged out of bed. Shuffling through the hall to the foyer, Julian leaned against the door to check the peephole. She stood straighter and gasped. She cringed and tried to smooth her wild hair down before opening the door. "Drake? What are you doing here?" she asked once she did.

He looked handsome as always in a pair of jeans, a form-fitted long-sleeved t-shirt, and a leather jacket. She noted the foil-covered plate. He smiled, and her stomach fluttered. "Our mothers decided you should have some of my mom's lunch even if you couldn't make it to the house." Without waiting for an invitation, Drake strolled past her into the house. He gave her a quick up and down glance. "I told Mom I was sure you were telling the truth about going back to bed."

Julian cringed again as he sauntered through the house to her kitchen, placing the plate on her counter. "Where are your forks?" he asked.

She closed the door and followed him apprehensively. "This really isn't necessary," she protested as he pulled a fork from the drawer.

He put the uncovered plate in the microwave. "Sorry, but I have been ordered to make sure you eat before I leave." He grinned, folding his arms and leaning against the counter as the microwave hummed. Julian took a deep breath and tried to pat her hair back down again. He waved at hand at her hair. "It's a good look for you."

Julian rolled her eyes. "Uh-huh. I'll be right back." She scurried into her bathroom to brush her hair and wash her face. She moaned at her still sleepy eyes and pale skin. Oh, well. She refused to slather on makeup when she would probably go back to sleep after Drake left. She found him placing the warmed plate on the table with a glass of ice water. "Thanks," she croaked and sat at the table. He poured his own glass of water and joined her. She started to eat as he watched. "Okay. You're making me nervous. I feel like a bug under a microscope."

"Sorry." He had the grace to look sheepish. "I ate at my parents' house." He looked around the room. "Where's that book?" He gave her a roguish smile.

She sighed in amusement, shaking her head. "Take it, if you want. It's on my bookshelf."

He crossed to the bookshelf and inspected her collection. She continued to eat as he perused the titles. "You have an eclectic library."

She murmured an incoherent response as she chewed.

He chuckled and picked up another of her novels. "Are these part of a series?"

Through a mouthful of food, she told him, "Yeah, but you don't have to read them in order. Each one is a stand-alone book, but all the characters know each other. Except my new one. It's a different series." With another forkful, she said, "This is really good."

Drake watched her thoughtfully then turned back to the books. "Mind if I borrow another of your books?"

Julian stopped chewing. "No, but they don't seem like your kind of books." He shrugged, and she put her fork down. "Your mom sent too much food."

He nodded. "I told her she was probably overdoing it, but you can save it for later." Drake had retrieved the plate, covered it, and placed it in her refrigerator before she could stop him. She sipped her water and rubbed her hands over her face. Drake said, "That's my cue to get out of your hair." He crossed to her and knelt by her chair. "Are you okay? Need anything else?" Muddled by how good he smelled, she mutely shook her head. Drake squeezed her hand with another smile. "All right. Call if you need anything." And he was gone.

Julian blinked. The man was a force of nature. He came, he saw, he conquered whatever task it was—training recruits, tending to Amerigo, corralling his parents, making sure she ate. She wondered what it would be like to date someone like Drake. She bet he was the kind of guy that filled your car with gas so you didn't have to. He probably took out the trash and killed the spiders. She sighed a dreamy sigh. Guys like that didn't look at her twice. To Drake, she was just another responsibility on his plate.

CHAPTER FOUR

Over the rest of the week, Julian walked each day to gradually work up to her normal distance and felt more like herself. She fought cabin fever by reading and writing, taking advantage of the time off work to plug away at the follow-up novel to her most recent release.

Thursday afternoon Mary called her, her normal casual tone tentative. "I have a favor to ask of you. You know you and Gale are invited to Drake's retirement party, right?"

Julian sat straighter. "Retirement party? Drake's not old enough to retire, is he?"

She could hear the smile in Mary's voice. "Sweetie, he enlisted at eighteen. He's been in the Marines for twenty years. He is, indeed, retiring. Thank God. Worrying about him overseas was awful."

"I can't even imagine." She shuddered thinking about the worry a mother would have for a child in a war zone, even a tough one like Drake. "Well, it's nice that he can retire so young. What's he going to do now?"

"He wants to help us with the vineyard. I thought at first he just hadn't decided what he wanted to do, but now I think he really likes the idea."

Julian blinked in surprise. "A vineyard?"

"That's the Salvatore family business, dear. They're winemakers back in Italy. It's been Anthony's dream to start a vineyard here so we decided to give it a go about ten years ago."

"That's fantastic!" Julian's genuine warmth for the notion came through her voice. "That's a nice idea for this area."

Mary chuckled. "We hope so. We've been at it for a while now, and it's going well." Mary paused then cleared her throat. "So, Julian, I do have a small favor to ask." Julian held her breath until Mary continued. "See, the retirement party's a surprise. We need someone to keep Drake away for a bit, then bring him to our house on the vineyard. You know, get him to go to coffee or something before the party to give us plenty of time to be ready."

Julian balked. "I dunno, Mrs. Salvatore. I'm not very good at subterfuge. Besides, I don't think Drake would take the bait."

A loud, annoyed sigh came through the phone. "Julian, how many times do I have to ask you to call me Mary? My name is Mary." Before Julian had the opportunity to apologize, she continued. "And don't be silly. Of course he'll take the bait. Pretty girl like you. He'll jump at the chance to take you to coffee or dinner."

"Mrs. Salva—I mean, Mary, I'm not—"

"So get him to go to coffee with you around six. I'll tell him to bring you by after to see Amerigo and have a quiet dinner," Mary instructed. She sounded gleeful when she said, "He won't suspect a thing."

Julian scrubbed a hand over her face. He would. He definitely would. Drake had no interest in dating her, and her invitation would sound like a date. What if she asked him to coffee and he said no? Her poor self-esteem.

Mary said, "You can do this, Julian. You're resourceful and smart and such a sweet girl. He'll take the bait."

Julian inwardly sighed. Mary and Gale really did seem cut from the same cloth. "I'll try, Mary."

After they said their goodbyes, Julian collapsed on her couch in exhaustion. Talking to her mother or Mary felt like a roller coaster ride. They took a person wherever they wanted, the other party hanging on for dear life. Julian smiled. At least the women generally meant well.

Glaring at her phone, Julian decided to get it over with. She called Drake and tapped her fingers on her left thigh. His deep voice sounded gruff when he answered. She gulped. "Um, hi. Is this a bad time?" she asked.

He exhaled noisily. "No. Sorry. You're fine. Just a bad day at work. I'm leaving now."

"When's your last day?"

"Tomorrow." A beat passed. "It's probably a good thing I'm retiring. It's time to shift gears."

Was he confiding in her? She hadn't expected that. "Looking forward to working at the vineyard?"

His voice brightened as he replied, "I really am."

Julian smiled. "I'm really happy for you, Drake." She decided to use the moment. "In fact, why don't you let me treat you to a celebratory coffee Saturday afternoon?"

Silence hung between them. She rushed to add, "I mean, you've been so nice to my mom and me. I'd like to at least buy you a latte or something and talk about something other than cars and car wrecks and doctors."

He chuckled. "All right. Coffee's good, but I'll treat. You'll be doing me a favor to get me out of the house."

She felt her stomach flutter again. "We'll see about who treats who. So how does six sound?"

"Sure. I'll be by to pick you up at six."

"Okay." She swallowed again. "Well, I won't hold you up since you're going home. If I don't talk to you before, I'll see you Saturday."

"Julian?"

"Yeah?"

"Thanks."

"Uh, sure thing. Bye."

Her hands shook when she pressed the end button. She pressed her fingertips to her lips. "Well, I'll be dirty doggone. Mary was right."

* * *

Friday, Julian went to see the surgeon she had been referred to for follow up care by the doctor in the hospital. She had already been once to have her stitches removed. After some cajoling, the doctor narrowed his eyes at her. "If I write the orders to release you back to part time work for a week earlier than normal, do you promise to take it easy?" She nodded.

"Dr. McKinley, I sit at a desk all day, but if I start to feel tired or bad, I'll just go home."

He frowned. "If you follow my directions, I don't expect to see you back here again." A smile replaced the frown. "Bravo for your courage, Ms. Fursey."

She blushed and left the office with a spring in her step. Julian had actually missed her coworkers. They had gone in together to send her flowers once she got home. She didn't have enough leave time for another full week, and her budget left little room for emergencies. Anthony had offered to subsidize her pay for the work she would miss when she first came home. Aghast, she had flatly refused. Her budget, though thin, would survive.

On her way home, Julian decided to treat herself to a latte and stopped at a local coffee shop, one of her favorites. As she sat at one of the tables reading the book she had downloaded on her tablet, she noticed a couple watching her. She pretended not to see them and tried to focus on the book. Having finished her friend's racy novel, she'd moved to The Chronicles of Narnia by C.S. Lewis for a change. Despite her love for the series, Julian found it difficult to concentrate with the two pairs of eyes boring into her. Finally, the woman and man approached her.

"Excuse me," the woman interrupted.

Julian forced a smile. "Hi?"

"Hi. I'm sorry to interrupt you, but aren't you the woman we saw on the news who rescued those guys in the river?"

At that, more people turned to look at her and whisper. She heard breathy comments:

"Oh, it is her!"

"I saw that on the news too."

She continued to force a smile and considered lying, but lying felt foreign to her. "I guess so." The couple sat at her table uninvited.

"That was amazing!" the man told her. "It's good to know there are still people willing to help others out there."

The woman agreed fervently. "We saw that and couldn't believe it. Good for you."

"So, how are you doing since the accident?" the man asked.

People were openly looking at her and listening by then. Julian felt her face turning scarlet with the attention. She cast a glance to the exit. "I'm good. Thanks. Just trying to get back to normal."

Someone from another table leaned toward them. "Were you scared?"

"Yeah. What were you thinking when the SUV rolled over?"

"Did you know how badly you were hurt?"

Julian felt exposed and tense. A tall, slender man close to

her age with light red hair, bright blue eyes, and a dimple when he smiled appeared at her side. "Sorry I took so long, darling. Ready to go?" He spoke with a proper British accent. He held a hand out to her.

She stuttered, "Uh... um... Yeah." She shoved her tablet in her purse, grabbed her cup, and stood, taking the proffered hand. The man led her outside into the crisp fall air. In the parking lot, he released her hand and faced her.

"I hope I didn't alarm you. You just had a panicked look on your face. I thought I could help."

Julian smiled with gratitude. "You did. Thank you. I was just about to run out screaming like a banshee."

They laughed together. She liked his smile as he admitted, "I do have an ulterior motive, though."

Julian tipped her head to the side. He held a bag from the bookstore nearby and opened it. He produced a hardcover book she instantly recognized, and her face went red again. He pointed to her picture on the back inside sleeve.

Then she laughed again. "Oh my word. Not a book I would expect you to be buying."

He grinned. "It's for my mom for Christmas. She's a fan of your work." With a sheepish expression, he said, "It would be great if you'd sign it for her."

She replied, "I'm happy to!" She dug in her purse and found a pen. He handed her the book, and she opened the front cover. "What's your mom's name?"

"Claudia."

She made the inscription out to his mother, thanking her for reading her books and signed it. She did the occasional signing at local bookstores, libraries, and conventions, but each time someone asked her to sign, it flattered her.

The man took the book back, and with a sly grin, opened it back up. "You could put your number right there if you want to as well."

She chuckled. "That's smooth," she admitted. Then she eyed him warily. "It's a romance novel, but you're aware it's not racy, right?"

It was his turn to chuckle. "Um, I just think you're beautiful and smart and might like to have coffee or dinner sometime. I can wreck my car and let you pull me out if that's how you prefer to meet men." He winked.

Julian belly-laughed then said, "You know my name, but I don't know yours."

He flustered in embarrassment and held out his hand. "Rob Overton. Nice to meet you."

She shook his hand with a shy grin. "Nice to meet you, too."

He gave her another pleading look. "So coffee? Lunch? Dinner? Tea? Snack?"

Julian had been approached by men before and asked out, but Rob Overton's charm disarmed her when she normally would have declined. Instead, she bit her lip in consideration.

Seeing her indecision, he pulled the bookstore's promotional bookmark from the bag and took the pen from her hand. "How about we exchange email addresses? Then we can arrange a meeting through email without exchanging phone numbers until you feel more comfortable." He wrote his email address and handed it to her.

"That's a really good idea." She ripped the bookmark in half and wrote hers on the other portion. Julian handed the half back to him and smiled. "I really need to be getting out of here, but thank you again for rescuing me. I hope your mom likes the book."

Rob nodded with a warm grin. "I'm sure she will."

She waved and left with another spring in her step. How flattering to have such a charming man ask her out! Then she thought of Drake, and a frown creased her brow. She was right when she told Hannah he didn't think of her that way, wasn't she? Drake had given her no reason to believe he thought of her as anything other than someone to whom he owed a debt. Rob's offer was a genuine date. Julian liked his accent and red hair, and she truly appreciated his assistance at the coffee shop. A surge of discomfort rose in her again as she thought of the unwanted attention from the other patrons. Her heart sank. Hopefully that would die out soon. Another news story would capture the public attention, and people would forget her.

Her phone rang. Hannah. Excitedly, Julian answered the phone. "You'll never guess what happened to me."

"The doctor said they'll have to cut out your kidney?"

"Cute," Julian replied. "He said I'm good to go back to work for half-days, but that's not what I was going to tell you."

"What then?" Hannah asked with the breathless energy Julian loved about her friend.

"These people started asking me all these personal questions about the accident until this cute British guy rescued me."

"Seriously?"

"Yup. He asked for my number and asked me out."

"What did you say?"

"I gave him my email address instead."

They giggled together like teenagers, then Hannah asked the same question Julian had been pondering. "How do you think Drake will react if you go out with this guy?"

"How many times do I have to tell you we're just friends? He's just being nice to me because—"

"You saved his life. I know, I know. I've heard you say it a hundred times now, but I'm not sure I buy it," Hannah replied. "I think he's more interested than you think he is. Didn't you say he took a couple of your books to read? Do you think a guy like that reads a lot of romance novels?"

Julian opened her mouth then closed it again before finally admitting, "I hadn't thought about it that way. I just figured he was curious as a friend to see what I write."

"That could be, I guess."

"In any case, Rob and I just exchanged email addresses, for goodness' sake. Absolutely nothing will come of that, either. I've been down this road before." She finally parked in her driveway and saw the email notification on her phone. "Hang on," she told Hannah and checked her email, the most recent from Rob Overton. She read it to Hannah. "Dear Julian, I would be happy to put my car in a ditch near Sweeny's Saturday evening around eight o'clock. If you help me, I'll buy dinner. Sincerely, Rob."

They laughed together. "Okay," Hannah said. "That is hard to resist. Are you gonna go?"

"No, I promised Mary I'd lure Drake to his surprise retirement party Saturday night, remember?"

"Ah, yes. The guy who's only going with you out of obligation. I remember."

Julian snickered. "I'm hanging up now."

* * *

When Drake had mentioned the coffee meeting with Julian to his mother, she'd pounced on him, making him promise to bring her to the house for dinner after. He'd called Julian and pitched the idea, surprised when she'd happily agreed.

"Your family's so nice, and I'd like to see Amerigo again," she had said.

Saturday afternoon, Mary called Drake. "Dress nice. We're all dressing nice."

"Okay. I guess I'll take off my hobo rags and put on something else."

Mary clucked her tongue at her son. "Don't get smart with me. Khakis, at least, please. Don't shame me."

Drake rolled his eyes. "Mom…"

"Don't you want to impress Julian?"

"Impress her? You know we're not…"

"I said dress nice, and I mean dress nice!"

"Good grief, Ma. All right." Drake made a face at the phone. What was wrong with his mother? What did she think he would wear? A sequined jumpsuit? Anyway, it was just coffee then dinner at their house. But he wore a pair of black slacks and a green knit shirt and tried to ignore the realization that he wanted to dress nice to see Julian again. He wouldn't admit to anyone how much he looked forward to their phone conversations. Her laugh always made him smile.

He left early and made his way to Julian's house, his conversation with his mother still ringing in his ears. He knew that tone, and it spoke of trouble-making. Maybe even matchmaking.

His parents liked Julian, and why wouldn't they? She had saved both their sons. He liked Julian. He had a lot of respect for her and admired her. As a Marine, he rushed into danger because he had been trained to do so. She did it simply because someone needed help. It took a special person to do that.

Drake clenched his jaw as he drove, suspecting their mothers might be trying to push them together. Meddlers. He considered the women he normally dated then rethought the word "dated." It probably made more sense to say he went on a couple of dates with women instead of saying he dated women. Dating implied some sort of relationship. He hadn't had an actual relationship since… Well, for a long time. He wouldn't lump Julian in with the other women he'd gone out with in the last few years. He liked her sense of humor and her spunk, and he'd been pleased by her invitation to coffee, happy to spend more time with her.

Drake pulled into her driveway, stepped out of his rental car, and went to the door to ring the doorbell. Julian opened the door and greeted him with a wide smile. He fought to keep his expression neutral, but his strong reaction to her caught him off guard. "You look beautiful," he said. She wore a long-sleeved, fitted black sweater with a scoop neck over a gray pencil skirt, black tights, and knee high black boots with a low heel. Her dark hair had been swept up in a clip. She wore delicate silver earrings, a thin silver chain with a heart charm, and a chunky ring on her right hand. Around her neck, Julian sported a long purple scarf which seemed as much for warmth as fashion. She topped the outfit with a gray and black twill trench coat.

She blushed a little. "Thanks. You look nice too."

He silently thanked his mother for warning him to dress nice. "Thanks." He smelled her subtle perfume as he opened the car door for her. She gracefully sat, and he closed the door for her. He crossed around the car and dropped into the driver's seat.

"Shall we?"

"Yes. Let's," she said with a grin.

The drive passed in surprisingly comfortable silence. At the coffee shop Julian recommended, they went inside and ordered. Julian ordered a fancy latte, and he ordered a plain black coffee, refusing to let her pay. When they sat with their drinks, Julian gave a hesitant look around then confided, "Last time I came here, people recognized me from the news."

Drake blinked in surprise. "Really?"

She nodded, her expression somber. "So embarrassing," she murmured then glanced at her purse when her phone gave a ding. Julian pulled out her phone to check the message. "Sorry." She gave him an apologetic smile. "I normally wouldn't mess with my phone when I'm out with a friend, but this is Mom. She's needy tonight."

"Do what you need to. I'm not offended," he said though he chaffed a little at the term friend. He silently chastised himself. They were friends, weren't they? He hadn't meant to give the impression he wanted more than that. He wanted to do the right thing by her, make sure she and her mother were all right, considering his family's debt to them. And if they could share coffee and laugh together, even better. Still…

She gave him a grateful smile. "Thanks for being understanding." Her eyes sparkled with mirth as she continued, "Of course, you've met my mom so you have reason to be more understanding."

He chuckled. "And you've met mine. I think we're even."

"Your mom is a peach, Drake. I love her. And your dad. And your brother. You have a fantastic family."

Her genuine warm expression pleased him more than he expected. "They're not too bad, I guess," he said with a grin. "Your mom's pretty amazing." He liked Gale and had been happy to see his mom getting away from the vineyard more with her new friend. "She's done my mom a world of good. She works too hard with Pop."

Another ding from Julian's phone, and she glanced at it again. "Well, your mom is definitely better with technology than mine. Each of these texts ends, 'Love, Mom.'" He chortled at that, and Julian laughed with him. After a moment, she asked, "So Mary said you're going to work on the family vineyard?"

Drake nodded. "I started helping on leave and found I missed it after a while. It's hard work, but it's worth it."

"I don't know much about vineyards or the winemaking process," she admitted.

He suggested, "It'll be too late tonight, but you ought to come out to the vineyard for a tour sometime."

Her eyes sparkled. "I'd like that." Then her eyes looked behind him and recognition lit her face.

She looked at Drake again and opened her mouth just as a pleasant male voice behind him said, "Fancy meeting you here again!"

Drake swiveled in his chair to see a lean, red-headed man standing by their table. He wore a bright smile, his curiosity obvious. Julian allowed the man to lean down and kiss her cheek, though he thought she looked the tiniest bit shocked by the action.

"Uh, hi," she stammered and motioned to Drake. "Rob Overton, this is Drake Salvatore. Drake, this is Rob."

Drake stood eye-to-eye with the newcomer. They shook hands, and the man gasped, "You're one of the men from the wreck!"

A couple of heads turned in the coffee shop, and Drake saw Julian glance around nervously. Drake's jaw tightened. "That's me," he acknowledged. Unsure what to do next, he offered, "Care to join us?" Please say no, Drake thought.

"It's kind of you to offer, but I was just on my way out." Rob nodded to Julian. "I'm looking forward to our lunch." To Drake, he said, "It was nice to meet you." They shook hands, and Rob disappeared through one of the exits. Drake sat down again, his eyebrows raised.

Julian's cheeks had turned pink, but she smiled with a shrug. "He rescued me when people started to recognize me the other day, and I agreed to lunch."

Drake narrowed his eyes at the door Rob had exited and made a mental note to Google the guy. He seemed nice enough, but one could never tell. Julian's mom gave her personal information out like candy. That guy could be anyone.

She chuckled. "Hey," she said, waving a hand in front of him to get his attention. "You okay?" She grinned, and Drake grinned back.

"Yeah. Sorry." He sipped his coffee. "Get asked out by total strangers a lot?" He tried to keep his face blank as he asked.

"Are you gonna do the overprotective brother thing?" Julian teased.

Drake bit back the snort he felt as he took in her beautiful blue eyes and pink, bow-shaped mouth. His mind immediately went back to the night at her house when she'd fallen asleep on the couch, so trusting she'd used him as a foot warmer. The corner of his mouth twisted upward. "Overprotective, maybe. Brother, no."

She blinked her surprise, her mouth gaping before she said, "Oh."

They sat in a suddenly awkward silence as Drake considered what to say next. He turned his cup around in his fingers on the table and inwardly cringed. He liked her more than he cared to admit, enjoying their easygoing phone conversations and the occasional text, but he didn't know exactly what he wanted from their relationship other than to not be a jerk to the woman who had saved him and his brother. He glanced up from his coffee cup to see her staring at him, her lips still slightly parted.

She clapped her mouth closed as her phone chimed with another text. Amusement twinkled in her eyes. "My mother needs help," she said with a snort. She turned the phone around and showed him the blurry, flesh-toned picture.

He squinted. "What is that supposed to be?"

"I'm pretty sure it's her cheek. Your mother is trying to teach her how to take a selfie."

They burst into laughter together, the awkward moment gone. Drake loved her laugh—not delicate or dainty, but still feminine. She wiped tears of mirth from her eyes and took a deep breath. "I think we should really worry about leaving them alone together," she said, still chuckling. "In fact, your mom sent me a text that dinner's almost ready."

"Guess we should get going then," Drake said. They stood, and Drake helped her with her jacket before donning his own, turning from her momentarily to shrug it on his shoulders. When he turned back around, he tensed at the expression of fear Julian's pale face.

He followed her gaze to a man entering the coffee shop. He was shorter than Drake with a receding, dirty-blond hairline and a weak chin. His brown eyes landed on Julian and stopped.

"Oh no," Julian whispered. She grabbed his arm and pulled

him toward the other door. "Let's go."

He didn't resist despite his curiosity, but the man caught up to them before they reached the door. "Julian!" he called and reached out as if to hug her.

The panicked look in her eye prompted Drake to step between them. "Hey, there, buddy," he said as the man stopped short. "Can I help you with something?"

The man tilted his head back, eyes defiant. "Who are you?"

"You first."

"I'm her husband."

"Ex!" Julian practically shouted from behind the wall of Drake's back. "Ex-husband." Drake glanced over his shoulder to see her straighten, her chin pushed up and steel in her spine. She stepped beside him. "Drake Salvatore, meet my ex-husband, Arnold Woodley."

Drake regarded the man, disliking him more than before. The man assessed Drake then plastered on a salesman's smile. He shoved his hand out. "You must be one of the guys from the accident."

Drake gripped the man's hand with more force than necessary, gratified when Woodley winced slightly. He could feel Julian's discomfort at this man's presence, the tension radiating from her in waves. Tension and fear.

"To what do we owe this pleasure?" Drake asked.

"I just happened to be on this side of town. Figured she'd be here. Thought I'd say hello." Woodley kept the smile plastered on his face as Drake waited for a cue from Julian.

"You said it. Now say goodbye," she said, her voice clipped and low.

Atta girl, Drake thought.

Woodley's smile slipped. "We need to talk."

"No," she said and turned away, one hand on the door.

The man grunted in frustration and reached for Julian's arm. Drake's hand caught his wrist. "Don't even think it."

Woodley snarled as he jerked his arm back. A few of the patrons eyed the scene warily. "We'll talk another time," the man spat and spun on his heel toward the other door.

Drake faced Julian, his chest tightening at the look on her face. "Wanna go?" he offered, motioning toward the exit.

"Yes. Let's," she said, her face stone, and Drake wished she still wore the bright expression from earlier when she'd used the same phrase. He held the door open and cast a glance over his shoulder to be sure Woodley didn't double back as Julian brushed past him. She waited as he joined her.

"Don't worry. He's not coming back," Drake assured her with an arm around her shoulders and led her to the car.

* * *

Julian's stomach roiled with nerves as she sat in the passenger seat of Drake's rental. Why was Arnold sniffing around? And introducing himself as her husband? She hadn't seen him in five years, and she had been thankful for it.

"No pressure," Drake said, and she nearly jumped at his voice. "But if you need to talk about it…"

She rapidly blinked away unshed tears, part of her desperately wanting to spill everything about her horrible ex to Drake, but she shook her head. Drake respected her. If he knew about Arnold, she'd lose that. She also didn't want to distract from his surprise party. Mary's texts exuded her excitement, and Julian wanted Drake to have a good time. He'd earned it for his service in the Marines. On top of that, she wanted to throw her arms around his neck and kiss him for being a buffer at the coffee shop. Without knowing any details, Drake Salvatore had been on her side the moment he'd seen her face when Arnold walked in. If she hadn't already found Drake attractive before—which she had—she would have after that. The man had actually sandwiched himself between her and

Arnold.

Julian forced a cheerful expression. "I'm fine, but thank you for the offer."

His look said he knew better, but he didn't push any further. Instead, he said, "I'm glad you agreed to come to the vineyard for dinner tonight. The folks are excited to see you. I think Amerigo even said he'd leave his cave to visit."

She grinned slyly. "I'm flattered."

"Yeah, he said he might brush his teeth and put on pants. We're all very excited."

Julian laughed in earnest. "I'm double flattered," she told him.

Drake smiled at her, a hint of concern in his eyes.

With a sigh, Julian told him, "I'm fine, Drake. Seriously." She knew it was a lie. She was pretty sure he knew it was a lie, but she wanted him to remember this night as his retirement party, not the night Julian got freaked out by her ex-husband. "Tell me more about the vineyard," she said.

He dove into a history of the South Carolina vineyard, established before he was born with just a vine and an idea, and the evolution of the wine it produced, a combination of multiple vines and new growing techniques. Julian expected to be bored, but Drake's enthusiasm infected her, and she watched him as he drove. She barely noticed the length of the drive into the countryside and found herself surprised to see a rustic house before her. The patio wrapped around the entire structure, and there was a porch swing by the front door. The light-gray wood exterior of the house was trimmed with darker wood and stone. Large windows lined the front, allowing them to see into the country-chic living room with plush, tasteful furniture surrounding a large stone fireplace.

As they parked the car, not a single person could be seen inside. Drake gave a grunt. "Weird. I figured Ma would be practically bounding out the door to see you. Wonder where everyone is."

Julian played dumb. "Maybe they walked to the vineyard or something?"

He gave her an incredulous look but grinned. "In the dark?"

She shrugged, also grinning. Her palms dampened anxiously, but her heart lightened. "Do you have a key? Couldn't we go inside?"

"Yeah," he replied. "I have a key for emergencies." They got out and made their way to the front door. "I can't see anyone," he murmured as he twisted his keyring around the right key. "I'm starting to get a little worried."

"Let's just get inside," Julian said in as soothing a tone as she could muster, earning a raised eyebrow from him.

Once Drake opened the door, people leapt from behind furniture all around. "Surprise!" a group of close to thirty people yelled simultaneously.

Julian laughed in glee as Drake staggered backward. When comprehension sank in, he guffawed and whirled on Julian. "You knew!" he accused.

"You bet your butt I knew," she said as guests swarmed him. She stepped back to make room and found herself next to her mother. They smiled together.

Gale said, "Good job keeping him away long enough." The older woman waved a hand toward the formal dining room and Julian caught sight of a spread of food and desserts as well as a separate table with gifts and cards. Julian bit her lip. Gale patted her arm. "I got the book you suggested and signed the card from both of us. Don't fret."

"I should have gotten him something separate."

Gale rolled her eyes. "Stop worrying. Just enjoy the party."

Julian tried valiantly. Drake's family made sure to speak to everyone, even Amerigo from his chaise lounge in the corner with his immobilized leg on the chair. He beckoned Julian over while Gale chatted with Mary. When Julian sat next to him, he put an arm around her shoulder and gave her a brotherly hug. "Thanks for helping out. We owe you even more now."

She squirmed. "You guys don't owe me anything."

He wrapped his arm around her neck gently and tilted her toward him to plant a peck on her cheek. "We owe you everything," he said.

What was with men she saw today? She hadn't even been kissed at all in so long she could scarcely remember, but now twice in one day? Granted, neither one felt lewd or uncomfortable or even sexual, but the thought of two men kissing her in one day caused her to chuckle. Amerigo loosened his hug and patted her shoulder. "I know you don't want to hear it again, but I don't care. Thank you."

Tears sprung to her eyes, her thoughts jumping to Arnold Woodley's face in the coffee shop. The contrast of memories of their relationship and the new caring friendships she had with Drake's family made her emotional. Amerigo looked horrified. "I'm sorry. Was that too forward? My dad's Italian. We kiss everyone on the cheek, but I should have asked first."

Julian gave a husky laugh, battling her watery eyes. "You're fine. I'm not offended."

Amerigo looked down his nose at her with a knowing glint in his eye. "Drake said something stupid, didn't he? He's like a bull in a China shop sometimes."

She shook her head. "No. He was perfect, actually. You guys all are. You're so sweet and considerate and nice to each other."

"Whoa there, Nelly!" he said. "I'm glad you have a high esteem of us, but we can be serious jerks." He pointed at Mary. "That one has to have her way, and she's not above manipulation to get it." He pointed at Anthony. "That one's still old school. He's the man of the house and what he says goes, regardless. He means well, but it gets old." He pointed at himself. "Spoiled." Then he pointed to Drake. "That one. I could spend all night. Over-protective, over-responsible, and over-bearing sometimes." Amerigo sighed. "But we all mean well." Then he chuckled. "Except me, maybe. I'm spoiled, remember."

Julian patted his arm. "There's more to you than you give yourself credit for." She folded her hands in her lap and stared at them. "What's going on with me has nothing to do with any of your family. I'm fine. Really."

She saw the disbelief written on his face, but he chose not to push the issue, for which Julian was grateful. Instead, he waved a hand to an older couple in the corner and beckoned them over. When Julian would have rose, Amerigo captured her wrist in a loose hold. "What are you doing? I want to introduce you to some people. Drake's the guest of honor, so he needs to mingle."

Julian sat back down as the couple approached and sat together on an ottoman the man pulled over. Amerigo shook the man's hand and gave the woman a one-armed hug. "Ted, Cecilia, meet Julian."

They shook hands. The woman gasped with a smile. "Oh! You're the one who saved the boys. We're friends with Anthony. These boys are like part of our family."

The couple was just the beginning. Amerigo beckoned over family friend after family friend to introduce Julian, including Drake's best friend, Martin, and Martin's wife, Jill. After introductions, they took the spot on the ottoman another couple had just occupied.

Jill smiled brightly as she shook Julian's hand. "Great to finally meet you. Drake has very nice things to say about you."

Martin nodded with a mischievous grin. "That was quite the feat, pulling these two degenerates from the wreck."

"I just did what I think most people would do," Julian said for what felt like the hundredth time.

Amerigo fake-punched her shoulder. "She's too modest."

Mary interrupted their conversation by bringing out a large sheet cake with flowery writing. After she cut the cake, and everyone had a piece, Julian sat next to her mother on the couch and lied, "I'm really tired. Mom. Do you mind taking me home?"

Overhearing, Mary said, "Oh no, dear. Did you overdo it today?"

Pushing aside her guilt at the fib, Julian nodded. "I hate to leave early, but I think I better get some rest." Guilt gnawed worse when she saw her mother's disappointed expression.

"Sure, honey. We can go."

Mary offered, "If you want to let Julian take your car, I'll make sure you get home."

"Perfect," Gale replied and disappeared to get her keys from her purse in one of the guest bedrooms.

Julian swallowed hard. "Thanks, Mary."

"No problem, dear. You are a little peaked."

She had no doubt. Despite the festivities, the scene at the coffee shop had replayed in her mind all evening though she tried to convince herself it had truly just been a coincidence.

Gale returned with the keys. "Are you okay to drive yourself home?"

"Oh, yeah. Just tired. I'll go to bed when I get home, but I can make the drive."

She made the rounds telling the Salvatores goodbye, stopping for a moment with Drake in the hall. "I'm sorry to leave early," she said.

He put a hand on her arm. "Please stay. I'll drive you home in a bit. Want to lie down in a guest room?"

She stifled a sigh. "Thanks, but I just want to go home and be in my own bed. It's not that late, and I'm fine to drive. I don't want you rushed. It's a great party."

"All right, but be careful. Text me when you're home, okay?"

Julian grinned, thinking of Amerigo's assessment of Drake. She agreed, "Sure thing," and hustled out the door.

CHAPTER FIVE

Drake watched her leave with trepidation. Martin handed him a bottle of beer and nodded his head toward the door. "You scare her off?" his friend asked.

"Thanks for the vote of confidence, Master Gunny." They chuckled together. Drake shook his head. "We ran into her ex-husband at the coffee shop before we came here, and she got really spooked."

Martin scowled. "How spooked?"

"It wasn't good." Drake took a long drink from the bottle then continued, "He tried to grab her arm when she went to leave."

"With you right there?"

Drake nodded.

"That's not a good sign."

"No."

Martin's wife, Jill, joined the men. She beamed at Drake and playfully punched his shoulder. Martin had often told Drake he didn't deserve this gorgeous woman—curvy with light brown skin and striking topaz eyes. She winked one of those gorgeous topaz eyes at Drake. "Gonna be lazy now that you're done with the Marines?"

"Yes, ma'am," he replied with a grin.

She made a clucking sound. "Yeah, right." She looped a hand in the crook of Martin's arm and asked, "Tell me about your lady friend. She's sweet."

Drake smiled. Sweet, yes, but also sharp, funny, and beautiful. "Yeah. She is."

Martin said, "Pretty sure she's too good for him."

Jill rolled her eyes. "Wow."

"Besides," he continued, "she's not his type."

Drake's eyebrows shot up. "Not my type?"

Jill agreed, "You've got a point."

"Wait," Drake said. "I've got a type?"

The couple exchanged a look. Drake placed his beer bottle on a nearby end table and crossed his arms over his chest as he waited. Martin shrugged. "Tall, leggy girls."

"Airheads," Jill added.

Drake's mouth fell open. "Don't hold back, folks."

Jill giggled. "Sorry. It's just nice to see you with someone with substance for once."

"We're not… together," he said slowly.

"Then you're dumber than you look," Martin accused with a grin.

"Remember the part where this is my retirement party? I'm the guest of honor. You should be nice to me."

Jill chortled. "We're helping you. That's how we're being nice."

They erupted into laughter together.

By the end of the evening, Drake had laughed till his jaws ached. As the last of the guests made their way to the door, he noticed Gale still sitting on the couch next to Amerigo, who looked a tad wan. They chatted amicably until Gale noticed Drake watching. She waved him over. When he joined them, she instructed, "You should help your brother to his room. I think he overdid it."

"Sheesh," Amerigo blurted. "You and Mom are like clones." But a smile softened his words, and Gale laughed.

"I'll take that as a compliment."

Drake obeyed Gale's order and settled Amerigo back in his room. Amerigo narrowed his eyes at his brother. "What was wrong with Julian tonight? She said you didn't do anything, but something must have happened."

"And you assumed I did something?" Drake asked.

"You just seem to run off the nice ones."

"We're not…" He broke off with a frustrated noise. "Don't worry about it."

"Drake, stop treating me like a kid. I'm a grown man—"

"Who lives with his parents and can't hold down a job."

Amerigo's face reddened in annoyance. "Here we go."

"I'm just saying, if you want to be treated like a man—"

"Stop." Amerigo held up a palm. "Enough. I have parents. You are my brother." He ran the same hand through his disheveled hair. "Can't you at least treat me like a brother instead of a kid?"

Drake mulled over Amerigo's words. The age difference had always created a gap between them. Then Drake had joined the Marines and been gone for extended periods of time. With Drake gone, their parents had tried to press his younger brother into the family business, but it chaffed him. Drake met Amerigo's eyes and saw the plea there. He cleared his throat. "I didn't do anything to her. We saw her ex-husband, and he acted like a jerk to her."

Amerigo's face hardened. "Did you knock some manners into him?"

Drake grinned. "No, but I wanted to."

"Oh." Amerigo dragged the syllable out. "You like her." He smirked. "I knew it."

"We're done here." Drake spun on his heel and left with Amerigo's laughter following behind him.

In the great room, Mary, Gale, and Anthony bustled around cleaning up. Not one to stand on formalities, even for a retirement party, Mary had used as many disposable items as possible so picking up didn't take long. Drake helped. When they finished with the last of the trash and washing platters, Mary wiped her hands on a dish towel. "Ready to go, Gale?"

"Sure."

Drake frowned. "It's kinda late. Why don't you let me drive Gale home, Mom?" He looked at Julian's mom. "Is that okay with you?"

"Sure," she repeated and disappeared to gather her purse and jacket.

Once on the road with Gale, Drake said, "Tell me about Arnold Woodley."

With a shocked expression, Gale asked, "Julian told you about Arnold?"

"He was at the coffee shop."

Gale gasped. "What? What was he doing there?" Drake relayed the encounter for her, and her fingers curled into fists. She turned in her seat to face Drake. "I'm so glad you were there."

"Was he abusive?" Drake asked bluntly.

The older woman stared ahead again, the silence between them heavy until she said, "Yes."

Drake felt his stomach knot as red hot fury rose in him. He muttered a string of obscenities to make his fellow Marines proud and cut his eyes back at Gale. "How bad was it?"

"Most of it was verbal and emotional. They were only married about three years before she finally left him."

Most of it. Drake's hands gripped the steering wheel like a

vise at the idea of someone putting their hands on any woman, much less someone he cared about. "I know it's none of my business, but—"

"It's okay. I know you care about my daughter." Gale unclenched her fists to pick at imaginary lint on her slacks. She took a deep breath. "I knew that guy was bad news, but Julian didn't believe me. He could be so charming. Julian's father hadn't been dead very long when she met Arnold. She was vulnerable and grieving. He swooped in and pretended to be this caring guy." Gale snorted. "If my husband had still been alive, it wouldn't have happened. I truly believe she wouldn't have married him, but she did. The honeymoon was over before they even got home from the honeymoon. He was already criticizing everything she did." She shook her head. "It didn't take long before he accused her of infidelity and called her all kinds of names. I told her that he was projecting his own guilt on her, but she said he was sick and needed help."

Drake clenched his jaw. "I bet he even went to counseling."

"Oh, yeah. But it was a scam. He didn't think he was doing anything wrong."

"What happened to make her leave?"

"It was a gradual thing. I convinced her to come to church with me since she'd gotten out of the habit, and she ended up joining. Then she showed up to a ladies Bible study with a bruise on her face. I almost had a heart attack." Gale trembled with rage. "And I knew. I just knew he'd hit her." She swiped at her eyes. "Thankfully, I wasn't the only one who'd noticed what was happening, and the entire group practically staged an intervention." Gale chuckled wryly. "All three of us." Her amusement fled. "When she left him, they had a huge confrontation. He actually balled his fist and punched her."

Sick to his stomach, Drake asked, "Was someone there with her?"

Gale nodded. "There was a church member named Randall.

We didn't know much about him at the time. He was new to our church, but he caught wind of what was happening and drove over."

"Please tell me he beat the crap out of Arnold Woodley."

A satisfied smile spread over Gale's lips. "I was outside when Randall pulled up. Julian had made me promise to wait in the car while she grabbed a couple of things. I heard the yelling and was running for the door when Randall stopped me to go first. Arnold was on the floor screaming for help. Julian had a baseball bat."

"A baseball bat?"

"Arnold played baseball with a local team and had left the bat next to the door. It was the first thing she saw when she picked herself up." Gale smirked. "He was a mess by the time we got in there, crying for his momma." Tears filled her eyes. "I knew I had my Julian back then."

Drake tried to imagine the graceful, gentle woman he knew standing over a bloodied man with a baseball bat. He had trouble reconciling the images, but he had no doubt she could be fierce. She had already proved to be deceptively tough.

He pulled into Gale's driveway and got out with her, walking with her to the door of her small condo. At the door, she unlocked her door then turned to Drake. "I know Julian says you don't owe her anything, but she's my baby, and I'm not ashamed to call in a favor from you for her."

He shook his head. "Not necessary. I'm already on it."

Gale hugged him, patting his back. "I knew you were a good boy."

Drake rolled his eyes over her shoulder but smiled. Back in the rental car, he looked at the time. He'd long since gotten Julian's text he'd requested when she got home, but he doubted she was sleeping. His car wound up in Julian's driveway almost of its own volition. He sat motionless for a moment. What could he say to her? Still, he wanted to see her.

He rang the doorbell and heard her shuffling to the door. She couldn't have been asleep to get to the door so quickly. After a moment, he heard her slip the chain off and unlock the deadbolt. The door swung open, and Julian stood before him in a pair of ratty sweatpants, and worn t-shirt, and thick socks. Her hair hung loose around her shoulders. She frowned. "It's nice of you to stop by, but I'm okay."

"Can we argue about that inside?" he asked. "It's cold out here."

* * *

Julian stepped back to allow Drake to come inside. She closed the door after him, watching as he strode into her living room and sat on the couch. If he had been anyone else, she would have told him to go home and mind his own business. Instead, she bolted the door and did the chain before following him. "Want some coffee or something? I have some sweet tea," she offered.

"Tea sounds good," he replied with a bright smile, and Julian's stomach flip-flopped.

Frustrated with herself for being weak, she made two glasses of iced tea and sat on the other end of the couch. She handed him the tea and curled her feet beneath her. "Did you enjoy your party? Your friends are really nice. I liked Martin and Jill."

Drake took a drink then placed his glass on the coffee table. "I had a great time. Thank you for helping keep it a surprise." He gave her an encouraging smile, and her heart sank.

"How did my mom get home?"

"I drove her."

She gritted her teeth. "Mom told you about Arnold."

His smile faded. "Yeah."

Julian swallowed hard. "Even the baseball bat?" He nodded.

"Great," she bit out. She wrapped her arms around her knees. "I really don't like people knowing about it."

"You didn't do anything wrong, Julian."

"I was so stupid."

"What he did was not your fault."

"I'd like to think that now I'd see someone like him coming a mile away, but back then, I just…" Her voice trailed off, and she took a deep breath before putting her cheek on her knees. "I know you're right. It's just hard when it happens to you. I would tell anyone I know exactly what you're saying to me were it happening to them."

Drake stood and resettled next to her. "I know." She stared at him as he put a hand on one of her sock-clad feet. He gave a half shrug. "I'm not even sure why I came over. I know you're all right. Guess I just wanted to see it for myself."

Julian allowed herself a half smile. "You know, you might be one of the good ones, Drake Salvatore."

He chortled. "I don't know about that."

She looked at the clock and heard herself say, "I know it's a little late, but we could watch a movie or something if you want."

Drake looked at her for a long moment. "Go on a real date with me, Julian."

"I—"

"A real date, but no pressure."

She blinked at the earnest expression on his face. "I dunno…"

He grinned. "You made a lunch date with a strange British man, but I can't take you on a dinner date? I've slept in the same room with you overnight."

Julian felt her face burning but giggled. "It's more complicated with you and me."

"Why?"

"Because our families are friends now. What if we go on a

date and things go really badly?"

"Then we won't make that mistake again."

She bit her lip. "You promise if it doesn't go well, we stay friends and no hard feelings?"

"Absolutely," Drake said.

"Okay. A real date." Julian folded her arms around her knees again. "I'm not canceling lunch with Rob, though."

"Fair enough," Drake replied then rose. "On that note, I think I'll say goodnight."

Julian rose with him and tried to keep the disappointment out of her voice. "Oh. Okay."

Drake tucked a stray lock of hair over her ear, the corner of his mouth twisted in amusement. "I have plans in the morning or I'd stay and watch a movie." He made his way to the door, Julian on his heels. He undid the chain and deadbolt before facing her. "Thanks again for tonight, Jules."

She pretended not to notice he'd used the nickname, but it warmed her. "I'm glad your party was a success." She smiled up at him, reminded of how tall and broad he really was. And attractive.

"Call me if you need me. Day or night," he told her.

Julian nodded as she looked at his chest.

Drake placed a finger under her chin to tilt her face upward. "I mean it. Weird phone call, dog barking when it shouldn't, anything. I don't actually live all that far from here."

Meeting his eyes, she said, "All right."

He looked indecisive for only a moment before he pulled her into his embrace. Julian sighed against him, grateful for his strength and warmth as she wound her arms around his shoulders. "I'll call you to set up a time," he said in her hair.

She nodded against him then stepped back with a smile. "Good." Then she gave him a dose of his own medicine. "Text me when you get home."

"Yes, ma'am," he replied with a smirk, then he was gone.

CHAPTER SIX

Julian smiled across the table at Rob as he scanned the brunch restaurant's menu. Accepting his invitation to lunch had been unusual for her, but his charm had worn her down. His emails had made her laugh, and she had found it difficult to resist someone who flattered her about her writing. She glanced at her own menu. When the waitress arrived, she ordered a skillet dish loaded with potatoes and cheese, and Rob raised his eyebrows with a warm smile. "That sounds delicious."

"It's fantastic."

He ordered a sandwich and a salad as Julian looked around the small café and grinned. "I'm so glad you suggested this restaurant. It's one of my favorites," she told Rob once the waitress left.

"Ah! One point in my favor already," he said, beaming.

Julian laughed. "What is a charming Brit like yourself doing in a boring place like this?" she asked with a wave of her hand.

He replied, "Work, but this place isn't boring. I like it here. People are friendly."

Julian narrowed her eyes. "Work? Care to elaborate?"

Rob grinned. "I work for Smithsburg Industries."

"Doing?"

"I work in sales."

Julian tilted her head. "Feel free to narrow that down even further."

He chuckled. "You should work for MI-5. I'm the Assistant Vice President of Marketing for this region."

"Oh." Julian sat back. "Wow. That's impressive. Why did you hem and haw about that?"

He shrugged with a grin. "It sounds dull, not sexy like being a writer."

"Oh no," she countered. "Trust me. I don't write full time. I have a boring day job and write on the side. Your job sounds important and impressive."

Rob gave her a wink. "Whatever you do for a 'day job,' you're really a writer. I read your book."

She grimaced. "Okay. You can be honest with me. Give it to me straight." She made a show of closing her eyes as she waited.

Rob chortled before telling her, "It's good. I can see why my mother likes your work."

Julian slowly opened her eyes. "Really?"

"Yeah. You should consider trying to sell the movie rights. It'd make a great romantic comedy."

She rolled her eyes with amusement. "Oh, now I know you're just trying to flatter me."

They laughed together. "I am trying to flatter you, but you deserve the praise."

Julian smiled. "That's a nice thing to say."

The waitress returned with their food. After she set the plates down, she leaned down to whisper, "Are you the woman I saw on the news?" Julian gave Rob an apologetic look and sighed.

"I am, but—"

The woman slid into the booth next to Julian, cutting her off to say, "That was the bravest thing I've ever seen. And the guy who carried you, he's hot!"

Julian balked despite Rob's amused expression. "I appreciate that, but I'm actually on a date… with someone who's not the guy from the accident." She motioned to Rob. The waitress turned scarlet and rose to her feet.

"Oh! I'm so sorry. That was so rude of me."

To Julian's relief, Rob laughed it away. "No harm done." He smiled again. She couldn't help but think how likeable the man was. The word rang through her head again. Charming. She wished she was as charming.

"Thank you for not being mad." The waitress scurried away, horrified.

Julian giggled at Rob. "I can handle that kind of thing about my book, but the attention from the news is just weird," she admitted. She gave Rob an assessing glance and told him, "She missed how good-looking you are. That's a shame."

Rob's laugh included a large, bright smile of perfect white teeth and the dimple again.

After lunch, Rob suggested her normal coffee shop, but Julian shook her head. "I'd love coffee but not there."

"Is something wrong with the coffee there?"

"No, I love their coffee. I just don't want to go in the building right now." Her chest tightened thinking of seeing Arnold there.

He tilted his head. "Why don't I go get us coffee, and then we can go somewhere else to drink it? Is there a park around here? It's chilly, but I'm game for a walk if you are."

"After that carb-heavy lunch, a walk sounds good," she replied, brightening. "There's actually some walking trails at the park across the street from here."

"Perfect!"

He quickly returned with coffee, and they drove their separate cars to the park. Once there, they found a short trail and started walking. Julian was grateful for her decision to wear a pair of flat boots and a thermal shirt under her sweater. As Thanksgiving approached, South Carolina had turned unusually cold this year. She tightened her scarf around her neck and kept Rob's leisurely pace.

"So tell me, Julian…"

"Yes?"

"The man I saw you with at the coffee shop, the one you rescued—is he competition for me?"

Julian stopped for a moment to look at Rob. "I'm not a prize that anyone should 'compete' for."

He met her eyes with a regretful look. "That's not how I meant it." They resumed their walk, and Julian hid the bottom of her face in her knit scarf as she thought how to respond. With a friendly smile, Rob told her, "Your silence answers that question."

She cringed. "I'm not sure what to say. He asked me on a date, and I agreed to it."

"That's what you were doing with him last night? You were on a date with him?"

Julian shook her head. "Not really. He just retired from the Marines, and his family threw him a surprise party. I was supposed to just keep him away from their house for a little while. He asked me on a date after the party."

Rob nodded. "I see." She could see the wheels turning in his head.

"Does that bother you? I mean, I've never been in a position in which two men I really find attractive asked me out at the same time." She had no idea how to handle the situation.

He shook his head in disbelief with a grin. "You want me to believe you've never been asked out by more than one man at a time?"

She grinned back at him. "Not that I considered saying yes to. I'm picky."

He looked almost smug as he replied, "I see."

The hair on the back of Julian's neck stood on end as if someone watched her. She glanced around but saw no one. Rob noticed the gesture and looked around as well. "What's wrong?" he asked, sipping his coffee.

She shook her head but continued to scan the trees around them. "I just had one of those weird feelings. It's nothing."

"C'mon. You look half frozen. We should probably get back."

Julian smiled at him and allowed Rob to take her free hand. He led her back to where their cars were parked. He stood before her with a look of concentration. "May I be honest with you?"

"Of course."

"Well, I saw you for a couple of minutes at the coffee shop before I spoke last night." He paused. "If you think there might be something with that fellow, I think you should explore it. I'd like to continue being friends, but perhaps we should leave it there until you know how you feel about him."

Julian gaped at Rob but smiled. "You have to be one of the most charming, considerate people I've ever met. Do you mean it when you say you want to stay friends?"

"Absolutely. I enjoy your company." His honest smile put her at ease.

"Well, all right. As long as you stay my friend."

He hugged her as they said goodbye and looked down at her with an open expression. "I do truly want to be friends, Julian."

"I'd like that too."

Once home, Julian removed her coat, gloves, and scarf. She plunked herself down in front of her laptop to check her email and work on some writing. She already had an email from Rob thanking her for meeting him for lunch. She really did like him.

Julian moved to the next email. She didn't recognize the address and almost moved it to her spam folder, but the subject line read, "How was the park today?" With nothing in the body of the email, Julian debated the wisdom of opening the attachment. Curiosity won, and she clicked on the file. A grainy cell phone video played of her walking with Rob in the park, both holding their coffee and Rob holding her free hand.

Her heart raced. She looked up the phone number to the local police, deeming this not worthy of an emergency 911 call, and asked how to file a report. She spoke to an officer who told her to come to the station. Julian grabbed her coat, gloves, and scarf again.

With trembling hands, she dialed Drake's number as she started the car. He answered on the first ring, and she blurted, "I need your email address."

"I'll text it to you. What's wrong?"

"Someone took a video of me at the park with Rob."

"When?"

"Just now. I just got home and already had the email. I'm on my way to the police station to file a report."

"I'll meet you at the station."

"No, you don't have to—"

"It's fine. I'm already out. I'll see you in five." The line went dead.

Drake waited in the parking lot as she pulled in. It eased her conscience a little to see him already there. He hadn't lied about being on this side of town. She parked next to his rental car and opened her door. He rounded her car before she could get out.

"You all right?" She nodded mutely. "Show me the video," Drake said.

Julian's hands still shook as she pulled out her smartphone, yanked off her gloves, and opened her email. She clicked on the video, and they watched it play.

Drake scowled. "Let's go see what the police have to say."

After Julian explained the situation to Detective Reynolds, an older, stocky man with silver hair and sharp hazel eyes, she told him about the phone calls as well. The detective listened carefully, asking questions and making notes. When they finished, he gave her his card and told her to call if anything else happened or if she remembered anything else. Julian took the card, and Drake asked for one of his own. As they stood to leave, the officer stopped them. "Ms. Fursey, it was a brave thing you did helping this man and his brother. We'll do everything we can to find out who's bothering you."

Julian gave him a grateful, if thin, smile. "Thank you."

Drake followed her home and walked with her to the door. She shook her head when he made to follow her inside.

"Really, I'm okay. You don't need to come in."

"You realize your mantra is 'I'm okay?'" Drake said and tilted his head to assess her. "Does it hurt to just let someone be present for you? People… I want to help."

Julian blinked. Her mother accused her of shutting people out instead of accepting aid. Maybe she did. But she didn't want to shut Drake out as he stood patiently waiting for her to make up her mind.

"I guess it doesn't hurt." She opened the door, and they stopped in the foyer. Julian removed her coat, scarf, and gloves, placing them on the bench by the door and ignoring the coat rack. She heard something in the living room and tiptoed down the hall as Drake placed his coat on the coat hanger. She rounded the corner and shrieked in shock. Another shriek matched her own, and Drake stood in front of her before she could digest what she saw. Then she expelled a noisy breath. "Hannah!"

Having almost fallen off the couch in surprise, Hannah struggled to compose herself. "I'm sorry. I didn't mean to scare you. We were supposed to get together this afternoon, remember? I thought I'd wait for you inside." She scrutinized Julian. "You're white as a sheet. You okay?"

Julian nodded. "I'm okay." She cringed and looked at Drake, who gave her an "I told you so" face. "I guess I do say that a lot."

Hannah grinned at seeing Drake. "We haven't met." She held out her hand. "I'm Hannah Cameron."

He shook her hand and said, "Drake Salvatore."

Julian offered, "You guys want something to drink? I can make some tea or coffee?"

Drake replied, "No, thanks. I just wanted to walk you in the house. I've got some more errands to run. Call me if—" Julian gave Drake a warning look. "Call me if you need me for anything."

Julian nodded. "Thanks again, Drake."

"Nice to meet you, Hannah," he said and left them alone.

Hannah grabbed Julian's hand and dragged her to the couch. "Spill."

"Spill what?" Julian asked, playing dumb to buy time.

Her friend glared at her. "You had a date with Rob but ended up hanging out with Drake? Spill!"

Julian rolled her eyes. She told Hannah about her lunch with Rob. "And we decided to just stay friends. He's so likable and charming. It's hard not to want to hang around him."

"Charming, huh?"

"If you met him, you'd see what I mean."

Her friend folded her arms. "Okay, so make that happen. I'm seriously curious."

"What do you mean?"

"I mean have a dinner party for a couple of friends and invite him."

Julian tilted her head at the idea. "Maybe."

"Woman, work it out. Now, stop holding out on me, and tell me how you ended up with Drake and why he had to walk you in the house."

Julian silently cursed Hannah's observant nature. "Oh, he's just old-fashioned."

"But you never explained how you ended up with him after your date with Rob."

"He was on this side of town running errands."

"Go on."

"You know, I think the dinner party thing should be really small. Just you and some coworkers and Rob. Not my mom."

Hannah's smile faded as she mulled over Julian's words. "You're probably right. I love Gale, but sometimes she doesn't have a filter."

"So next Friday night?"

"I'll check my schedule, but I think I'm free."

"I'll make something simple. It'll be fun."

Julian congratulated herself on successfully diverting Hannah, who pulled a book out of her purse. "Here. I bought this for you." The she smiled wickedly. "I know how much you enjoyed her other book."

They laughed as Hannah gave her a romance novel by the same author that had horrified her and enthralled Drake. "You're bad. I probably won't ever read that."

Hannah shook her head. "Don't read it if you don't want to, but it's yours now." She tossed it on the coffee table and looked at a text on her phone. "Shoot. It's work. Last minute paperwork on a divorce. This one's ugly." She rose. "Sorry, Jules. Rain check on this afternoon?"

"Of course."

As she hustled to the door, Hannah called, "Don't think you got off so easy. I'll find out later what happened with Drake today."

Julian groaned.

* * *

Flowers, plants, and balloons awaited Julian at her cubicle when she returned to work. Coworkers stood and applauded her as she made her way through the department, her face on fire. She thanked them all and then hunkered down to get caught up. After an hour, Julian's manager stopped by her desk and checked on her. "We're glad you're back, Julian, but don't overdo it. I farmed out some of your work so nothing's getting too far behind. Don't worry." The older woman gave Julian a kind smile and patted her shoulder.

Julian had not anticipated how tired she would feel by lunchtime. She closed her eyes and leaned back in her chair. When she sat forward again, the coworker in front of her had turned around to face her. "You look tired."

Julian laughed. "That's a nice way of saying, 'You look awful.'"

The younger woman smiled at her. "You don't look awful. You look tired."

"Well, it's time for me to leave anyway. I'm going home to take a nap," Julian told her. She collected her coat and purse and headed home, the drive something of a blur. Her stomach growled as she drove, and she scowled. Her phone dinged with a text as she pulled into her driveway. Drake.

Feel like lunch? I can pick you up from work if you're interested. We can discuss plans for our date.

Her stomach growled again. Maybe she could go to lunch before her nap.

Pick me up at home, she wrote back.

She waited inside while playing with her phone until she heard a knock on the door. Julian hurried to meet Drake, not even letting him in the house. "I'm so hungry," she muttered and closed the door behind her. She turned and stopped short when she saw the shiny black truck in her driveway.

"Got tired of the rental," Drake said sheepishly.

Julian oohed and aahed over the vehicle as she circled the large truck, obviously meant to be a work vehicle. "Nice," she said with a smile.

Drake surprised her by looking pleased with her assessment. "I thought it would be more useful for the vineyard than an SUV." He opened the passenger side door for her, and she climbed in. It had the new car smell she had never experienced, having only ever bought her cars used. The dealerships tried to replicate the smell, but nothing matched the real thing.

"This is new-new," she said as he slid behind the wheel.

"Yeah, well, I'm gonna need it for years," he explained and turned the key. "So where to?"

Julian suggested a local deli, and Drake backed out of her driveway. She tried not to be obvious as she stared at him, but he looked ruggedly handsome in his work boots, jeans, worn t-shirt, and flannel jacket. He raised an eyebrow at her, and she turned away. To his credit, he chose not to call her on it, but she noticed his smirk as he drove.

The drive to the deli was less than ten minutes, and was spent in comfortable silence. They ordered at the counter, both opting for the deli's signature roast beef sandwich piled high with a creamy pink sauce and potato chips, then found a table near the window. Drake smiled at her as he asked, "What were you doing home? I thought you went back to work today."

"I did, but the doctor only released me to half days."

"How was your half day?"

"Okay. Everyone embarrassed me, but they meant well."

Drake chuckled. The girl behind the counter called their order number, Drake having refused once again to let Julian pay, and Julian moved to go get the food. "I got it," Drake said with a hand on her arm. "You look tired."

Julian sighed as he left the table. Tired. She dug in her purse for her plastic pill container and fished out two tablets for the headache forming.

When Drake returned, he handed her one of the baskets and said, "Why the long face?"

"Tired is code for awful."

He laughed. "I'm not that diplomatic. If you looked awful, I'd just say it." He gave her a once over. "Actually, I like your prim business outfit. You look like a sexy librarian."

Julian's stomach did the little flip-flop she had started to expect around Drake as she glanced down at her outfit. Nothing special about her black skirt and flats or the soft pink sweater she wore. She had twisted her hair back in a clip to keep it out of her face as she entered invoices.

With a shrug, she pretended not to be affected by his flirting. "Well, when you're as sexy as I am, you make everything look good." She took a huge bite of her sandwich and made a serious face.

He burst into laughter. "Yes, that is definitely sexy," he chortled as she struggled to chew the too large bite while fighting her own giggles.

"Mmph," she grumbled around the food.

"Just spit it out," he teased and handed her a napkin.

She held up a hand shaking her head. After a few more seconds of struggling, she finally finished the bite and giggled again, her eyes watering as she did so. "That went horribly awry," she said. She scrubbed a hand over her face. "I think I'm so tired I'm punchy."

"Maybe this isn't the best time to plan our date," he said with a grin.

She wiped her hands on a napkin and said, "Did you really take me to lunch to discuss our 'date?'"

Drake told her, "I was already out and about getting supplies for the vineyard and thought you might like to go to lunch."

"I see," she said and took another, reasonably-sized, bite of her sandwich and chewed thoughtfully.

"How about Saturday night?"

"I'm having some friends over for dinner Friday night. Would you like to come to that?" she offered.

Drake narrowed his eyes at her. "That's not a date."

"It can be."

"Not for us. I want our first official date to be just you and me."

Julian smiled softly. "Okay. You're still invited Friday night, though."

"I already have plans, but thank you." At her curious expression, he said, "Not another date. I promised to help one of Pop's friends clear out his garage, and Friday night was the only night that would work. What about Saturday night?"

"Sure. That's good. Anything special in mind?"

"Dinner and a movie?"

She shrugged. "Okay."

He grinned. "I know. Not very exciting, but I remembered you saying you wanted to see the new comic book movie, and it opens this weekend."

Julian knew she grinned like an idiot, but she couldn't stop. "I've been waiting forever to see it."

"Should we go opening night instead?" he asked.

"No. Saturday's good. I can wait 'til Saturday."

They finished lunch and returned to Drake's truck. With a full belly and a smile on her face, Julian closed her eyes as the heater warmed the cabin. "I like your new truck," she heard herself slur.

She dozed on the way home, comfortable and exhausted. When the truck stopped, she blinked, battling to open her eyes. Drake reached down by her leg and messed with her purse, but she couldn't bring herself to care. He disappeared for a moment, cold air slipping in the truck when he opened his door. Julian tried to open her eyes again, but she was so tired.

What was wrong with her? She had just taken a couple of over-the-counter pain killers at lunch. Why was she so dopey?

Her door opened, and Drake reached inside to unfasten her seatbelt. He slid his arms under her and lifted her from the seat. She wanted to protest, but she didn't want to have to open her eyes.

Drake kicked the truck door closed. "What did you take at the restaurant, Jules?" he asked.

"Just some Tylenol," she murmured.

"Are you sure?"

"I thought so."

He carried her into the house and to her bedroom where he placed her on her bed and pulled off her shoes. She hadn't made it that morning in her rush to get to work, and he easily pulled the covers over her. "I'm gonna check your purse," he said.

"Whatever," she said into her pillow, rolling onto her side and tucking her hands beneath her cheek.

She heard a bottle rattling, and Drake said, "I don't think this is Tylenol. You have it in an unmarked bottle. I think this is some of your prescription stuff."

Julian fought to open her eyes with a frown. "No. I'm out of that." He held the pink plastic container in front of her and opened it. Sure enough, she saw the small tablets from her prescription. She had thrown some in her purse when she first came home from the hospital and had forgotten them. "Crap," she sighed. "I thought it was the Tylenol." She tucked her hands beneath her cheek again. "I hate how those make me feel. Flush them or something, will ya?"

Drake disappeared again, and she heard him rifling through her bathroom. Despite her drugged state, she had a flash of realization. He thought she was abusing her prescription drugs. Why that struck her as funny, she couldn't say, but she smiled. The pills in her purse had to be all she had left. She'd never refilled the prescription and most of them went the first week.

He returned and sat on the edge of the bed. "I took care of those. I didn't see any others."

"Nope. They're gone. I'm not addicted. I forgot I had those in my purse."

She could feel his eyes on her even though her own were closed. "Sorry," he said. "Someone I…" His voice trailed off. "Nevermind. Get some sleep. I'm taking your spare key to lock your deadbolt."

"Okay," she said.

She wondered if he thought she wouldn't remember the conversation later when he brushed her hair from her forehead and told her, "I'm sorry for all of this. It's my fault. If I'd just stopped to get some sleep instead of letting Amerigo drive…"

Julian fought the fuzziness to say, "It's not your fault, Drake. Life just happens. Don't own something you didn't cause." Then she drifted back to sleep.

* * *

Drake pulled up to his parents' house still chewing on what Julian had said. Life just happens. Seeing her pale face and the dark circles under her eyes had bothered him. He felt responsible. He always felt responsible. Her words came back to him again. Life just happens. It seemed so fatalistic, but maybe she had a point. A dozen different variables could have changed what happened the day of the wreck, but none of them did, and because of it, he had the fortune to meet Julian Fursey.

He found Amerigo sleeping in the chaise lounge of the main room with the television tuned to a ridiculous reality show. Drake rolled his eyes and used the remote to turn it off. Amerigo stirred and muttered, "I was watching that."

"Boy, you were watching the back of your eyelids."

Amerigo smiled and opened his eyes. "How's Julian doing?"

"You mean the other invalid? Sleeping like you."

Drake sat on the couch next to Amerigo and propped his feet up on the ottoman. "Where's Mom and Pop?"

"They're overseeing the pressing of the grapes today." When Drake started to rise, Amerigo added, "They said to tell you they don't need you today." He grinned and added, "I think Mom's exact words were, 'Let him be retired for a couple of minutes before we work him like a slave.'"

Drake chuckled. "How are you feeling today?"

Amerigo shrugged. "My leg's kinda swollen again, and the brace itches." He looked thoughtful for a moment and asked, "How do you think Mom and Pop would react if I found a normal job but tried to do some local theater here? Maybe took some acting classes? Really see if it's worth pursuing?"

Drake chose his words carefully. "I think they'd be proud of you for putting in the effort to learn the craft. No one doubts you have the ability if you want to do it. I bet they'd even help pay for classes."

Amerigo surprised Drake by shaking his head. "No. I don't want them to pay for that. They already let me stay here rent free. It's not fair to them. I should be pulling my weight."

"I'm glad to hear you say that, brat." He ruffled Amerigo's hair.

Amerigo grimaced and pushed his hand away, hiding a smile. He sobered as he asked, "You find out why Julian's ex-husband had her so spooked the other night?"

Drake said, "Let's just say I'd like to break his arms." Amerigo's eyes widened as Drake gave him an abridged version of what Gale had told him.

"What kind of a coward hits a woman?"

"Arnold Woodley."

They sat in silence before Amerigo ground out, "So she's got her crazy ex-husband hanging around and some weirdo taping and calling her."

"Yeah. Except I think the calls have stopped since she changed her number."

"How's she holding up?"

"Pretty well considering. She's tough."

"Not hard to look at either."

"Watch it," Drake jokingly warned.

"So when are you two going on a date?"

"Saturday night."

Amerigo narrowed his eyes at Drake. "Didn't you say some other guy is in the picture now?"

"Rob. Rob, the British guy. Rob, the likable British guy. Rob, the guy holding her hand in his likable British paw in that video."

Amerigo snorted at his brother's discomfort. "Oh, c'mon. U.S. Marine trumps British guy."

Drake shook his head and grinned. "I dunno. Even I liked Rob, that's how likable he is." They laughed together.

"Hang tough, Marine," Amerigo said and slapped his shoulder.

* * *

Julian stirred the tomato sauce for her signature pasta dish and thought of Drake taking her on a date the next night. Her stomach got that light, strange feeling again, and she rolled her eyes. She was being silly. She had already spent a lot of time with Drake. No reason to be nervous around him now. Julian pushed those thoughts away and focused on her current mission—the dinner party.

She smiled in anticipation of Hannah and her coworkers meeting Rob. When the doorbell rang, Julian wiped her hands on a dish towel before hurrying to look thought the peephole. She saw Rob holding flowers and a bottle of wine. She smiled and opened the door. "Hi!"

"Hi!" He kissed her cheek and presented her with the flowers and wine. "I'm so glad you took me seriously about being friends and invited me to your dinner party."

"Of course," she replied with a bright smile. Julian ushered him into the house and smelled the bouquet of mixed flowers in autumn colors. "These are beautiful. Let me get them in water." She pulled a vase from the top shelf with Rob's help and put the flowers on the counter.

The doorbell rang again. "Be right back," she told Rob. She used the peephole to see Hannah, who carried a bakery box. When Julian opened the door, Hannah shoved the box at her.

"A cake. I didn't have time to bake something," she said, her face a mask of annoyance. "Please tell me there's wine."

Julian pulled Hannah inside and asked, "Where's Ray?"

"Busy," Hannah said, her eyes flashing a warning. Julian wanted to sigh in relief. Ray sometimes acted as a date for Hannah for events, but Julian had never liked him, suspecting Hannah had a crush on him and that he took advantage of it.

"Well, there is wine. I'll pour you a glass." She led Hannah into the great room, Rob standing in the kitchen opening the bottle of wine. She introduced Hannah to him. They shook hands as Julian's cell phone rang. "Excuse me." She took the phone in the other room and answered.

"I'm so sorry, Julian. I don't think we're gonna make it for dinner."

She recognized her coworker's voice and frowned. "Oh no! Why not? Everything okay?"

The woman sighed. "Yeah. We just all decided to ride together and had to drive out to the boonies to pick up Sally, and we got a flat in her driveway. And wouldn't you know it? Brittany doesn't have a spare. So we're scrambling to get this sorted out." Julian could hear the aggravation in Allison's voice.

Julian felt panic set in as she realized there would only be three people at her dinner party—a terrible, awkward number, but there was nothing to be done about it. "You guys just take care of yourselves. If there are any leftovers, I'll bring them to work."

Allison replied, "Oh, thank you. I hate to miss your cooking."

They ended the call, and Julian sat on her bed, wringing her hands. Now what? She glanced at her phone and saw she had a text. Drake's text told her he hoped the dinner party went well. She smiled thinking of the effort that must have cost him since he knew Rob would be part of the get-together when she had neglected to tell him about their "just-friends" conversation. She shot back a text telling him he jinxed her and now only three people remained.

Julian walked back to the kitchen where Hannah and Rob stood laughing and talking together over glasses of wine. Hannah had stirred Julian's sauce in her stead. Julian placed her phone on the counter and took over the sauce and pasta. "So my whole group of coworkers just called to say they're not coming." She explained the phone call and looked at the guests standing before her.

To her surprise, she found the pair laughing together. "You look horrified," Rob said, his grin making Julian grin.

She looked at Hannah whose eyes glittered with amusement. "It's fine. We'll have fun. It'll be easier to gossip without your work harpies and there will be more food for us."

Her phone buzzed with Drake's reply text.

Ha ha. Good luck with that.

Julian chuckled as she could almost see his amused grin at her expense.

She shrugged and looked at her guests. "I appreciate y'all being good sports." She strained the pasta and started making plates. "By the way, I'm not fancy enough for appetizers so we just have salad, bread, and pasta."

Hannah took the plates from Julian and placed them on the table while Rob sliced the garlic bread. He teased Julian, "We're all going to have garlic breath, you know."

"We'll just chase it down with the wine you brought, and then no one will care," Hannah tossed over her shoulder.

The meal went smoothly. Julian watched with growing fascination as Hannah and Rob joked and chatted easily. If she hadn't been the hostess, she would have felt like the third wheel as she had feared Hannah or Rob might. Rob explained his job at Smithsburg Industries. In turn, Hannah talked about her job as an attorney with a firm downtown.

Julian listened to them with envy. She always told people she was happy with her job. Most of the time, she felt content, but sometimes, she thought she should have a more professional career. She might be a published author, but she did that on the side. Her job at the electric company paid the bills. After the meal, Julian offered everyone a second glass of wine. As she did, she inspected the label. A smile crossed her lips. "Rob, did you happen to notice who makes this wine?" He shook his head. "This is from the Salvatores's vineyard."

"Really?" Hannah came to the kitchen to take the bottle from Julian's hand. "How about that?" She grinned. "Oh, send Mary a picture of the bottle!" Rob looked confused.

Julian explained, "That's Drake's mom. She loves the texting. She's like a sixteen-year-old girl with her smartphone. My mom calls the phone I bought for her 'the devil.'" He laughed. Julian snapped a picture with her phone and sent a text to Mary. Then she sent the picture to Drake as well. They settled into the living room area. Julian offered to put a movie on, but Hannah and Rob preferred to just talk with the music still in the background. Julian merely listened as they enjoyed a lively conversation. She excused herself to slice the cake Hannah had brought. "Wine and cake. Sounds like the perfect night to me."

Eventually, Hannah noticed the time. "Oh! I didn't realize how late it was getting. I have somewhere to be early in the morning."

Rob appeared doubtful. "On a Saturday?"

"Hannah volunteers with an organization that helps distribute food to low income families in the area. It's their monthly planning meeting."

He raised his eyebrows in appreciation. "Good for you."

Julian ran with the opportunity. "Hannah's too modest, but she supports a lot of charitable causes. She's got a big heart." She grinned at Hannah who's cheeks pinked. Julian suppressed her giggle. She rarely saw poised, sophisticated Hannah blush.

Hannah tried to wave it away, but Rob's impressed smile seemed to affect her ability to collect herself. Soon after, they all said goodnight and her guests walked outside. Julian watched through the peephole as Rob and Hannah continued to talk in her driveway. When Rob offered her his number, Hannah looked torn.

Do it, Julian silently ordered, hoping Hannah would let go of her ridiculous crush on the guy who obviously stood her up for the party. When Hannah accepted the number, Julian heaved a grateful sigh. She shuffled to the kitchen to clean up and considered texting Drake with the turn of events then decided against it. She worried he only showed interest in her out of gratitude for the wreck. Maybe if he thought she had interest in Rob, he could make a decision based on his real feelings instead of a misguided notion. She rolled her shoulders back and loaded the dishwasher.

CHAPTER SEVEN

Saturday evening came too quickly for Julian. Her nerves felt raw as she ran errands and did chores to stay busy. After going to the grocery store, returning books to the library, cleaning her kitchen, and doing two loads of laundry, she finally stepped into the shower and dressed for her date. Every time she thought of the word date, her hands trembled slightly. She felt ridiculous. She and Drake had spent a lot of time together since the day of the accident. He had sat with her overnight at the hospital. He had brought her dinner. He had taken her to lunch and gone with her to the police station. They had talked on the phone and sent each other texts. But calling the time they spent together an actual date felt somehow different. She reminded herself to be prepared. If things went poorly, she would need to figure out how to remain friends for the sake of their families. Gale and Mary had already started planning Thanksgiving together, and that was only a week away.

Ever punctual, Drake rang her doorbell right on time. Julian had been digging in her closet for the right shoes to go with her jeans and violet sweater. She scrambled to her feet and ran to the door. She flung it open, aware that her hair had become disheveled as she had gotten tangled up with the clothes when rising to her feet.

"I'll just be another minute. I'm so sorry I'm running late." Her nerves felt scrambled at the sight of him, clean-shaven in a pair of jeans, a long-sleeved, gray cotton shirt, and a black leather coat. She could smell his soap and forced herself not to lean closer for a better whiff of it He gave her an easy smile.

"Come on in for a sec," she ordered and grabbed his hand to pull him in the house. Then she noticed the bouquet of yellow roses he carried. She closed the door behind him, still clutching his hand. Julian took a deep breath and smiled. "Those are beautiful. I should put them in water." She nervously took the roses and made her way to the kitchen. She flung the cabinet door open and looked up. Her normal vase still had the flowers from Rob and the other rested on the top shelf. "I forgot the step ladder," she muttered and turned only to bump into Drake's chest.

He grinned down at her. "I got it." He reached around her and plucked the only other vase in the house from the shelf. Julian stood motionless as he held the vase toward her.

"Th-thanks." She smiled hesitantly and took the vase from his hand. He stared down at her with dark eyes, and her breath hitched. Inwardly shaking herself, Julian slipped around him to go through the same motions with the roses as she had with Rob's bouquet. When finished, she held the vase triumphantly and placed it on the counter. "Perfect. I'll be right back." She dashed back to her bedroom and dropped back to her knees to dig in the closet again. Julian cursed herself for not having organized her winter shoes sooner. Finally, she found the short boots she wanted. "Aha! I am victorious!" She clumsily pulled the boots on from a standing position. When she turned to hurry back to the kitchen, she slammed into the wall of Drake's chest again. "Whoops! Sorry!"

Drake grabbed her shoulders to steady her. "I'm trying to figure out what's wrong with you."

Julian cringed. "I know. I'm acting like something crazy."

He laughed at her. "Yeah, you are. It's just dinner and a movie, Julian. I didn't even think of something clever."

"Ha! Considering how we met, dinner and a movie sounds great." They chuckled together. Julian gently stepped out of his grasp and grabbed some jewelry. She then grabbed her scarf and coat. "Okay." He rewarded her with a smile and held out his arm.

They had a quiet dinner with mindless small talk at a casual restaurant not far from the movie theater. Once in the theater, Drake produced the tickets he bought online to avoid the wait at the ticket window. They stood in line at the concession stand. Julian looked at a woman across the room then at Drake with a scowl. "I bet that's the kind of girl you're used to going out with, huh?" They looked at the supermodel-thin woman walking by them at the concession stand. Julian shook her head. "What's up with that? I mean it's one thing to be naturally skinny, but it's another to starve to look like that."

Drake chuckled at her. "You know, maybe she is naturally skinny."

Julian watched as the woman passed up her date's popcorn, candy, and even drink. She sipped at a bottle of water and ignored the man with a bored expression. Julian snorted. "Naturally skinny, my butt." She held her fingers up to her eye so that it looked like the woman was between her forefinger and her thumb. "I could break her like a twig." She made a snapping noise and closed the gap between her fingers. When Julian turned back to Drake, he started laughing.

"Behave or I'm taking you home."

She rolled her eyes. "Spoilsport," she muttered with a grin. Then she frowned. "No, you're right. I shouldn't be like that.

Making fun of someone for being skinny is as bad as making fun of someone who's plus-size."

Drake gave her a long, thoughtful look before he smiled. "Wise words, ma'am."

They reached the front of the line. Drake ordered popcorn for them to share and two drinks. With snacks in hand, they entered the theater and found seats in the middle. Julian leaned back in the reclining seats with a sigh. "This is how to watch a movie."

Drake agreed. "I would have gone to a chick-flick with you to be nice, but I'm glad you suggested this movie instead."

"Action, special effects, explosions. That's what a movie theater is for. Everything else is for watching at home in a pair of sweats and a t-shirt." She shamelessly dug her hand in the popcorn and tossed some in her mouth. "Mmm…butter."

Drake leaned close to Julian and whispered, "Your friend is here." He nodded toward the entrance where the thin woman and her date stood deciding on seats. She still looked bored.

"Poor guy." Julian sighed again. "I hope the movie is good, at least. She looks like a pill."

He raised an eyebrow at her. "A pill? Who says that? When were you born again?"

She slapped at his leg with a grin. "Oh, shut it, you." Drake tugged at a lock of her hair in response to her slap. She hit him again, and he tugged her hair again. They dissolved into laughter until the lights went down and previews started. Julian watched with rapt attention. One of the previews highlighted a superhero movie, and she sat up straight. "Yes! I can't wait for this one! We have to see that one." From the corner of her eye, Julian caught Drake watching her. She looked at him, and he turned his attention back to the screen. She did the same. After a few minutes, she stealthily gazed at his profile, taking in his rugged good looks. He caught her staring this time and smiled as she turned her head back to the screen as well with an innocent face.

By the end of the movie, the popcorn no longer existed, and Julian held her hand over her stomach with a groan. "Ugh. Why'd you let me eat so much?"

Drake grinned. "I liked watching you enjoy it."

Her stomach fluttered at his smile. Unnerved by how he affected her, she stood as the aisles emptied, raising her arms over her head to stretch her back. She picked up her coat and tugged it on as Drake rose to his feet as well.

"So, what now? Coffee?" he asked.

She nodded with enthusiasm, deciding to chance the possibility of being recognized again or running into a familiar face.

"Okay," he said. "I'm just going to the restroom first. I'll be right back."

Julian sat on a bench in the lobby to wait. She turned her phone back on and checked for messages. Sensing someone standing in front of her, she asked, "Ready to go?" She looked up to see a familiar face other than Drake's. "John?" The thin, dark-haired man smiled shyly as Julian forced a return smile. "Sorry, I thought you were my date."

"You're on a date?" He looked around nervously, his dark, brown eyes darting from one end of the theater to the other. "I didn't mean to interrupt."

"It's okay. He's in the bathroom. What brings you to Columbia? I think I remember you saying you live in Atlanta."

"Researching a book. It's set here."

She raised her eyebrows in surprise. "Really? Not much of a hotspot for a book. What's it about?"

He inspected his shoes. "Oh, there's no special reason for Columbia. I just thought downtown is pretty. I was looking for Southern charm."

"It is pretty, isn't it? You could also use Savannah's historic district down in Georgia if you want old school Southern. And

Greenville is great, too. Lots of character downtown. It's like modern Southern, kinda bohemian." Her mind instantly imagined a road trip to either of those locations with Drake, and she smiled before she reined herself in. This is just a first date, she chided herself. You could still make the trip as friends, though, she thought.

Drake appeared from nowhere. "Who's your friend?"

Julian stood and introduced him. "John, this is my date, Drake Salvatore. Drake, this is a writer I met at the last convention, John Hatcher." The men shook hands. Julian thought it seemed like Drake shook the man's hand harder than necessary. She gave Drake a tight warning smile, and he dropped his hand. Julian told John, "It was nice seeing you again. Good luck with the novel."

"Thanks. See you soon," he replied as Julian and Drake headed outside and to his truck.

Once they were settled inside the cab, Julian glanced slyly at Drake. "Trying to break his hand?"

Drake's lips thinned a little. "There's something odd about him."

"I don't really know him," she admitted. "He seemed a little lost at the convention and followed my friend and I around. He's harmless. Just awkward."

"Harmless, huh? Kinda creepy to me, and I bet you thought so at the convention, too."

She shrugged. "I couldn't be mean to him."

Drake turned fully toward her. "It's not being mean to listen to your gut telling you someone's weird. It's okay to put your safety first."

Julian swallowed hard, conceding Drake had a point. Ignoring warning signs had led to an abusive marriage. She looked away from Drake and noticed John standing on the sidewalk in front of the theater, watching the truck.

Drake's set jaw revealed he saw John too, but he put the

truck into gear and pulled out of the parking space. He drove them to the coffee shop where he bought her a fancy latte and himself another black coffee. They sat at a small table to sip the hot drinks and saw the same couple from the theater. The man seemed to be working so hard to please his date that Julian felt sorry for him. Drake noticed the couple too. "It shouldn't be that hard."

She shook her head. "Neither one of them looks like they're having a good time. It's too bad. I'm surprised they came for coffee. I would have just gone home after the movie."

"I guess that means you're having a good time?"

Julian grinned. "Yes, I am."

He chuckled at her. "Me, too."

The other couple sat on one of the soft leather loveseats with their coffee. The man excused himself for a moment. As soon as he left, the woman's expression changed, and she slid a mirror from her purse to check her hair and lip gloss. She quickly stowed the mirror and makeup back into her purse and fidgeted.

Julian smiled. "Look at that. She's nervous. Maybe I misjudged her. She's putting on an act."

Drake made a sound of disgust. "Why do women do that? Why do they play games like that?"

Julian narrowed her eyes. "That's not just women, buster. Men do the same crap, just in a different way."

He tilted his head. "Maybe." He met her eyes so intently she thought there must be something on her face. "You're not like that, though. You're very open and honest. I like that about you."

"Thanks." She suddenly felt shy again. "I guess I don't have much of a filter. I come by it honestly, at least. Mom's got no filter at all."

Drake chuckled. "No, she doesn't, but I like her a lot."

"Me too," she laughed. "But you… You're a tough nut to

crack, I think."

Drake's eyebrows shot up. "Really? I feel transparent."

"Sometimes, but other times you have this tough Marine persona. You look like this." She made a stoic face. He laughed at her imitation as she continued, "I like it better when you're smiling. I doubt you do that enough."

* * *

Drake thought about that. Maybe what he had seen in the war had quenched some of his joy. Nothing made him laugh during his tours. He had been a leader and lives depended on his decisions. If a man or woman in his unit was injured or killed, he had felt the weight of it on his shoulders. Drake knew he had been fortunate, as it had happened to his units infrequently, but it had still been a heavy load. He reined in his thoughts and looked back at Julian. She wore the same stoic expression she had teased him with, and he chuckled again.

She asked, "What are you thinking about when you do this?" She made the face again.

He shook his head. "I was thinking about how I'm not used to anyone other than my family being so honest with me."

"I like being the harbinger of truth sometimes. Well, if it's helpful, anyway." She took his hand to turn his wrist and glance at his watch. With a mournful sigh, she said, "I promise I'm having a good time, but it's getting late, and I've got church in the morning."

"Let's get you home then."

They took their coffees with them and made their way to his truck. They chatted amicably as he drove her back to her house, but he could sense her tension. Once he parked the truck, she practically jumped out with a quick, "Good night."

He hurried after her as she put her key in the lock. "Whoa. What kind of man do you think I am not to walk my date to the door? Especially this late?"

She looked guilty. "Sorry, I..."

He could see her struggling to find the right words. He cocked his head at her. "Are you worried I'd try to kiss you?"

Julian bit her bottom lip and met his eyes. "I was worried you wouldn't." At that he stepped a little closer to her. She stood her ground, still looking up at him with the height difference. "I thought it'd be less awkward to avoid the moment."

"Hmm. How'd that work out for you?"

"Umm..." She gave a nervous laugh.

Drake closed the distance between them but avoided any contact, still trying to gauge her mindset. The wind picked up a little, and Julian shivered, pulling her coat closer around her against the chill. "I'll put the question to rest." He put his hand on the back of her neck and softly kissed her. She put her hands on his chest and leaned against him as she returned the kiss. Drake pulled her closer, and Julian slid her arms up and around his neck. He inwardly smiled at her response. After a moment, he leaned his head back and looked down at her. "Mystery solved." Then he kissed her again.

Julian giggled against his mouth then pulled her head back to meet his eyes. "My nosy neighbor is probably watching us with binoculars."

He laughed at that and pushed a stray lock of hair behind her ear. "We're not doing anything wrong, Julian."

"You don't have to be for her to be judgmental." She rolled her eyes in exasperation. "Mean old lady," she muttered then gave Drake a smile. "I really should go."

Drake slowly released her and grinned. "Okay." He cleared his throat. "Is this the time during a real date when we can plan our second date?"

She chuckled at him. "Mighty sure you're getting a second date."

"Well, you did say we have to go see that superhero movie together. Seemed like a clue," he said. He knew she hadn't even realized how telling the statement was when she said it, but it had warmed him. He liked Julian Fursey. A lot.

Julian giggled. "You've got a point. I guess we can plan our next date tomorrow at your parents house over lunch since your mom insisted my mom and I come over." She ran a hand over his jacket. "Which I love about her, by the way," she told him with a grin.

Drake returned the grin. "Pop said you're one of ours, remember? The Salvatores take that seriously."

Julian's eyes clouded slightly, but she smiled. "Okay. Well, goodnight then." She said and disappeared behind the door. He wondered about the look, but for the first time in a long time, Drake looked forward to Sunday dinner.

CHAPTER EIGHT

After the church service, Julian and her mother climbed into Julian's car and headed for the Salvatore's house. Julian had only been vaguely paying attention the night of the party and had to use the GPS application on her phone as they drove. Gale casually said, "So you and I haven't had much time to talk for the last couple of days."

Julian knew that tone and prepared for the inquisition.

"Yeah. Sorry, Mom."

"How was the dinner party?"

Good."

"Sounds like Hannah is smitten with this Rob fella."

Julian glanced at her mom. "She called you, eh?"

Gale pursed her lips. "She did."

"What else did she tell you?"

"You and Rob are just friends, and he asked her out instead."

"That's true."

"Are you okay with that?"

"Of course. I gave them my blessing, not that they needed it. I like Rob a lot, but it just wasn't going to progress past friendship for us, and you should have seen them together." She grinned at her mother. "It was so obvious that there was a spark. They were cute."

Gale smiled. "I'm glad. He sounds like a nice man."

Julian's shoulders relaxed a little, glad the questioning hadn't been too severe until her mom asked, "So are you and Drake an item now or what?"

"We've had one date, Mom."

"Sometimes that's all it takes. Your father and I got married a month after we met."

"I remember the story."

"Oh, he was so romantic, your father. Is Drake romantic?"

"Mom…"

"He come from good stock, Jules. Don't let this one get away."

"Mom!" She ran a hand over her face. "He's not… It's probably not gonna work out, so let's just try to remain calm, okay?"

"But he's not like Arnold, sweetie. Drake's a good guy."

Julian took the opportunity to turn the tables on her mom. "Speaking of Arnold, why did you feel the need to tell Drake about Arnold?"

Gale sputtered a little. "I… felt like he should know."

"I don't like anyone knowing about Arnold."

"Well, Drake met him that night, so it wasn't a big secret."

"My marriage and divorce isn't a secret, but I don't like anyone to know the details. I'm humiliated enough that I made the bad decision to marry him."

"You have nothing to be embarrassed about. I told Drake because he's a good boy."

Julian shook her head. "Mom, you have got to stop telling

people everything about me. There's a… Someone is…"

"I know about the phone calls," Gale told her. "And I'm not an idiot. I don't tell everyone everything." She folded her arms. "It's a good thing Hannah lets me know what's going on with you, or I'd never know anything."

Julian sighed. "I just don't want you to worry."

"You're my daughter. I will always worry. I'd rather know what's going on so I'm prepared to help."

Julian felt guilty then. "I meant well, Mom."

"I know, sweetie."

"Does Drake know?" Gale asked.

Julian cut her eyes toward her mother for just a moment before turning them back on the road. "Yes…"

"Interesting," Gale said as they pulled off the road and onto a long driveway lined with large trees and a rustic wooden fence. In the light of day, Julian could fully grasp the beauty of the house and land around it. She loved it. "Have you been out here since the party?"

"Oh, yeah. Mary and I play cards together a couple of nights a week."

Julian gave her a look. She turned the GPS off and asked, "Why didn't you just tell me how to get here instead of letting me use the data on my phone?"

Gale shrugged. "Well, you like playing with your devil phone so much I didn't want to stop you."

"Oy, Mom."

Julian parked next to Drake's truck and came around the car to take the pan of food from her mother, kissing the older woman on the cheek. She put her free arm around Gale's neck and told her, "You make me crazy, but I love ya." They smiled together.

Mary met them on the porch before they could reach the door. "I'm so glad you two came. We're almost ready. Let me take that." Mary took the pan of macaroni and cheese from

Julian's hands despite her protests and waved them into the house. They walked past the open living room to the kitchen with the breakfast nook. Once there, Mary turned and shooed Julian out to the living room. "Gale and I will take care of the food. Go see the boys."

Julian obeyed meekly and entered the living room. A fire burned in the fireplace, and Amerigo sat on the chaise lounge next to it. His face brightened when he saw her. She walked over to him and hugged him around the neck. "How are you feeling today?"

He smiled. "Okay. The leg's not too bad right now."

"Pain meds?" She sat on the couch next to him.

"Only to go to bed. They just make me so groggy." They looked at his leg in its large cast, grimacing as he shifted.

Julian squeezed his arm as the doors on the other side of the room opened, and Anthony and Drake entered.

Anthony rushed to Julian, who rose and hugged him. "I'm glad you came, Julian. Where is your mother?"

"She's helping Mary with the food. They ran me out."

"Sounds like Mary and Gale," he said with a chuckle.

Julian met Drake's eyes and smiled. He smiled back at her. Anthony released Julian and turned to Amerigo. "Give me the remote," he ordered and held out his hand.

Amerigo held it away and shook his head. "Ma said not till after lunch."

"But the game—"

"I'm just following orders," Amerigo replied, his expression firm.

Drake rolled his eyes then stretched out a hand to Julian. "C'mon. You can see the vineyard from the back porch."

She took his hand and let him lead her outside. The cool November air slipped through the knit of her sweater, and she shivered as they rounded the corner of the house out toward the back. She clung to Drake's warm hand and practically ran to keep up with his long stride.

Drake turned and saw her shaking with the cold. He stopped and took off his jacket, throwing it over her shoulders. "You can just see it from here. The grapes have already been harvested, but you can still see the vines." From the porch at the back of the house, Julian could see the rows of vines growing over strategically placed posts and wire. "Now it's time to prune and winterize the plants. The grapes have been pressed and are fermenting." Drake gestured toward the porch swing, and they sat, his arm across the back behind her. "When we have more time, I'll give you a real tour."

"It's beautiful out here." Julian scanned the area thoughtfully. "I imagine it's a lot of hard work, though."

He nodded, his expression open and satisfied. "It's worth it."

"From what I can tell, your family seems to do well with the winemaking business. It must be wonderful to support yourself doing something you love."

Drake chuckled. "They do something they love, but it just began to be profitable. Pop brought old family money with him when he came to America. It's probably a good thing Amerigo can't get to his trust fund yet or he'd have drained it completely already."

Julian blinked. "You two have trust funds?"

"Yeah. I was able to access mine years ago, but Amerigo can't yet." Drake looked embarrassed, and Julian didn't press the issue.

Instead, she looked at the beauty of the vineyard from their seats and pulled her phone out of her pocket. She clicked a picture of the scenery then turned the camera on Drake. He grimaced playfully and put a hand up to cover his face. She refused to be thwarted and continued to take pictures. "I have a lot of storage on this camera. I can do this all afternoon."

Drake rolled his eyes then caved in with a smile. "Fine." She took the picture and grinned triumphantly.

Mary called out from the side of the house. "Come eat."

They stood, but Julian noticed the email notification. Though not completely unusual with the amount of emails she received in a day, a sense of dread crept over her. "Hold on." She opened the email entitled, "Lunch." Attached to the email, Julian and Drake looked at twenty pictures of them, eating lunch together at the deli. "My God," Julian whispered.

"You need to forward this to Detective Reynolds."

Julian swallowed around the lump in her throat and forwarded the email with an explanation to the email address Reynolds had given her. She met Drake's eyes and saw concern. He cupped the back of her neck and gently ran his thumb along her jaw.

"It's going to be all right, Jules."

"Don't tell anyone, okay?" she pleaded, shivering uncontrollably. "I don't want to spoil everyone's lunch. Can we pretend this didn't happen?"

Drake nodded. "Let's get you out of the cold."

* * *

Once everyone had eaten all they wanted, Mary and Gale began clearing the table. Drake watched with amusement as Julian stood to help only to be shooed by the older women again. Julian put her hands on her hips and said, "What are y'all doing in the kitchen that I'm not allowed in there? I'm starting to get a complex."

Drake blinked in surprise when Mary nodded her head toward the kitchen. Julian grabbed some plates and followed their mothers. She had spirit, he'd give her that. Even he avoided his mother's wrath when possible. He turned to Anthony and Amerigo, who had been plunked into the wheelchair so he could prop his leg up. He saw surprise on their faces as well. Drake shrugged and rose from the table. He grabbed the rest of the dishes from the table and made his way to the kitchen as well. Gale rinsed dishes and handed them to Julian to load into the dishwasher as Mary put food into storage containers, some for the fridge and some for Gale and Julian to take with them. He handed the plates to Julian.

She met his eyes with a look of triumph and winked. Drake smiled in response. He returned to the table, helping Amerigo back into the living room and onto the chaise lounge that had become his permanent daytime residence. They propped his leg up on some pillows in its bulky cast. Amerigo grimaced at the pain.

"Mind getting me some aspirin? I have some on my nightstand," Amerigo asked.

"Sure." Drake went to Amerigo's room to get the bottle of medicine and noticed one of Julian's books on his nightstand. He smiled and picked it up. Drake recognized it as the second book in her series. Did that mean Amerigo had read the first? He chuckled to himself and returned to the living room with the bottle of pills. "That's interesting reading on your nightstand."

Amerigo turned a shade of red and leveled his gaze at his brother. "I happen to know you read one, too. Besides, I've read everything on my bookshelf. Mom bought all her books, so it was something new."

Drake cocked his head at that revelation. "Mom bought all her books? How many are there?"

"Eight."

The women joined them in the living room. Anthony also joined them from wherever he had been and sat on the couch near Amerigo.

Mary announced, "Gale and I are going to go shopping."

"Julian, mind if we borrow your car? Mary doesn't want to drive, and I don't feel comfortable driving her car. I won't feel so bad if I wreck yours." Gale gave her an innocent smile.

Drake shook his head. Did these women really think they were subtle? He grinned at Julian. "I can drive you home if you want to let her use your car." He could see amusement in her eyes as well.

"Thanks. Let me get my keys." She retrieved her purse from the bench by the door and dug around for her keys. She found them and handed them to her mother.

Gale reached for her purse. "Here, let me give you my keys so you can use my spare to your house."

"It's all right. I have a key." Drake regretted the words instantly. Every eye in the room landed on him then turned to Julian, who glared at him.

Julian placed her purse back on the bench and held her hands up to their families. "It's not what you're thinking. I… just needed some help one day, and, uh… let Drake use the key."

They all looked back to Drake.

Anthony looked the most skeptical. His father narrowed his eyes. "Then why didn't you give it back once you helped her?"

Drake looked at Julian. He had genuinely forgotten to give it back. He assumed she'd forgotten, too, now that he thought about it. But she looked panicked now, trying to figure out what to tell their families. Obviously she was not ready to admit to the phone calls or email. Mixing up her medication and practically passing out in his truck probably didn't rank high on her list of things she wanted to share either. Her eyes pleaded with him, and he wanted to laugh. She was a horrible liar.

In an effort to save her, he said truthfully, "I just forgot to give it back." He looked at Julian and dug in his grabbed his keys from the hook near the door, pulling her spare key from the jumble. "Here ya go." He handed her the key.

"Thanks."

"What did you help her with?" Anthony persisted.

Drake resisted the urge to remind their family that he and Julian had long since passed the age of needing to explain themselves and said, "She had a leak in her bathroom, and since we all told her to call one of us if she needed anything, she called me."

Anthony eyed Drake suspiciously. "Should I send a plumber?"

Drake shot his father a warning glance. "You don't think I can handle a leaking pipe? I took care of it." He saw relief on Julian's face and gave her an encouraging smile.

Accepting his response, Mary and Gale grabbed their coats and purses. "Don't look at the bags when we come back. This is Christmas shopping," Mary warned.

Drake saw a look pass between Gale and Julian. Gale's skepticism showed, but she said nothing before turning the same look to Drake. She and his mother left without another word. He turned to Julian and offered, "Want me to take you home now?"

She grabbed her own coat. "Sure." She hugged Amerigo and kissed Anthony's cheek. "Thanks for inviting us." Anthony patted her hand and glared at Drake again, which annoyed him. What kind of letch did they all think he was? Amerigo looked ready to burst with laughter.

His tone was gruffer than he meant for it to be. "C'mon, Julian."

Julian followed him outside to his truck. "Don't get grumpy with me. I'm not the one who blurted out you have a key like we..." Her voice trailed off as she looked for the right words.

"Hook up?" He held the truck door open for her and watched her frown. She climbed in without a response and pulled her seatbelt on. He rounded to the driver's side and joined her in the truck, worried his tone might have reminded her of the treatment from her vile ex-husband. "I'm sorry," he said. "I didn't mean to snap at you."

She looked out the window. "It's all right. Guess I can cut you some slack for being human," she said with a grin. As if reading his mind, she told him, "I know you're not like Arnold, Drake." Then she chuckled. "Boy, everyone sure was ready to believe the worst of us. I think your dad was really offended."

Drake gave a grunt. "I saw that. I'm a little offended myself."

"Only a little? Do they have reason to expect that kind of behavior from you?"

He grinned mischievously.

Julian held up her hands with a small laugh. "I don't want to know. Let me just think the best about you."

"My reputation is more hype than reality," he assured her, though he left out his track record with women over the last few years. A few dates, a little fun, then moving on.

Julian sighed and leaned her head back. "This sucks." She glared at her phone. "This is an awful feeling. I just want to go home and lock my door. And I had planned to do some Christmas shopping myself." With another frown and glance out the window, she said, "I'm gonna nix that idea today."

Drake's hands tightened on the steering wheel. If he ever found out who was doing this… "I don't have any real plans this afternoon. I can go with you, if you want."

She shook her head. "No, thanks. It's above and beyond for you to offer, but I'm really not in the mood now. I'll go with Hannah sometime this week." She pointed to the stereo. "Mind?"

"Help yourself."

Julian tapped the power button and left the dial on the station he had last tuned to which played Christmas songs by traditional crooners. "A little early, but nice."

When he pulled into her driveway, he walked with her into the house and looked around while she placed her coat and scarf on the coat rack.

"Want something to drink? Coffee? Tea?" she asked, her eyes pleading.

"Coffee sounds great," he replied, happy to be able to do anything to make her feel more at east. He removed his jacket and placed it on the coat rack as well.

Julian went in the kitchen and pulled out two mugs near the single cup brewer. She pulled open a kitchen drawer and waved a hand for him to look inside.

He joined her then balked at the contents. "I've never seen so many coffee choices outside of a store."

She grinned. "Pick your poison."

He grabbed one of the dark roast coffee packs and handed it to Julian. She turned and set the brewer to work. He watched her graceful movements and smiled. Sometimes she moved like a dancer, and sometimes she surprised him by how awkward she could be. She gave him a mug of coffee and then fumbled with her own, muttering under her breath. Drake approached her, placing his cup on the counter. As her cup brewed, she turned around and gasped at how close he stood. "Y-you take your coffee black, right?"

He grinned down at her and nodded. He was glad to see his nearness affected her because it affected him too. Drake could smell the floral shampoo she used as she stared at him from beneath lowered lids. He slipped her mug from her hand and set it on the counter next to his own. Julian leaned toward him, and he slid an arms around her waist as he brushed his fingers over her smooth cheek. She placed her hands on his chest and closed her eyes, her head tilting up slightly.

With a smile at her movement, Drake kissed her. He intended for it to be a gentle, reassuring kiss, but it heated the moment his lips touched her. He splayed his fingers into the hair at the nape of her neck as she snaked her arms up and around his neck. Drake felt his pulse leap as she clung to him, a tiny moan of appreciation escaping her.

It had been a long time since a simple kiss warmed his blood so quickly. He lifted his head from hers to look in her eyes. "I've wanted to do this since last night."

"You did this last night." The corner of her mouth turned upward at him.

He smiled. "Not enough." He bent down and kissed her with more urgency. He wrapped both arms around her waist and hauled her closer to him. When her phone played its irritating ringtone, he muttered breathlessly against her mouth, "Ignore it."

She giggled at him but replied with the same breathlessness, "What if it's Detective Reynolds?"

Drake groaned and released her. She grabbed the phone from her purse and looked at the number. "It's Mom. I'll call her back." Julian placed her cell phone on the counter and smiled at him. "Our coffee's gonna get cold." She opened the refrigerator to grab the creamer and picked up her mug. Drake sipped the black coffee from his mug and watched Julian add sweetener and creamer to her drink. She beckoned him to join her on the couch and sipped her own coffee.

He sank down on the cushions next to her and said, "You just ignored a call for me. I'm flattered."

Julian hit his arm. "Oh, and the ego rears its ugly head once again." They laughed, and Julian kicked off her shoes. She pulled her sock clad feet onto the seat and propped herself against the arm of the couch to look at him. "But that's all right. Guess attractive men like yourself have to fight that demon all the time," she said, her voice dripping with sarcasm. Julian made a face at him and poked her finger in his stomach. He tugged at a lock of her hair. She gasped and poked him in the ribs this time. He tugged the same lock of hair again. Julian gasped again in mock indignation. "Don't pull my hair!"

With a smirk, Drake narrowed his eyes. "Or what?" When she would have poked his side again, he grasped her wrist and easily twisted her arm around her back, careful not to hurt her. He grabbed her other wrist before she could counter and held it behind her as well. "What could you do now?"

"Well, if I really felt it necessary, I'd knee the family jewels."

He smiled at her. "That's pretty ruthless." His smile faded. "What would you do if someone truly did grab you like this?"

"I wasn't kidding. The family jewels are target number one. After that, anything is fair game."

He met her eyes, and the protective impulse surged within him again. "Good. Bite, scratch, kick, hit. If it's you or them, do whatever it takes."

Julian's eyes clouded. "You're starting to scare me, Drake."

He instantly released her wrists. "I'm sorry. Was I hurting you?"

She shook her head. "That's not what I meant." Julian looked away from him. "You really think this guy's gonna come after me."

Drake sat back. "I don't know, but it never hurts to be prepared."

They returned to sipping their coffee, this time in silence. Julian's hand shook slightly, and Drake saw it. In an effort to divert her attention, Drake inquired, "Mind if I ask about your dad? You and your mom never talk about what happened to him." He quickly added, "If it's none of my business, just ignore the question."

Julian smiled as she shook her head. "It's fine. He died a few years ago. Cancer. He was in the hospital for a long time before he passed. It felt like we lived there for awhile."

"That's why you hate hospitals."

Julian frowned. "Yeah."

"I'm sorry about your dad, Julian."

"Thanks. Me, too. He was a great dad. I miss him."

An insistent ringing of the doorbell interrupted the

conversation. Julian left the couch and hurried to the door. Drake followed close behind, alert. She looked through the peephole and heaved a sigh. "It's my mom." Drake remained behind her as she opened the door.

Gale demanded, "Why didn't you answer the phone? Did you forget something?"

Julian looked confused.

"I used your car. You need to take me home."

Julian narrowed her eyes at Gale. "That didn't take long. Is everything okay?"

Gale said, "Oh, everything's fine. We just decided since we both want to go to church tonight that we could finish shopping another time. We felt rushed. Mary's waiting in the car. We hoped you wouldn't mind dropping her off." Gale looked at Drake. "We didn't realize you would still be here."

He looked at Julian and felt a small moment of victory to see her disappointment. "I can take my mom home, Gale. I'll be out in just a minute."

Julian's shoulders slumped almost imperceptibly. "Let me grab my coat, Mom."

Gale called, "We'll be waiting in the car."

When Gale pulled the door closed behind her, Julian's face showed astonishment. "Huh."

Drake laughed. "I guess this is goodbye for now. You go back to full days tomorrow, right?"

She nodded. "Released to full duty."

"Feel like doing lunch tomorrow? My parents keep running me away from the vineyard. They said they want me to enjoy retirement before I really dive in."

"It's so weird to talk about your retirement. You're too young to be retired."

Drake smiled at her. "You didn't answer my question."

"Oh. We're having our pre-Thanksgiving luncheon tomorrow, so I really can't."

"Dinner tomorrow night."

"I promised Hannah a girls' night in."

He rolled his eyes. "Dinner Tuesday? How about you come to my place, and I'll cook for you?"

"Sure. Sounds nice."

"Good. Let's get these schemers home, shall we?" He gave her another quick kiss and turned to leave, but she grabbed his lapel.

"Wait," Julian said. She retrieved the spare key he'd returned from her purse and handed it to him. "I know it's completely stupid, but I feel a little bit safer if I know you have one."

Drake wrapped his fingers around the hand holding the key, his gut twisting at the look in her eyes—trust. "I'm happy to do anything that will make you feel safer," he said, hoping she heard the sincerity in his voice before he dropped another soft kiss on her lips and hurried outside.

* * *

Julian scowled at her mother as she drove. "Are you sure you and Mary didn't come back early to check in on Drake and me?"

Gale sucked in a deep breath as if offended. "Julian Fursey! I would never…" Julian gave her a look. Gale turned away from her with annoyance. "Think what you want." After a quiet moment, Gale continued, "I would like to know what happened. He obviously kissed you."

"What?"

Gale smirked. "Your father may have died years ago, but I still recognize that look." She held her chin up with an air of superiority then added, "Plus your lip gloss is a mess, and Drake had some on his lips too."

Julian gasped and checked in the rearview mirror. She hastily wiped the smeared portions away and sighed. "Okay.

Yes. He kissed me."

Gale clapped her hands together. "Oh, this is wonderful! We'll all be part of the same family. We can have dinner together every Sunday and big holidays—"

"Whoa, whoa, whoa! Put the brakes on, Ma. It was just a kiss, for goodness sake!"

But Julian didn't completely believe what she was saying. Her mother definitely put the cart before the horse, but that kiss was not just a kiss. Drake made her feel safe and beautiful. The chemistry that she and Rob lacked certainly existed between her and Drake. But chemistry wasn't enough to make a relationship. She figured he had no lack of interested women. Who could resist a man that good-looking, especially if he was a Marine? Julian made an effort not to think of who he might have dated or been in a serious relationship with before now. Once the novelty of her and their situation wore off, he'd get over the idea of dating her and move onto his normal type—not her, for sure.

"You got really quiet."

Julian jumped at her mother's voice. "Sorry. I was just thinking about stuff."

Gale smiled softly. "He's a good one, Julian."

She cast a sideways glance at her mother while still watching the road. Gale had been brutally honest about Arnold when their relationship changed from casual to serious. She knew he hid a different side from them, but Julian refused to believe her mother. In the end, though, Gale's instincts had been accurate. "He's not the problem, Mom. I'm not his type. I hate it, but I think he's just fascinated with me because of the accident, and with the emails, he's in protective Marine mode." Julian clamped her mouth shut, realizing her error.

"Emails?" Gale's face became stormy. "What emails? What are you talking about?"

Julian stifled a groan of annoyance with herself. "I've gotten a couple of emails with videos and pictures someone took of me doing stuff."

Gale shifted her whole body in her seat to stare at her daughter. "What kind of stuff?"

"Going to the park with Rob, having lunch with Drake, just stuff."

Her mother's face drained of color. "How many emails?"

"Two."

"Have you contacted the police?"

"Yes. Drake went with me." She bit her lip and thought hard. "That's the reason I gave the key back to Drake."

Gale pursed her lips together, and Julian could feel her rising anger. "When were you going to tell me?"

"Ma, I didn't want to worry you. There's nothing you can do. I asked Drake not to say anything to his parents either."

"That's just dumb. Don't you think they should know so they can help keep an eye out for anything out of the ordinary? And are you still going for walks in your neighborhood alone?" When Julian remained silent, Gale folded her arms. "You're getting a gym membership. You can't go walking in your neighborhood alone with some strange person spying on you."

"I hate going to a gym. I hate it." She felt grumpy and aggravated. "I don't want to change my life because of this idiot."

Gale put a hand on her arm. "It's not fair, but you're too smart to put yourself in danger if you don't have to."

Julian ground her teeth together as she pulled into her mother's driveway. Even in a short amount of time, Gale had accrued several bags. Julian got out of the car to help her mother carry them in. She placed the bags on her mother's bed as instructed. Then she sat on the edge of the mattress and sighed. "Mom, I…" No other words came out. She closed her eyes in frustration.

Gale sat next to her daughter and put her arms around her

shoulders. "I know." They sat in silence that way for a long time.

* * *

"I like Julian." Drake caught Mary's smile as he drove. "She's a nice girl."

Drake nodded. "What's not to like?"

"She's not your normal type."

Uh-oh. Where was this going?

Drake asked, "I have a type?"

"Yes. Dumb airheads."

"What? That's not—"

"You normally date airheads because you know it won't go anywhere."

"I don't—"

"Jessica?"

He gave a half laugh. "Okay. Betty was a little vacant."

"Tara."

"Tara was smart."

"The only smart thing she ever did was try to get her claws in you."

"Ma!" Drake rolled his eyes.

"After your divorce from Mariella, you've only ever dated dummies."

He made a frustrated sound. "That's mean, Ma. Stop calling them dummies and airheads. Those women are real people."

Mary looked sufficiently chastised but also undeterred. "None of them were right for you."

"That would be why I'm no longer dating them."

She huffed at him and looked out the window. "I like Julian." Then she glared at him. "What were you really doing with a key to her house? Are you sleeping with her? You have a key so you can just go over any time you want? I raised you better than that."

Drake's indignation colored his response. "I'm starting to get the impression my family has a pretty low opinion of me. Do you really think I'd take advantage of her?"

Mary narrowed her eyes and reached over to swipe her fingers across his lips. "It's not your color." She held her fingers up to show him the faint remnants of Julian's lip gloss. Drake felt his cheeks flush and wanted to curse aloud. He dug in the truck's console to grab a napkin and wipe the rest of Julian's lip gloss away. Only his mother could elicit that kind of a reaction in him. He had spent his entire adult life with Marines and soldiers on military bases at home and abroad. He's been in combat zones and had been unwillingly stuck listening to some of the most graphic, salacious stories his brothers-in-arms shared with each other. But his mother's current interrogation caught him off guard and made him feel like a fifteen-year-old boy caught making out with a girl in his bedroom.

"I kissed her. I don't think that makes me some kind of jerk. I have a key because she's scared, and it made her feel safer." He cringed.

Mary's response was as expected. "Scared of what? Is she getting more phone calls? I thought that stopped when she changed her number."

Drake took a deep breath. Julian had kept her mom and friend out of the loop, and he understood it, but he didn't like it. And he didn't like lying to his family. "Someone's been following her and taking videos and pictures of her. Before you ask, she went to the police and filed a report."

Mary fell silent then asked, "Do you think it's her ex-husband?"

He shrugged. "I really have no idea, but it's scared her. I think it makes her feel better for me to have a key."

His mother looked worried. "What do we do?"

"There's not really anything you can do."

"I'll add it to my prayer list."

Drake thought about that. "That's a good idea."

Mary prodded, "Why don't you come to church with me tonight? We have special prayer services on Sunday nights."

"Just add her to the list, okay?"

Mary sighed. "Drake, there's a trend to the women you've dated since your divorce. Julian won't fit that trend. If you're only interested in something physical with her, you should break it off now, or you'll be disappointed. Very disappointed."

"This is not a conversation I want to have with my mom."

"Want me to have Pop talk to you?"

"Mom, I'm a grown man. I think I understand the birds and the bees. I just wish my family had a better opinion of me. I'm not just out for sex with women."

Mary folded her arms and glared. As Drake turned down the long driveway to her house, she opened her mouth to speak several times but said nothing else until they exited the car, and she could look him in the eye. Standing in front of him, she placed her hands on her hips and said, "I know you're a good man, and I love you." She tugged him into a tight hug.

Drake patted her back with a smile. "I know, Mom." He grabbed her shopping bags, and walked in the house with her. Amerigo and Anthony watched a movie and laughed together at the comedy.

When they saw Drake and Mary, Anthony stood and held his hand out to her. "Feel like going for a walk?"

Drake watched her take his hand for their daily ritual. They walked every evening as the weather permitted. He felt a pang of envy. Their relationship set a high standard. He'd heard them fight, but they always worked it out. They sometimes raised their voices, but they avoided name calling or cruel comments. He thought of the nasty break-up with Mariella and the terrible things she had said. They still stung, though the initial hurt had faded through the years. As his parents left the house, Drake sat next to Amerigo.

"Do you think I have a 'type' of woman I normally date?"

"Yeah."

"Oh, really?"

"Yeah, sexy and shallow."

Drake's eyebrows shot up. "Wow."

"Hey, I'm not judging. My type's not really different except you normally like blondes. I like brunettes."

"I don't believe you guys. Mom told me the same thing."

Amerigo gave him a pointed look. "Well, Mom doesn't like anyone either of us dates."

"She likes Julian." His brother seemed surprised. Drake asked, "What's that look for? Are you surprised Mom likes her?"

"No, I'm surprised you lumped her in with women you've dated. So you guys are dating?" Amerigo elbowed his side with a smirk.

Drake blinked. He'd asked Julian to consider him and convinced her to go on a date with him. They talked and texted regularly. He had already been thinking about what to cook Tuesday night. His attempts to stop thinking about kissing her repeatedly failed. Amerigo chuckled at him. "Your face tells me all I need to know."

Drake shrugged. "We went on a date, and I like her, but I don't know what's going on with this Rob guy." He thought of Rob holding her hand, or worse, kissing her and frowned.

"Well, you'll get a chance to figure it out," Amerigo said. "Evidently, since neither Julian's friend, Hannah, nor Rob have any local family, Gale and Mom invited them to Thanksgiving with us."

"Are you kidding me?" Drake asked.

He shook his head. "I tried to tell her it might be weird,

but…"

Drake cringed. "This might be the most awkward holiday ever."

Amerigo laughed. "It might, big brother, but you'd better behave or you'll have three very angry women after you. Oh yeah, and a likable British guy too."

Drake warned him, "You better help me."

His younger brother sobered. "You really like Julian, don't you?"

"I really do."

"Good. Don't screw this up."

"Thanks for the vote of confidence."

CHAPTER NINE

Julian handed a glass of wine to Hannah and giggled as she turned the movie back on. She curled up on the end of the couch in her pajamas, holding her own glass of Salvatore Vineyard wine purchased specifically for their grown-up slumber party. Julian thought of the countless sleepovers she had enjoyed with Hannah growing up. As adults, they kept the tradition alive once a month. Sometimes their girls' night in fell on a weeknight due to their weird schedules, but they rarely missed a month.

Hannah laughed at Julian. "So what did Drake say when they all wanted to know why he had a key?"

Julian made a frustrated sound. "Oh, he's a horrible liar. He said I had asked him to help with something at the house and forgot to give it back. I wish you could have seen their faces." She shook her head. "Then Mom gave me the third degree about it later." Julian stopped laughing and took a deep breath.

"Hannah, I need to tell you something." Julian explained the emails. Hannah's eyes widened in horror. When she opened her mouth, Julian held her hand up. "I've already gone to the police. They're documenting everything, but I have no idea who it could be to even point them in a direction."

"Arnold, maybe?"

She shrugged. "I don't know. Doesn't seem like him."

Hannah shuddered then threw her arms around her friend. "Poor Julian."

Julian laughed at Hannah's dramatic reaction and patted her arms. "Oh, I'm all right. I just didn't want you to hear about the emails from Mom. The calls were bad enough, but the emails are a new level of creepy." She leaned her head against Hannah's and appreciated her friend's concern.

"I wish there was something I could do," Hannah said.

"You can pretend we didn't talk about it so we can enjoy our movie."

They sat back from each other and noticed a funny moment, laughing at the same time.

Hannah sipped her wine. "I haven't had time to talk to you about your date with Drake. We skipped right to Sunday dinner."

"It was fun." Julian took a sip from her own glass.

Hannah gave Julian a skeptical look. "That burly hunk of man took you on a date, and the word you use is fun?" Julian shrugged, a flush creeping up her neck. Hannah giggled. "That's what I thought."

Julian kicked her friend. "What about you? Did Rob call you?"

"He did."

"And?"

"We went for coffee."

"And?"

Hannah sipped her wine again. Julian was glad Hannah wouldn't be driving later. Her friend's eyes twinkled with barely contained excitement. "I really like him."

"He's a really nice guy."

"Ha! Nice? He's better than nice. I find you weird for having only ever used the word 'charming' to describe that man. He must not have kissed you or you'd never use that calm word again."

Julian gasped but then laughed at Hannah as her phone dinged with the text message alert. She placed her glass on the coffee table and looked at her phone. "It's Drake." She read the text and smiled. "He wants to know if I eat pork chops."

"Tell him something crazy like you only eat chickens because they hatch instead of being birthed."

They giggled together. "You're so weird." She snorted gracelessly as she continued, "No. I'll say…" She read each word as she typed it. "I. Love. Pork. Chops." She typed more then read all at once. "Now shush. Girls only. No boys allowed."

The women dissolved into hysterical laughter together. Julian looked at her second glass of wine and put it back on the coffee table. "Okay. That's enough for me. I'm not drunk, but I'm definitely feeling too good or that wouldn't be so funny."

She read the reply text aloud with a deep macho voice when it came. "I'm not a boy, I'm a man." They roared at that. Julian fell over on the couch convulsing with laughter while Hannah laughed so hard no sound came out of her mouth, just wheezing. Julian sat back up and shoved Hannah's phone toward her. "Text something to Rob so we can read his texts with his accent."

Hannah gasped. "No! I can't do that. You do it."

Julian sighed and grabbed her phone again. "Fine." She wrote a quick text asking how his weekend had been.

When he responded, Julian read with an overly exaggerated British accent. "My weekend was brilliant. Met Hannah for coffee. She's a lovely woman."

Hannah leaned close. "Really? Does he know I'm here?"

"I haven't talked to him. Did you tell him?"

"No. I just told him I had plans."

"Hmm." Julian tapped another text to Rob.

"What are you writing?"

Julian just smirked. "I asked him if his ears are burning since we're just talking about him."

His reply came quickly. Julian read with the accent again. "Only good things, I hope. Don't forget my dashing good looks."

Hannah grimaced. "Are you sure you're okay with this? I feel like a terrible friend."

"For what? We decided to be friends well before he ever laid eyes on you. My only goal now is to convince the two of you to fall in love."

They giggled together again. They quickly abandoned Rob as they had Drake to gossip about together and watch their movie before they finally called it a night.

When Julian's alarm went off in the morning, she was glad she'd stopped at two glasses of wine. Hannah's firm closed the week of Thanksgiving and the week of Christmas, and she slept soundly in the guest room while Julian dragged out of bed. She went through her normal morning routine as quietly as possible in an effort not to wake Hannah. Just as quietly, she finally slipped out to her car and headed to the office.

As the workday neared its end, Julian found it increasingly difficult to concentrate on her tasks as she thought about meeting Drake at his house for dinner. A few minutes before she would have normally gathered her things to leave, Julian's manager called her into her office. "Close the door," the older woman instructed.

Julian felt her heart sink. She obeyed and sat at her manager's request. The older woman's grim face worried her. "I don't even know how to say this." She took a deep breath. "You know, with the economy and the company's financial problems, upper management is trying to find ways to save money."

Julian felt lightheaded. "I'm being laid off?"

Her manager fought tears. "Yes."

Julian's throat tightened in concern. "Effective when?"

"Today. I have your severance package here. A month's worth of pay and your remaining leave time."

The manager frowned as she handed the paperwork to Julian. Julian accepted the paperwork mutely. When she found her voice, she asked, "They made you tell me two days before Thanksgiving?"

Her manager burst into tears. "I know. I'm so sorry."

Julian stood and hugged the older woman. She forced a smile on her face. "I'll be all right." After completing the paperwork, Julian returned to her desk and collected the few personal items she used to decorate—a couple of framed pictures of her parents and one of her and Hannah as kids, and a small plant she struggled to keep alive. The rest of the office had already emptied. Julian was glad. The last thing she wanted was to have everyone telling her goodbye and getting upset. She just wanted out of the building.

Julian used her phone's GPS app to find Drake's house and let her jaw drop as she entered the neighborhood. While Julian was familiar with the exclusive area, she had never been there. She drove through the town square designed for the lakefront community which housed small coffee shops, boutiques, an upscale sports bar, and more. All around the square sat townhouses. A little further out from the square were rows of Charleston-style single-family homes–narrow, multilevel houses with very little yard. Drake's two story house was gray-blue with white trim. Julian parked and took a deep breath. Using the visor mirror, she brushed her hair and freshened her lip gloss. She then grabbed the plant from the passenger seat along with her purse. Julian walked up the stone path to the door and rang the doorbell. She forced a pleasant expression onto her face.

When Drake opened the front door, Julian felt the familiar flip flop of her stomach at seeing him. He looked relaxed in jeans and a black knit shirt. He smiled, but it faded with a hard look at Julian's face. "What happened?"

She gave up the pretense, sighed, and shoved the plant at him. "Maybe you'll have better luck keeping this plant alive than me. I don't need it at work anymore."

Drake ushered her inside and closed the door behind her. He took the plant, her coat, and her purse and led her into the bright, open living area with a similar concept to hers. The kitchen, dining area, and living room all sat in one large room with a fireplace. Julian could smell the food waiting for her, and her stomach growled despite her state of concern over her job. They chuckled at that. Drake put the plant on a shelf and asked again, "What happened?"

Julian shook her head. "Can we eat first? I'm not ready to talk about it."

"Sure."

They sat at the dining table and ate. "This is really good." Julian meant it. She figured Drake would be one of those annoying people who would excel at anything they chose to undertake.

"Thanks."

She saw him watching her carefully as they ate. She asked about the vineyard and his parents and Amerigo. He casually answered her questions and carried the conversation as they finished dinner. After they ate, Drake took their plates to the kitchen and started to open a bottle of wine. Julian held up a hand. "None for me. Thanks."

Drake abandoned the bottle with a thoughtful look.

"C'mon. I'll show you the rest of the house."

He showed her the back patio with the bistro table and

chairs. Then they went upstairs. The house had four bedrooms. He occupied the master and had a guest room ready for visitors. The other two rooms had been set up as an office/library and a home gym. Julian gave Drake an impressed look. "You really have a nice house." She glanced in the room with the treadmill and weights and grinned. "That figures." Drake laughed and shrugged. Then he followed her to the other room as she gazed at the desk and walls of bookshelves. Julian scanned the titles with a genuine smile. "This room I wouldn't have expected. You boys really like to read."

Drake feigned insult. "What? I'm a jarhead so I don't know how to read?"

"I didn't mean it like that," she said, embarrassed.

He just chuckled and took her hand, leading her back down the stairs to sit on the couch in front of the fireplace. "All right. You've put it off as long as I'll let you. What's wrong? Did you get another email?"

Julian shook her head. "No, thank God. It's simpler than that." She retrieved her purse and pulled out the first paper of the packet her manager had given her. "I was laid off today."

"What?" He took the paper and looked at it. "When's your last day?"

"Today. My manager—well, now former manager, I guess—told me at the end of the day. I came straight here." She explained the severance package with dry eyes. Then Julian muttered, "Two days before Thanksgiving. I guess I should be happy they didn't do it right before Christmas."

Drake frowned and pulled her into his embrace. "How long did you work there?"

"Ten years, two months. I just got my ten year plaque." She leaned gratefully against him and started anticipating the conversation with her mother.

"Will you be okay?"

She nodded against his shirt. "I'm sure I'll find something."

She sighed when he stroked her hair. "I'm sorry to be such a downer on our second real date." Julian leaned back to grin at him.

Drake laughed. "You shouldn't ever worry about that with me."

She sighed again. "Why are you so nice to me?"

"You saved—"

Julian held up a hand with a frustrated sound. "I know. I saved you and Amerigo. I got it." Why had she even asked that question? She'd already suspected that reasoning was the root of why Drake spent time with her. Sheer gratitude. Duty. He would eventually get over this silly notion and move on. She stood, snatched up her coat and purse, and headed for the door only to have Drake intercept her with amazing speed.

"Julian, you didn't let me finish."

"It's all right. I understand. I'm not your type, but I helped you guys so—"

He interrupted her, his jaw tight. "Why does everyone keep talking about my type? I'm starting to get a real complex." Julian saw frustration etched in his features. "How shallow does everyone think I am?"

Julian stopped short and clapped her open mouth shut. "I don't think you're shallow, it's just—"

"It's just what? Why shouldn't I be interested in you? Because you're intelligent? Because you're intuitive and understand family? Compassionate. Articulate. Funny. Beautiful."

She stared at him. He meant what he said.

With a grunt, he said, "Maybe you're the one who shouldn't be interested in me. Evidently I'm about as deep as a puddle of water according to my family."

"What in the world are you talking about?"

"You should have heard the interrogation about that key when I took my mom home Sunday."

Julian rolled her eyes. "Ugh. From my mom too."

Drake grunted again. "Then she and Amerigo gave me this same drill about my type. I really believe they don't think I'm good enough for you."

Horrified, Julian felt tears threatening. "They don't really think that. It's just—" Words failed her. She felt exposed by this conversation. A strangled sound left her as she fought to control her emotions. "Drake, I'm pretty sure I don't look like the kind of woman you normally date. Sometimes when I'm with you, I feel beautiful and sexy. Then I'm reminded how I saved your life, and how you think you owe me something. Then I feel like the nerdy girl the quarterback takes pity on after she helps him with a test. Eventually, he ends back up with the homecoming queen."

A muscle worked in Drake's jaw as he stepped closer to her. She forced herself not to back up when he towered over her.

"Julian, we met under unusual circumstances. You saved me. You saved Amerigo. I will always owe you for that, but that didn't obligate me to ask you out or want to see you or want to kiss you." Julian swallowed nervously but stood her ground as he continued, "And for the record, you are beautiful and sexy. I'd have to be dead not to notice it, and it's your fault I'm not dead." Julian's hands shook and threatened to drop her purse. He cupped her face and tilted her head toward him. "I can prove I'm not dead."

His mouth descended on hers. Julian put one hand against his chest to steady herself as he kissed her with a tenderness she hadn't expected. When he raised his head, she looked into his dark eyes. She dropped her purse and coat as they collided, her arms around his neck and his around her waist. The tenderness was replaced by an urgency that she felt, too. Julian's head emptied of rational thought as she clung to him.

They staggered together in the foyer until Drake urged them back to the living room as they kissed. He steered them around the armchair and table until their legs met with the couch. Julian yelped as they tumbled onto the cushions together, ungracefully sitting, him pulling her across his lap. They sat still for a moment, the action jolting them both back to reality.

"See? I'm not dead."

Julian laughed and then took a deep breath. "No. Neither am I." She raised a shaky hand to touch his dark hair with a grin then frowned and scooted off his lap.

"There's something else, though." Her heart thudded. She took another deep breath and expelled it noisily.

Julian opened her mouth, but Drake announced, "You're not going to sleep with me."

She sat back, stunned. "How did you know I was going to say that? I mean, I was looking for a delicate way to put it, but it is what I was going to say."

"It's something my mom said Sunday." He grinned and mimicked his mother's voice. "If you're only interested in something physical with her, you should break it off now, or you'll be disappointed."

Julian's shoulders slumped in thought as she looked at the floor. "Wow. I never even had a conversation remotely close to that with your mom." She turned her eyes back to Drake, her heart in her throat. "Okay. So it's out there. I understand if that's a deal breaker." She held her breath as she watched him.

He gave her a wry smile. "Despite the reputation I evidently have with friends and family, sex is not my ultimate goal in life." Julian felt hope bloom and smiled. He held up a hand. "Don't get me wrong. It caught me off guard. I thought about it a lot." Julian's palms still felt damp as she listened. This was the conversation that normally ended up with a polite goodbye, a harsh goodbye, or a lie to respect her decision then the attempt to seduce her anyway. She knew him well enough to expect a polite goodbye if he couldn't deal with the decision. Instead, he continued, "I'm physically attracted to you, but if that's the decision you've made, well, then that's how it is." He put an arm around her and pulled her close to him. "I won't pretend it won't be a challenge though."

Julian grinned and ran her fingers over his clean-shaven jaw. "Stop talking about what people think about you. You know what you are better than anyone else."

"Okay. Then you don't ever try to imply you're not attractive again either." He kissed her softly and asked, "This is still okay, though, right?"

She caught his teasing tone and smiled. "It's more than okay." Drake smothered her next comments with his mouth. Julian closed her eyes and realized for the first time in a long time, she'd need all her resolve to maintain her decision.

* * *

Julian's alarm went off early in the morning as normal. She rolled over and turned it off with a grimace, wishing she'd remembered to deactivate it the night before. She had binge-watched a television show with Drake on Netflix then called it a night, deciding to wait to tell Gale and Hannah until the next day about her job. She had just wanted to think about anything but that for the rest of the evening. Sitting next to Drake and laughing with him at one of her favorite shows had chased all other thoughts away.

As the sunlight filtered into her bedroom, the unwanted thoughts furiously rushed back. Julian ran a hand over her face and moaned. She would tell her mom first, but she decided to eat breakfast before calling.

Julian toasted a bagel and spread cream cheese and jelly on top. She ate the bagel while she perused some social media websites and her email. Thankfully, her email only contained some newsletters and a quick note from her friend, Jodi, her fellow author thanking her for reading her latest book. Jodi's email then indicated she had received a call from John Hatcher. "He's a sad, weird little man," the email said. Julian chuckled and wrote back to tell Jodi about seeing John at the movie theater. She also told Jodi about Rob and Drake and losing her job. She enjoyed their friendship. They mainly only saw each other at conventions, but when they saw each other, they talked as if no time had passed since the last convention.

Since she had eaten breakfast, she might as well have some coffee before calling her mom. She brewed a cup of coffee and sat at the kitchen table with her laptop again. Her cell phone dinged with a text from Drake: Call your mom before mine does. Julian groaned and replied she would. She then dialed her mother.

Gale gasped. "Two days before Thanksgiving?"

"I know. That's what I said."

They chatted for a little while about nothing, but the talk comforted Julian. Her mom always made her feel better when something bad happened. When they finished their call, Julian steeled herself and called Hannah.

Hannah's reaction included a few choice words that made Julian cringe. When she calmed down, she asked, "Why don't you let me take you to lunch?"

Julian agreed to meet Hannah then spent time praying about the things worrying her—the calls, the emails, now her job, and even her relationship with Drake—and the prayer time encouraged her. Feeling better, she decided to take advantage of the free morning before lunch.

Instead of her normal shower, she took a steaming bubble bath. Then she touched up the paint on her toenails. She used a mud mask and drank some herbal tea while listening to music on her phone. After that, she washed off the mask and blew her hair dry. Then she applied her makeup and dressed in a pair of jeans, a nice blouse, and a pair of tasteful boots. Julian stood in front of the bathroom mirror and checked the time. She had just a few minutes before she needed to leave. Still in front of the mirror, Julian pulled her hair back and looked at the scar at her hairline. It had healed well but not yet faded. The ugly scar stared at her. Julian pushed her chin up and gave herself a defiant look. Life beat her up sometimes, but she faced it and the scar proved it.

Hannah waited at a table in the Asian bistro, one of Julian's favorite places. She rose from her chair and hugged Julian harder than normal. They sat down and placed their orders with the server. When he left, Hannah gave her a sympathetic smile. "How are you feeling?"

"Well, I woke up kinda depressed, but I spent the morning primping, and now I feel better."

They laughed together. Hannah agreed, "Yeah, doing that kind of stuff always makes me feel better too. So what now?"

Julian shrugged her shoulders. "It's only been a day. I think I'll just try to make it through Thanksgiving tomorrow, and hope the sympathy doesn't depress me too much."

Hannah folded her hands on the table. She fidgeted. "I'm nervous about tomorrow. Are you sure this is okay?"

"Of course it is. You'll love Drake's family, and they'll love you."

"I hope you're right. I'm nervous about seeing Rob, too. I have no idea why."

Julian looked at her friend's worried face and patted one of her hands. "If he doesn't show the proper attention to my best friend, I'll kick him out. Even if it isn't my house."

Hannah smiled at her. "You're the best friend a person could have, Julian."

CHAPTER TEN

Drake arrived early at his parents' house Thursday morning to help prepare for guests. As was tradition in their home, his mother had prepared a light breakfast so they would be hungry for their Thanksgiving dinner, normally served at lunch time. Amerigo hobbled through the house on crutches but soon rested on the chaise lounge again. Drake watched his younger brother's pinched face and felt his chest tighten. Poor Amerigo. His improved prognosis had not eradicated his current pain or need for physical therapy. Amerigo could look forward to a lengthy recovery. Drake helped his mother cook while his father started a fire and set the table. Anthony joined them in the kitchen and offered his services. Mary set him to work peeling potatoes. While Anthony had only come to the United States in his early twenties, Mary's family had been in America for generations, most of that time in South Carolina. She believed in a hearty Southern Thanksgiving meal with mashed potatoes and gravy, baked macaroni and cheese, sweet potato casserole, cornbread, among other heavy dishes. Gale had offered to cook and bring the turkey while Julian would bring a ham. Hannah and Rob were tasked with bringing extra desserts but were warned not to bring pie. Drake would make pies. No one remembered how the tradition started, but each year, Drake made homemade pies from scratch, even the crust. He had made them all the night before, and they would just need warmed.

Julian and Gale arrived around eleven. Drake met them at the car and carried the turkey for Gale. He met Julian's eyes and gave her a warm smile over the roof of the car and out of Gale's sight. She blushed but returned the smile. As they walked toward the house, Gale went ahead of Drake and Julian to hold the door. Drake murmured, "Brace yourself. Mom and Pop are in full on fix-it mode about your job."

He heard Julian groan then laugh. "Your family is good people, Drake."

Drake nodded. "I'm really lucky… Even though they could drive me to drink the entire vineyard dry sometimes."

She giggled as they walked by Gale and through the door. Drake noticed an unknown car approaching. He continued to the kitchen to deposit the turkey then returned to the porch. He recognized the two people once the car parked. Rob and Hannah. They carried two cakes and a covered pan. Drake took one of the cakes from Rob, and they shook hands. Hannah gave Drake a one-armed hug as each of them held a dessert. "It's good to see you again, Drake." He returned the embrace with a grin.

"You too, Hannah. Hi, Rob."

Rob smiled his likable smile, and Drake felt a snake of jealousy coil in the pit of his stomach. "Thanks for having me over today. Your family was very kind to invite me," Rob said.

"Not a problem." Drake led them through the house and cast a look of disdain at Amerigo as he passed. Amerigo smirked from the chaise lounge. Drake told them, "The food's basically ready so we're getting right to eating, it seems."

Julian joined Rob and Hannah in the kitchen. Drake forced himself not to grind his teeth when Rob embraced Julian. Mary and Anthony appeared from nowhere, and Julian introduced them to Rob. She then introduced Rob to her mother when she entered the kitchen as well. Gale held his shoulders as she met his eyes. "I've heard a lot about you. All good."

Mary made a clucking sound. "Too many cooks in the kitchen. Everyone take a dish and put it on the table in the kitchen. We'll make plates in there and eat in the dining room." Drake went into the living room and helped Amerigo into his wheelchair, propping his leg up as everyone else obeyed Mary's command.

Amerigo spoke under his breath to Drake. "You're right. He's likable and good-looking, but you've missed something important, and I'm not gonna tell you. You'll have to figure it out on your own."

"You're such a spoiled brat."

"Ha! You love your favorite brother. Admit it."

"Favorite brother? You're my only brother."

Amerigo laughed at his own joke.

Everyone loaded a plate buffet-style from the table in the kitchen then headed to the dining room. Once everyone sat with their plate and drink, Anthony held out his hands to those to his left and right. Once everyone held hands around the table, Anthony said a heavily-accented prayer for the food and fellowship. Afterward, Gale asked Amerigo how his leg felt to start conversation.

"It still hurts, but it's a lot better. My prognosis is good. I'm very fortunate."

"I'm so glad. My women's group at church has been praying for you," Gale told him.

"Thank you," he replied, a genuine smile on his lips. Amerigo's positive attitude encouraged Drake. Amerigo added, "I figured while I'm stuck here, I would let Julian's example inspire me."

Julian's head snapped up from her forkful of macaroni and cheese. "My example?"

"I'm taking an online creative writing class."

She beamed at him. "That's great. Have you already started?"

He nodded. "I'm working on a short story right now."

Drake grinned at her as she clapped her hands together excitedly. "Good for you. When can I read it?"

"Never." His tone held a shy note. "I just thought you'd be interested in knowing about it."

"I won't pressure you. It's hard to let people read your writing when you're first starting. I still get nervous when someone I know is reading one of my books." She cast a glance at Drake.

"I love your books," Mary told her.

Hannah nodded. "Me, too."

Rob smiled broadly. "Just out of curiosity, how many people at this table have read at least one of Julian's books?"

Everyone raised their hands. Julian turned scarlet. "Really?" She gave Anthony a skeptical look. "Even you?"

The older man confirmed it. "It was good. I liked the hero and how he fought for justice for his family"

Mary added her opinion. "I like all of them, but I especially like the one where the main character trips over her own feet all the time. I really cheered for her."

"I like the one with the woman who plays video games all the time." Amerigo took a bite of his mashed potatoes.

Drake grinned as he ate, listened, and watched Julian squirm in the seat next to him. His grin turned into a grimace when Gale said, "Well, you can get more writing done now that you're not working—at least until you find another job."

Rob looked confused. Julian took a deep breath. "I was laid off this week."

"Oh no!" he said, a look of horror on his face. "I'm so sorry."

Drake reached under the table and squeezed Julian's hand. She plastered on a smile. "Thanks."

Mary astutely changed the topic. "What do you do for a living, Rob?"

"I'm the assistant vice president of marketing for my company."

"How nice!" Mary said.

Gale turned to Drake. "How are enjoying retirement, Drake?"

Drake chuckled. "I'd enjoy it better if I was actually able to do something around the vineyard, but it's good. Thanks for asking."

Mary tsked at him. "Plenty of time for that soon. Enjoy the down time while you can."

Conversation continued in a light vein as Hannah answered questions about the law firm and her job there. Everyone talked about life in general as they ate. Drake watched Julian, exchanging smiles with her often at different points of the conversation. Amerigo gave Drake a pointed look and motioned his eyes toward Rob as subtly as possible. Drake glanced in Rob's direction attempting to be discreet and finally figured out what Amerigo saw that his older brother had missed. Rob's eyes stayed glued on Hannah, and Hannah reciprocated.

Upon the realization, Drake glanced at Julian, her eyes full of mischief. She winked at Drake, and he shook his head at her with a grin. That little minx, he thought but couldn't bring himself to be angry, not when she looked so relentlessly cheerful.

After dinner, everyone gathered in the living room. Drake helped Amerigo back onto the chaise lounge then sat next to Julian, flanked on her other side by Gale. Anthony opened a bottle of wine and served everyone in the room. Then he stood near the fireplace. "Every year, we share a bottle of our best and tell why we're thankful. I'll start. I know she hates for us to bring it up, but I'm thankful to Julian for my sons. Without her, this holiday would not be the happy occasion it is today."

Julian gracefully accepted the praise, obviously prepared for it. Drake smirked at her. She poked her elbow in his ribs. "Your turn to be embarrassed will come eventually." He casually stretched his arm across the back of the couch and tugged at a lock of her hair in response. She elbowed him again, and he tugged her hair again.

Gale slapped Julian's thigh and hissed at the pair. "Behave."

Drake chuckled but stopped. Julian folded her arms petulantly but then smiled.

They went around the room allowing everyone to speak, but almost all of their turns sounded much similar—gratitude for friends and family.

Rob glanced around the room. "I like Thanksgiving." They all laughed at that.

After a moment of amiable silence, Mary clapped her hands and grinned. "Well, now Thanksgiving dinner's over. Do you know what that means?"

Drake and Amerigo looked at each other and groaned as Mary hurried to the other side of the room. Rob looked bewildered. "What does it mean?"

In unison, the men announced, "Christmas music."

Mary toyed with a stereo, and Elvis began singing "Blue Christmas" through speakers mounted in the room. Julian roared with laughter. "You're a woman after my own heart."

Mary reminded everyone, "Don't forget we have dessert in a little bit."

The room of people broke into smaller conversations as the music played around them. Drake turned to Julian and rubbed his stomach. "I'm not ready for dessert. That was way too much food." He smiled. "You know what we should do?"

"Take naps? We could pull out mats like in kindergarten, and everyone take a nap," she said, her eyes sparkling with humor.

"Funny," he replied and tweaked her nose. "I was going to say we could walk down to the vineyard and look around. That would help."

Julian's face lit up at the idea. "That'd be nice."

Drake stood and announced, "We're walking to the vineyard." He reached a hand out to Julian, who took it with a grin. "Anyone joining us?"

Rob turned to Hannah. "Want to go?"

"Sure. I need to move around, or I'll be asleep in five minutes."

Mary looked at Gale. "I see the vineyard all the time. Want to play cards?"

Gale nodded and followed Mary to the small table with two chairs in the corner.

Anthony took her vacant seat next to Amerigo. "I think we'll turn the game on with the sound off."

Drake, Julian, Rob, and Hannah all slipped into their coats and headed outside, Drake leading the way. Late November in South Carolina tended to be a grab bag of temperatures. Thanksgiving had turned cold for the state, and they could see their breath. Julian had wrapped her black and purple scarf around her neck and donned her matching knit gloves. Her half-hidden face amused him. Rob and Hannah walked next to them but far enough away that their conversation could not be overheard. Drake appreciated that as he leaned closer to Julian. He spoke to her under his breath. "You neglected to tell me something about Rob."

She smirked at him. "Oh yeah. We're just friends. Evidently, he and Hannah really hit it off after we decided that."

Drake cast her another sidelong glance. "You could have

told me that. How long ago has it been?"

Julian shrugged sheepishly.

"You had multiple opportunities to tell me, Julian."

She gave him a pretty smile and batted her eyelashes. "Well, when I'm with you, I'm not thinking about Rob."

He laughed at that and put an arm around her shoulders. "That was smooth."

Julian pulled her collar up around her face and said, "Yup."

They chuckled together. She put an arm around his back as they walked. He glanced over his shoulder at Hannah and Rob, who talked quietly while walking hand in hand. Drake smiled down at Julian, who smiled up at him from behind her scarf. The wind caught her hair, and he saw the red line of the cut at her temple. His smile faded as he wished it had been him that had been injured in the wreck instead of her or Amerigo. He'd rather bear it himself than see either of them hurt. He ran the fingers from the arm around her shoulders over the scar. "It doesn't still hurt, does it?"

"Nah. It's fine. Just not attractive."

He kissed the top of her head. "You're beautiful."

They walked the rest of the way in comfortable silence. When they reached the rows of vines, Drake pointed out how the vines had been pruned and winterized. The three visitors listened with genuine interest as he explained some of the process of wine making. Rob asked good questions, showing sincere interest.

Julian tilted her head. "I've never thought to ask if you if do tours and samplings here."

Drake shook his head. "No. My parents thought about it, but they didn't want to deal with the headache by themselves. It's something we've talked about again now that I'm here to help."

Hannah looked around appreciatively. "That's a great idea. It's really beautiful here."

Rob added, "The nearest vineyard to you isn't close. There's a good market here."

Drake thought about it for the umpteenth time. The idea seemed nice, but the amount of money, time, and even renovations needed would be enormous. They would need more staff. He looked at the old barn in the distance and thought how it could be converted for visitors. The idea had not yet been put to rest. "It's a possibility."

"What time is it?" Hannah asked, and Julian dug her phone out of her pocket to check.

"It's two o'clock." She pulled off one of her gloves and touched the screen. Then the color drained from her face. Drake pursed his lips.

"Show me."

Julian tapped the phone then turned it around to reveal the screen. The video showed Julian leaving her car and entering the restaurant where she had met Hannah for lunch. Hannah gasped, and Rob narrowed his eyes.

"What are we looking at?"

Drake explained, "Someone's been following Julian and sending her videos and pictures of herself."

Hannah added, "We think it's the same person that had been calling her before she changed her phone number."

"My God," Rob whispered.

Julian released a pent up breath. "I'm forwarding it to Detective Reynolds now." She tapped the phone again then forced a smile. "I'm sure it's a harmless crackpot, but better safe than sorry, right?"

Rob met Drake's eyes. Drake gave him a slight nod. Rob cleared his throat and suggested, "Hannah, let's go see if anyone's ready for dessert." Hannah allowed Rob to take her hand and lead her away.

Drake turned to Julian. "Are you okay?"

"No." She ran her hands through her hair. "I want to know how he knows where I am all the time. How does he know where to be?"

Drake wanted to know, too. "We'll figure it out."

Julian walked a few paces away then turned and walked back. "When will I figure it out? When he's hurt someone? When he's hurt me?" She balled her fingers into fists. She looked at Drake with a helpless expression. "What do I do?" Tears welled in her eyes. He pulled her into his arms and smoothed her hair away from her face as the tears spilled over her cheeks.

"I didn't say you'll figure it out. I said we'll figure it out."

Her voice came out as a whisper when she said, "It's gonna get worse before it gets better."

Drake's heart sank. She was probably right. He felt Julian trembling, and his protective instincts, already focused on her, kicked into high gear. He tightened his embrace as she sobbed He avoided platitudes. She needed to cry. Drake let her. When her tears slowed, he pulled her back to look his her red-rimmed eyes. "I'll do whatever is in my power to protect you." She blinked as she looked at him.

"That's what I'm worried about. I'm afraid someone else will get hurt. I couldn't stand it if something happened to my family or your family. And if something happened to you…" She choked back another sob.

He smiled at her. "I'm not helpless, Julian." She laughed through her tears.

"No. I guess a career Marine probably doesn't need a bodyguard."

Drake sobered then. "Look, South Carolina is a concealed weapons state. Why don't you let me teach you how to use a weapon, and you can get your permit to carry something with you?" He had been toying with the idea for a few days.

Julian opened her mouth to answer but closed it again as she turned the thought over in her head. "Okay."

CHAPTER ELEVEN

Julian still had trouble believing she agreed to this. She stood in the firing range with a pistol on the platform in front of her. Her heart thudded wildly in her chest. Her hands shook a little. That probably needed to stop before she picked up the gun. She turned to face Drake fully. He grimly met her eyes. "You can do this."

She smiled at him resolutely. "I know. I just want to make sure you don't turn into a drill instructor and start yelling at me. I'm not a Marine, okay?"

"I wasn't a drill instructor," he told her with a grin.

"But you did train, right?"

"Yes."

"Did you ever yell at the trainees?"

His response came through the grin. "Maybe."

"Ha! See? Don't yell at me." She gave him a pleading look.

"I won't. I promise."

She sighed and some of her shaking subsided. Drake began explaining gun safety tips, such as only putting her finger on the trigger when she intended to actually fire and how to properly use the safety feature on the gun. He showed her how to load the ammo and remove it. She watched closely, actively trying to commit everything he showed her to memory. He had her repeat the steps to him. They reviewed everything again. With a stern look he told her, "If an assailant comes at you to take your gun, make him reach you through a wall of bullets."

Julian set her jaw. "Drake, I would do anything I could to protect the people in my life, but make no mistake about it. If I think someone will hurt me, I will also zealously defend myself."

He smiled. "Good girl."

It took a long time before Drake would let Julian actually fire the pistol. Julian appreciated the ear protection when she used the gun. Drake corrected her stance a little and had her fire again. She bit her lip and imagined the target to be the man sending her emails. Anger rose, but she took a deep breath to use it as fuel instead of letting it ride her. Drake whistled after her shots. "Impressive, Julian." She looked at the cluster of holes in the paper target surrounding the center circle. "Have you ever practiced marksmanship before?" Julian shook her head. "What about video games? Ever play first person shooters?"

"Oh yeah. I used to play a lot when I was younger. I still like it, but the consoles got so expensive I couldn't keep up with the latest technology."

He looked at her. "Now I know what to get you for Christmas." Drake chuckled with pride. "I wish some of my trainees picked this up as quickly as you are. You still need to practice, but that's really good for your first time." She blinked at him, and he admitted, "Okay, well, it's good for anytime, but there's always room for improvement. Plus, you don't want to forget or lose your familiarity with the weapon."

Julian handed him the pistol. "Let me see you do it." He

shrugged and took the gun. He held it up and fired several shots together. Drake pushed the button to bring the paper close to them. Julian gasped. His shots had been so accurate they had created a single hole in the center of the target's forehead. She gawked. "I guess I do have room for improvement." He handed the pistol back to her.

"I'll get a new target, and let's see you try again."

As Julian continued to practice, Drake continued to give her advice. "If you're ever in a really dangerous situation, try to think. Tell yourself to think. You're very intelligent. Use your brain." Julian stopped firing for a moment.

"What if I'm scared beyond reason?"

"It happens, but I think you could push through it. It's how you were able to help Amerigo and I in the accident. You didn't freeze up."

Julian shrugged. "That was different."

"Why?"

"Because the danger was to you guys, not me. At least, not at first."

Drake nodded. "True, but you put yourself in danger when you came to help us."

It still seemed different to her. She hadn't realized the danger until it actually happened. Then Drake had gotten them out of the SUV and towed her to the shore. All she did was unfasten their seatbelts. But Drake's face indicated how futile arguing would be. Julian took a deep breath and returned to practicing.

After a long time, Drake suggested they get something to eat. Julian had been enjoying the practice, but her stomach rumbled in protest of its neglect at the mention of food. "Food sounds great," she laughed.

They drove to a nearby casual restaurant, chatting comfortably about nothing as they ordered burgers and fries. Julian considered how different her life had been not even two months ago. She'd been content as she worked at her boring day job and wrote fiction on the side, not looking for a relationship or to change her circumstances. Then came the accident, and suddenly everything felt upside down in both good and bad ways.

She smiled at Drake as she thought about how much knowing him and his family had enriched her life. And her mother's life. Even Hannah had been affected. Things looked promising with Rob, but Julian wouldn't have met Rob if it hadn't been for the story on the news that led to that day in the coffee shop that led to Hannah meeting him. Funny how things worked out.

Drake reached toward her plate for a sweet potato fry. Julian swatted at his hand. "Excuse me, but I offered you half of these and you said, 'Sweet potato fries are an abomination.'"

He laughed at her imitation of him then the amusement fled from his face as he looked past her.

Julian turned to look at what he saw. A beautiful couple waited at the hostess stand to be seated. The man looked like he belonged in a magazine perfume advertisement except he was fully dressed. The woman looked older but still gorgeous. Whippet thin and tall with sleek, shiny blonde hair expertly worked into long waves down her back, the woman glanced around the room as if she had stepped in something unpleasant. Then her eyes locked on Drake, and Julian saw recognition. Julian's stomach knotted. The woman's mouth curved into a cruel smile as she approached their table. Julian turned and saw Drake's face, a set of hard lines. That couldn't be good. The woman stopped by their table.

"Hello, Drake."

"Hello, Mariella. I wouldn't expect to see you someplace so far beneath you."

"I'm slumming it with Raoul over there. He might have bad taste in restaurants, but he's a cash cow."

Drake snorted derisively and looked at Julian. "Julian, meet my ex-wife, Mariella Cortez. Mariella, this is Julian Fursey." Before Julian could greet the woman, he nodded his head toward the younger man now waving to Mariella to join him. "So you represent him?"

"Yes. Among other things I do with him." She gave Drake a lurid smile. "The clients love his look."

Julian remained silent as she continued to digest how Drake had introduced this woman. His ex-wife? She hadn't even known he had been married before. He looked like he could barely contain his disgust with her. Without glancing at Julian, he explained, "Mariella modeled until she couldn't. Now, she runs an agency." He narrowed his eyes at the woman. "What are you even doing in town?"

"Well, it's the holidays. I came to see my family."

"Did they actually want to see you?"

She laughed a light, bright laugh Julian imagined she used with clients and suitors alike. Julian felt sick to her stomach. Not only had Drake been married, but he'd actually been married to an actual, freakin' model?

Mariella said, "You're still so funny, Drake. It was nice to meet you, Julian. Enjoy your meal." She walked away without ever really looking at Julian.

Drake frowned and swigged his tea. Julian cleared her throat.

"Well. That was… awkward," Julian muttered.

Drake looked sheepish. "I should explain."

"No," Julian replied quickly. "Not here." Julian caught Mariella still watching Drake and smiled cheerfully. Through her smile, she said, "Don't worry. I'll give you the third degree in the car, but right now, I won't give your heifer ex-wife the pleasure of thinking she ruined our meal." She ate one of the sweet potato fries and continued to grin. Julian wanted to be angry and jealous, but she sat across from a man who had promised to do anything he could to protect her, had spent his morning helping her learn how to protect herself, and had instantly disliked Arnold before he knew anything about him other than Julian didn't like him. Fair was fair. If Drake disliked Mariella Cortez, then she did too. "Is she still watching?" Julian asked.

He looked annoyed when he replied, "Yes."

The server stopped at their table to check on them. "Will there be anything else?"

"Just the check."

Julian caught him. "Do you have a dessert menu?" He nodded. She flashed her brightest smile at him. "I'd love to see it."

Drake raised an eyebrow at her. "I'd rather just go."

Julian batted her eyelashes at him and smirked. "Oh, c'mon. It won't take long. We'll share it." The server brought the dessert menu, and Julian scooted into Drake's side of the booth, allowing them to both see the table where his ex-wife sat with Raoul. She held up the dessert menu and whispered in Drake's ear, "I won't order anything if you really want to leave, but if you want to be disgustingly happy in front of her, I'm game to play it up." She gave him a pouty grin, her mouth still very close to Drake's ear. "I can be much more diabolical than I get credit for."

He cleared his throat as the server returned and said, "We'll have the strawberry shortcake."

Julian genuinely giggled at his response. "That's the spirit." She stayed close and placed an arm around him to run her fingers through his thick hair. Julian grinned when he put an arm around the back of her chair as well. He rubbed his hand over her shoulder possessively and gave her the first smile she had seen from him since Mariella had entered the restaurant. Julian crossed her legs so that her whole body shifted toward Drake, her left calf resting over his under the table. Julian knew

Mariella could see this action as the side of their booth faced out toward Mariella and Raoul's table. She lowered her lashes to give Drake a heated look. He grinned.

"You're not kidding about not getting enough credit for knowing how to use your feminine wiles."

She laughed. "Just because I choose not to use them doesn't mean I don't know how to." He gave her an appreciative look, and she chuckled. "I'm glad you're enjoying this." The server set the strawberry shortcake on the table in front of Drake and Julian with two spoons. "Thanks," Julian told him.

Drake let his gaze wander from Julian's face for just a moment as she lifted a spoon. "Interesting," he said under his breath, but Julian eyed the strawberry shortcake with glee.

"Strawberry shortcake's my favorite," she said with delight.

"I know," Drake replied. "I remember overhearing you tell Mom at Thanksgiving."

Julian stopped short to blink at him. "You remembered that?" He shrugged almost shyly. Julian smiled and cut a bite from the dessert, hoisting it to her mouth.

In a low voice, Drake said, "Raoul is fascinated by you."

"Oh yeah?" she asked, too distracted by the light strawberry goodness and whipped cream to pay attention. She took another bite and closed her eyes again with a moan of genuine pleasure, forgetting the task at hand. "This really is good. Have some. This restaurant gets it right. Not too sweet. Not too tart. Just the right combination." She swallowed the spoonful and opened her eyes to see Drake staring at her, his eyes heavy-lidded and dark. Her breath caught in her throat. "Is Raoul still fascinated?"

"I don't know." She could feel his breath on her lips with his nearness.

Julian discreetly and reluctantly cut her eyes toward the couple on the other side of the restaurant. Mariella and Raoul scrutinized her and Drake. Julian dropped her spoon to cup

Drake's face. She kissed him assertively, confidently. When she would have released him, his hand at the back of her head held her captive for just a moment more. Then they broke apart with goofy smiles.

Drake took his wallet out and threw enough cash on the table to cover their meal and tip. He urged her out of the booth. She gave the other couple a small wave as Drake took her hand and led her out of the restaurant.

Outside, they got into Drake's car and laughed. He pulled her toward him for another kiss, one that took her breath away with its intensity.

"What was that for?" she panted.

Drake held her face between his hands and smiled broadly at her. "You took my side even without knowing the full story." His smile dimmed as he said, "I should have told you I'd been married before."

She sat back in her seat. "I didn't tell you about my ex-husband until you met him. I don't really have a right to be too angry about Mariella." She said the woman's name as if it tasted bad in her mouth. "Mariella, the model. Tall, thin, perfect hair Mariella."

Drake started the car and drove as he said, "She's a sad woman with problems, but that doesn't excuse her behavior when we were together." When he fell silent, Julian wanted to prompt him for more information. Instead, she waited. Eventually, he continued, "We were still pretty young and dumb. I'll admit, I loved the idea of being married to a model, but Mariella loved the perks of being a model. That included other men and drugs. I tried to get her help. We went to counseling. I paid for rehab, but she didn't really think there was anything wrong with what she was doing so she didn't get any better. I was still trying when she took off with her agent and filed for divorce."

Julian rubbed a hand across his back and felt his tense

shoulders. "I'm really sorry, Drake."

He smiled gratefully at her. "It was a long time ago." He remained quiet for awhile then started to snicker. "Maybe it was mean, but I have to admit their faces were priceless." He raised an eyebrow with a grin. "And I really enjoyed seeing another side to Miss Proper Julian."

She chortled at him. "I'm not a huge fan of public displays of affection so enjoy your moment. I did that because you stood up for me with Arnold. And..." She hesitated. "And because I just wanted to do something for you." She wondered if he felt as vulnerable when he had told her his interest was more than simple gratitude. She felt exposed and silly, but Drake had carried her out of that river, slept in her hospital room, protected her from her ex-husband, comforted her as she cried, and taught her to shoot a gun. If ever there was someone with whom she should feel comfortable enough to be honest, it had to be Drake Salvatore. When she put her hand back in her lap, Drake reached over and squeezed it.

"Thank you." He returned his hand to the wheel and smiled. Drake noted the time and said, "I forgot I told my friend and his wife I would stop by their house to drop off some paint supplies this afternoon. Their house is on the way to your house. Do you mind?"

Julian shook her head with a small laugh. "It's not as if I need to rush back to work."

Martin and Jill Patterson met them outside of their new two-story house situated in a newly-built neighborhood. Julian remembered them from Drake's retirement party, and was happy to see them again. Drake and Martin brought in the paint supplies while Jill offered to show Julian around. They ended up on the second floor where Jill showed Julian the mural she and Martin had started. The room obviously was intended to be a nursery.

Julian gave Jill a pointed look, and she smiled shyly. "This will be our first." She placed a hand over her still flat belly then put a finger to her lips. "We haven't told Drake yet. We wanted him to guess when he saw the nursery."

With a gleeful squeal, Julian reached in her pocket for her cell phone to take pictures of the nursery and realized she left it in Drake's truck.

"I'll be right back."

* * *

Drake and Martin laughed at Drake's tale of Julian's behavior upon seeing Mariella. Martin took a drink of his beer and offered one to Drake. "No, thanks. I can't stay. I need to get Julian home. Speak of the devil…"

Julian rushed downstairs toward him. "Can I borrow your keys? I left my phone in your truck, and I want to take some pictures." He pulled the keys from his pocket and handed them to Julian.

She rushed outside, and Martin grinned. "I like her."

Drake laughed. "Everyone likes Julian."

"I can see why. Hard to find someone loyal these days."

They heard Drake's truck start as Jill screamed from upstairs, "Someone's taking Julian!"

Martin and Drake instinctively ran toward the sound of his truck. He saw Julian's phone and purse dumped on the ground by the passenger side door as the truck pulled out. He could see a man's head in the driver's seat with a baseball cap.

Drake cursed. "He took her in my truck!"

Martin produced his car keys as Jill called 911. Drake took Martin's car without hesitation. Peeling out of the driveway after the truck, he hurried to catch up to his truck and popped open Martin's glove compartment to find the pistol he knew Martin kept there. Still in the neighborhood, his truck came into sight. Drake considered firing at the driver but decided not to risk the driver losing control of the truck. He held the gun ready instead, focusing on keeping up.

The truck sped through the suburb wildly in an attempt to lose Drake, but Drake kept pace with the driver as he looked for a way to stop the vehicle. At the next corner, the truck slowed just enough to make the turn, and Drake watched in horror and relief as the passenger door opened. Julian tumbled out. Seeing his chance, Drake hung his left arm out the window and fired at his own truck. The bullet shattered the glass of the rear window, but the man ducked in time. Drake could smell the rubber of the squealing tires as the man sped away.

Drake pulled off the road, parked the car, and tossed the gun onto the passenger seat. He ran to Julian, kneeling next to her as he dialed 911 on his cellphone. He put the phone on speaker and dropped it on the ground next to her while he inspected her. Blood ran down the side of her face at the same place she had been cut in the accident. Drake cursed again then asked, "Julian, are you hurt anywhere other than your head?"

She muttered incoherently, her eyes fluttering open and closed. He finally understood, "My head hurts."

Drake ripped off the button up shirt over his t-shirt and pressed it to her head. He detailed their location to the 911 operator as Julian's eyes closed. "No, Julian. Stay awake, girl. Stay with me. An ambulance is coming." Julian moaned but he could see her fighting to stay awake. "Good girl. Hang on, Julian." He talked back into the phone. "My friend was calling, too. If he's on another line, could you tell him I found her?"

Julian attempted to roll on her side. Drake touched her shoulder. "No, Julian. Stay still. You fell out of the truck."

"Jumped," she murmured.

"What?"

"I jumped."

Drake smiled at her. "You're a pistol, Julian Fursey." Her head rolled to one side again, and her eyes clamped shut. "No, no, no, Julian. C'mon. You're tough. Stay awake." Fighting to keep panic out of his voice, he held Julian's hand and continued to encourage her despite her closed eyes. The eight minutes it took for an ambulance to arrive felt like an hour. Paramedics moved him back to carefully put a brace around Julian's neck and place her on the back board. Drake turned off Martin's car and locked it, placing the keys in his pocket as the paramedics loaded Julian into the ambulance.

"You gonna follow us?" the female paramedic asked.

"No. I'm coming with you," Drake said and climbed in behind them.

CHAPTER TWELVE

Her head pounded. Julian forced her eyes open and tried to remember what had happened. She felt the cold pack on her head and realized she wore a hospital gown with her jeans. A doctor come in—a short, round man with dark eyes and a receding hair line—asking her standard questions about her pain and vision. She attempted to answer, but she could see Drake talking to a uniformed police officer and Detective Reynolds in the hall. She looked at the doctor before reaching up to feel the new bandage over the cut at her temple. She really just wanted to go back to sleep. He asked more questions. This time he asked the day, year, and president. Groggily, Julian found the answers to the simple questions. The doctor turned and told the three men in the hall they could talk to her. Julian moaned. She didn't want to talk to anyone. She wanted to sleep so her head would stop hurting.

"How are you feeling, Julian?" Detective Reynolds asked.

She licked her dry lips and sighed. "I'm really thirsty. And my head hurts." She pointed to her temple and the bandage with a frown. Drake asked a passing nurse for a drink. Even in her muddled state, Julian could see his expression—a mix of anger and concern.

Detective Reynolds said, "Ms. Fursey, tell me what happened as well as you can remember."

She closed her eyes and tried to think. "I went to get my phone out of my purse in the truck. I was digging in my purse when everything went black. I guess that's when the guy hit me. When I came to, I was on the passenger seat of the truck, and the guy was driving."

The nurse returned with a cup of ginger ale. Julian gratefully sipped it through the straw.

Detective Reynolds wrote in his notepad. "Did you get a look at his face?"

"He was wearing a mask, like one of those stupid Halloween masks that just stay on with a rubber band. It was Santa Claus."

The detective wrote it down. "Go on, Ms. Fursey."

"I tried to pretend I was still unconscious so he wouldn't pay any attention to me. As soon as I thought the truck slowed down enough, I opened the door and jumped out. I thought it was better to take my chances."

"Good instincts. Can you tell us anything about what he was wearing and his build?"

Julian narrowed her eyes in thought. "No. I should have paid better attention, but I only really thought about how to get away."

He shook his head. "You're a smart woman, Ms. Fursey. Escape should have been your first priority."

Julian bit her lip and fought tears. "He's gonna try again, isn't he?"

The men all exchanged glances. The detective said, "We're doing everything we can to catch him. We're working on tracking the emails. The phone calls you described came from different disposable phones. And we're looking for the truck. Can you tell us anything else?" Julian shook her head and blinked hard. Detective Reynolds put a hand on her shoulder. "If you think of anything else, call me. Even if it seems like nothing."

"I will."

Drake shook hands with the two men as they left.

Gale arrived as they left, rushing to hug Julian. "How badly are you hurt?"

Before Julian could answer, the doctor returned and examined her again, checking her eyes and motor skills. He removed the cold pack and looked at her head. "Ms. Fursey, you have a concussion and seven stitches. I'm gonna keep you in the hospital for observation for a while, but I don't think your concussion is too bad."

She could feel her lips trembling. "Do I have to stay?" Her voice shook. "I really want to go home. I want to sleep in my own bed."

Drake asked, "Can she go home if someone stays with her?"

The doctor took a deep breath and looked at Julian. "Only if someone stays with her for the next twenty-four hours. I'll get some care instructions together for you." He put a hand on Julian's arm before he left and told her, "You're gonna be all right."

Within a few minutes, a nurse appeared with discharge instructions and paperwork. Drake waited in the hall as Gale pulled the curtain closed and helped Julian put her bra and top back on. Julian cringed at the bloody knit shirt.

"Don't worry about that. You can change when you get home," Gale said. Once dressed, she opened the curtain again. Drake waited with a wheelchair and asked Gale to bring her car to the ER doors. She walked ahead of them. Julian could see Martin and Jill through the double doors, waiting with her purse as Drake stopped at the check out window. The woman explained Julian's copay with her insurance, still in effect. Drake paid the bill and wheeled her out.

She sighed. "You don't have to do that."

"Stow it."

Jill hugged Julian. "I'm so glad you're okay." Martin patted her shoulder.

Julian forced a smile at them. "Thank you."

They helped her out of the chair and into Gale's car. Jill placed Julian's purse on the floorboard by her feet in the front seat. "Let us know if you need anything."

Julian nodded weakly. She slept almost as soon as the car door shut. Julian woke to Drake unbuckling her seatbelt. "Can you stand?" She saw her mother already opening the door to the house.

She scoffed. "I'm not that bad off." She gently swung her legs from the car and pushed herself up. The world jumbled around her as Drake caught her. He slung her arm around his neck and lifted her.

"I gotcha."

Julian rested her head against his shoulder and fought nausea. This pose always looked so romantic on book covers, but Drake had carried her like this twice now, and neither time had been pleasant. He placed her in a sitting position on her bed as Gale met them. Julian heard them talking but paid no attention. Drake left the room, and Gale rummaged through her dresser for pajamas. Her mother helped her change again and urged her into bed. "Thanks, Mom."

Drake knocked on the door then entered with another ice pack. Gale gingerly placed it on her head. "Honey, we have to wake you up every now and then so don't get mad. The ice pack should help the swelling."

"Okay."

Gale kissed her uninjured forehead and left Drake with her. Julian noticed he carried two pills and a glass of water. "They said to give you more of this for the pain once we got you home," he explained. She sat up enough to swallow the medicine and drink some of the water. Then she leaned back onto her pillows.

Drake turned to leave, but she grabbed his hand. "Thanks for coming for me."

He rounded the bed and sat next to her. He put his arms around her again and nearly crushed her in his embrace. Julian felt his warmth and sighed against him. He held the icepack to her head and settled into place with her leaned against his chest. "Go to sleep." Julian placed her arm around his waist and drifted off.

* * *

A gentle hand on Drake's shoulder shook him awake. He opened his eyes to his mother's concerned expression. He glanced at his watch. They had only been sleeping for about thirty minutes. He gingerly slipped from Julian's side and followed his mother into the hallway. She burst into tears as soon as he closed the door to Julian's room. Drake put his arms around his mother and patted her back. "She's okay, Ma. She's all right."

Mary wiped her nose on the tissue she held. When Drake walked into the living room, he blinked in surprise. Gale had wasted no time spreading the word. Hannah and Rob waited on the couch as Gale cleaned Julian's kitchen. He raised his eyebrows at her. She waved him away. "It's how I cope. I clean."

Hannah jumped up and ran to hug Drake. "Thank God you were there."

Rob stood as well. "How is she?"

"She's still sleeping. The doctor said she'll be okay, though. Concussion and stitches."

Mary sniffled into her into her tissue and took a deep breath. "Amerigo really wanted to come, but your dad insisted he stay put and stayed there with him."

Gale shook her head as she dried a glass from the dishwasher. "He didn't need to come. The doctor said she needs to sleep." Her hands shook as she put the glass in the cabinet. She turned around and faced them. Drake saw the same struggle in Gale that he had on occasion seen in Julian—that strong will to avoid tears in front of others.

Drake put his hands on her shoulders. "We're all friends here, Gale."

Her face crumpled, and Drake hugged her as she cried. His mother handed him some tissue which he gave to Gale. She stepped back and wiped her eyes and nose. "I know she's okay, but there's some crazy man out there just waiting for the right moment to snatch her again." She shuddered. "Why Julian?"

"Does it matter?" Julian asked, staggering toward the living room.

Drake moved to prop her up against his side. "Okay. Take it easy now."

"I'm just looking for my phone to call Detective Reynolds."

Gale picked up the phone from the kitchen counter and handed it to Drake, who ushered Julian back to her room and onto the bed. Once situated, Drake dialed the number then handed the phone to Julian.

"Voicemail," she whispered. "Hi, Detective Reynolds. This is Julian Fursey. I remembered something. The guy had a pistol on the seat next to him with blood on the handle. Guess that's what he hit me with. And he was wearing cowboy boots and a ball cap. Hope that's helpful somehow, but if not, sorry about the call. Thanks." She pushed the end button and looked at Drake with a small smile. "At least I remembered something else." She shrugged. Drake put the phone in his back pocket.

When Julian protested, he told her, "You don't need anyone

bothering you right now. I'll man the phone for you." He smiled at her and touched her cheek. Fury rose in his gut and threatened to choke him as he glanced at the bandage over the cut at her temple. He struggled not to think about what her captor had planned for her.

Julian met his eyes. "Everyone's pretty freaked out, huh?"

He frowned. "They love you." She sighed and looked away from him. He asked, "Can you go back to sleep?"

"I think so. I'm still kinda drugged up." She grasped his hand. "This is karma for the way I acted at the restaurant."

Drake balked. "No one deserves what happened to you today. Besides, you don't even believe in karma."

"How do you know if I believe in karma or not?"

"Oh, trust me. I have been briefed on your core values from my mother who got them from your mother. You know the meddlers had to compare."

"Really?" Her eyes looked tired but curious. "What did the meddlers have to say?"

"We share the same doctrinal Christian beliefs even through I've slid into heathen ways." He grinned at her as she rolled her eyes.

Once Julian slept once more, Drake returned to the living room. Hannah and Rob had left, but Gale and Mary remained. The three of them sat in the living room. Drake tapped his fingers on the arm of the chair he was seated in as his mind raced with thoughts. Before the stalker had taken Julian, the idea seemed like a worst case scenario that felt unlikely. Now, everything had shifted. Not only had that happened, Drake knew the man would try again. And next time, he would probably have a better plan. Drake took a deep breath and thought about his years of training. He needed a plan, too. But short of keeping her cooped up in a bubble, it was impossible to make her perfectly safe. Still, he could try to minimize the threat.

"Drake, are you listening?"

His head snapped toward the women on the couch at his mother's question. He shook away his thoughts. "I'm sorry. I missed what you were saying."

Mary told him, "I said maybe Julian should come stay with us for a little bit. This guy probably doesn't know where we live."

Drake narrowed his eyes at the thought. "I hadn't planned to go to Martin's house. I didn't even tell her until we were on the way there, but that's where he showed up." He ran his hands over his face. "How did the guy know to be there?" Drake rose to his feet and paced. "Staying at the house with you and Pop won't keep her safe. It will just put you in danger with her. There's some way he knows. But how?" He stopped pacing and started to look around Julian's house for anything that might be used to track her. "Maybe her phone?"

Gale shook her head. "She keeps her privacy settings pretty tight on that phone. It hardly ever leaves her hand or pocket."

He stopped walking and straightened. "The first video was taken at the scene of the accident. She dropped her phone on the ground when she helped us. It would have been easy for someone to mess with it then." Drake pulled her phone from his back pocket. He poured through the apps and settings. She had a lost phone/back-up program on her home screen. In the complete list of her apps, however, he found another similar app. He couldn't imagine why Julian would have a second application with the same purpose. She didn't lose her phone. In fact, he noticed she rarely misplaced things. So why would she have an app to find and track her phone above and beyond the one he saw on her home screen? He looked at his watch to see how long they should wait before checking on her again.

In an effort to distract each other, Gale and Mary chatted about goings on at their individual churches and their shopping lists. Then they moved on to talking about their shared favorite

TV shows.

Drake mulled over the phone apps. As soon as enough time had passed, Drake returned to Julian's room with a fresh ice pack and her phone. He touched her shoulder, and she hissed in pain.

"I'm sorry!" Drake gasped. He gently tugged at the collar of her pajama top. The skin had already discolored, and the bruises would deepen. The doctor had warned them that while the concussion caused him the most concern, Julian would be banged up. Drake grimaced.

"Poor Jules," he whispered. He saw her faint smile.

"You've never called me Jules before."

He touched her face as he sat on the edge of the bed. "Is it okay?"

"Yeah."

He pulled the app up on her phone and showed it to her. "Is this an app you normally use?"

She sat up hesitantly and blinked against the pain in her head. Julian took the phone from Drake and scrutinized the screen. "I've never even heard of this. Did you download it?"

"No. It was already on your phone."

Comprehension lit her eyes. "Think he's using this to figure out where I am?"

Her ability to reason that out even with a concussion impressed Drake, but her intelligence had always impressed him. "Maybe. Can I delete it?"

"Please do."

He did so and put the phone in his back pocket once more. Julian met his eyes with a worried look. He asked, "Interested in a new phone?"

She shook her head. "Not really. I can't afford to get a new phone right now. I just lost my job, remember?"

"I'll buy it for you."

Julian jerked the rest of the way up to look at him then

groaned at the pain in her head. "Drake, you're already going way above and beyond to help me. I can't take your money too. You've already spent too much with my hospital bill. I can take the phone to the store and have them restore it to factory settings. That should get everything out of the memory."

He scowled. "I don't know. I'd feel more comfortable if you had a completely new phone."

She sighed and placed a hand to her head. "I feel kinda sick."

Drake held her upper arms and helped her recline onto the pillows again. "Rest, Julian. For now, I'll just turn your phone off. That should take care of it."

Julian looked at him with wide eyes. "If he's been tracking my phone, he knows everywhere I've been—your house, your parents' house, my mom's house…"

Her breathing came in short gasps. Drake grabbed her hand and met her eyes.

"Look at me. Take a deep breath." He slowed his breathing so she could follow his example.

Her eyes filled with new tears. "Everyone I know is exposed. Everyone I care about is at risk."

Drake rounded the bed, kicked off his shoes, and took up the spot he had occupied earlier in the afternoon. He gently pulled her against him, conscious of her injuries. She grunted in pain but strained to help him haul her close. Once she rested against his chest again, Drake kissed her temple, placed the ice pack on her head, and gave her a soft smile.

"I promised we'd figure this out together, and we will."

Julian's panicky breathing slowed as he held her. "Okay," she whispered.

"That's better," he said as he stroked her hair. "I'll stay here with you as long as you need me."

"I'm selfish enough to take advantage of it," Julian said, and Drake chuckled at her.

A knock at the door interrupted their conversation. Mary opened the door and popped her head in the room, holding a cellphone to her ear. "Is Julian awake? Anthony wants to talk to her." Drake waved Mary in, who handed Julian the phone.

Julian put the phone to her ear and said, "Hi, Anthony."

As Julian spoke to Anthony on the phone, Mary leaned close to Drake and lowered her voice. "Your friend, Martin, stopped by just a little while ago. He assumed you might be staying here for a bit so he went to your house and packed a bag for you. I put it in the guest room."

"Thanks, Mom."

Mary patted his cheek and looked at Julian still speaking to Anthony, barely able to get a word in edgewise. Mary grinned. "You take good care of her."

Drake smiled back. "I will."

"You're a good boy, Drake."

Julian gave the pair a desperate look. "But I… No… It's really sweet of you, but…"

Mary rolled her eyes and took the phone from Julian's hand. "Enough, Anthony. The girl has a concussion. Leave her alone." She looked back at the couple and said, "Gale and I will make some dinner whenever you're hungry."

Julian put a hand to her stomach, her face turning slightly green. "Please don't wait on me. I'm still nauseous." She sat back and closed her eyes.

Mary looked nervously at Drake.

"I'm not really hungry either, Mom. You guys go ahead and eat."

Mary nodded and put the phone back up to her ear. "Anthony, I told you she wanted to stay home."

When the door closed again, Drake and Julian laughed quietly together. She held a hand over Drake's holding the ice pack as she grimaced then smiled. Drake tweaked her nose and ordered, "Close your eyes, and go back to sleep."

* * *

When Julian next opened her eyes, night filled the room. She rested on her back, the uninjured side of her head buried in her pillow and Drake's arm slung around her waist. She saw him sleeping face down next to her. A blanket covered them, and Julian's face flamed thinking it might have been one of their mothers to provide it. She would have assumed one of them would have been indignant enough to run Drake out of her room. Instead, they had made them more comfortable? Not that anything sordid would happen while Julian still suffered the effects of the concussion. She felt better, but still fuzzy and tired.

Curious about the time, Julian tried to remember where she'd put her phone. The last she saw it, Drake had placed the phone in his back pocket. In the dark and in her awkward position, she could barely make out his shape. As delicately as she could, she reached down to attempt to get the phone. Her mouth went dry as her hand hovered over the pocket. She gingerly tried to reach in the pocket. No phone. Perplexed, she stretched further over him to try for the other pocket. Swallowing hard, Julian tried the other pocket. No phone there either. She held her breath. Julian might have resolved to wait before having sex again, but Drake's description of waiting rang through her head. It'll be a challenge. She remained motionless, one hand in his back pocket, her heart racing. She shook her head and jerked her hand away. Julian expelled the breath she had held and covered her face with her both hands.

"Find what you were looking for?"

Julian jumped when Drake spoke. Her face turned five shades of red she hoped he couldn't see. "I was trying to find my cellphone so I could check the time."

"If you say so." She could barely see his smirk in the dark.

"It's on the nightstand next to me. You're welcome to crawl over me to reach it."

Julian laughed. "Nice. Convince the injured person to crawl over you for a cheap thrill."

Drake chuckled and raised himself up enough to reach his phone. He checked the time. "You're phone is still turned off, but my phone says its 1:13 a.m."

She gasped. "Oh no! Do you think our moms are still here? They've got to be exhausted." She struggled to sit up. Drake put his arm back around her waist to stop her.

"They both went home. Stop fretting, and go back to sleep." He snuggled down next to her under the blanket again.

Julian chortled. "For a big, bad Marine, you sure enjoy sleeping in a cozy bed."

"Yup. Doesn't hurt to wake up next to a beautiful woman even if it's in the midst of horrific frustration."

She giggled. "That makes me feel guilty… And frustrated, too." To add insult to injury, Julian's stomach rumbled with hunger. "We haven't eaten since lunch."

Drake sighed with resignation. He removed his arm from her waist and sat up, rubbing his face with his hands. "I guess I'm kinda hungry too."

They staggered into the kitchen. When they flipped the light on, a figure on the couch rose. Julian shrieked and jumped what felt like three feet off the floor. Drake shoved her behind him. With her hands against his back, she looked around Drake's shoulder and narrowed her eyes. "Rob?"

Rob wiped his hands over his eyes and flung the blanket away. "So sorry. I hope this is okay. Hannah's in the guest room. She couldn't sleep because she was so upset and wanted to come over. I didn't like the idea of her traipsing around at midnight by herself." Julian felt Drake's muscles relax against her palms.

She stepped around him. "It's fine, Rob. Thank you."

"How are you feeling?" he asked.

"We're scavenging for food," Drake explained. He turned around in the kitchen and opened Julian's refrigerator. When she moved to help, he gently wheeled her around and winked at her. "I got this."

While Drake pulled out leftovers from the meal Mary and Gale had prepared, she leaned against the counter and propped her head up on her hands. She met Rob's eyes. "You like Hannah," she said in a sing-song voice. She grinned at him as he chuckled.

"I really do."

Julian noticed Drake's smirk out of the corner of her eye as he made a plate and placed it in the microwave. "I'm so glad. But I should tell you that Drake taught me to shoot a gun yesterday so be warned." Drake laughed.

Rob chuckled again. "Thank you."

With a grin, Drake added, "It's not an idle threat. As long as I'm here, she'll have access to a gun, and I'm sticking around for a while."

CHAPTER THIRTEEN

Julian had thought Drake's comment was an exaggeration, but the next couple of days proved him a man of his word. After two days of mostly sleeping and half-watching movies with Drake hovering, Julian still nursed bruises and creaky muscles, but her head felt much better. It felt so much better, in fact, that after she and Drake had gone to their separate rooms the third night, she stared at the ceiling unable to sleep. Julian rolled onto her side and tried to imagine the characters of her latest novel escaping the quandary in which she'd placed them. Instead of her characters, she saw the masked face of her stalker. Julian's eyes popped open, and she sat up. She sipped from the glass of water on the nightstand, unsettled by the idea that Santa could look so evil to her now.

She shook her head to dislodge the image and closed her eyes again. This time she saw the gun on the seat of the truck and the cowboy boots. Julian gasped, her eyes flying open. Giving up, she threw the covers back and rose to her feet. She grabbed her robe and slipped it over her pajamas then padded down the hallway to the living room.

Julian sat on the couch and picked up one of the magazines on the coffee table. A throw blanket had been left on the cushions, and she pulled it over her legs as she flipped through the glossy pages. She scanned the self-help articles and recipes. After a few, she tossed the magazine back on the coffee table. Julian turned on the television and the game console then snatched up the controller. She could work out some frustration by killing video game villains.

The game loaded, and Julian concentrated on the objectives so intently, she didn't hear Drake approach until he touched her shoulder. Julian yelped then sighed when she saw him.

"You nearly scared the life out of me."

"Sorry." He sat next to her as she paused her game.

"Did I wake you up?" she asked.

"I heard you moving around and thought I'd check on you when you didn't go back to bed."

"I can't sleep."

Drake put his arm across the back of the couch. Julian leaned back and against his shoulder, controller still in hand. He rubbed her non-bruised shoulder and kissed her forehead. "Feel like getting out of the house tomorrow?"

"Yes."

He laughed at her quick response. "Getting stir crazy?"

"Yes," she said. "And you have to be, too." While her Mom, friends, and church members came in and out of the house to visit and bring food, Drake rarely left. She felt selfish, and had been grateful when Martin came to sit with her while Drake went home to gather more of his clothes and toiletries or when he went to the store. Having an armed Marine around the house tended to make one feel more secure against a bad guy.

"I'm all right, but I need to do some Christmas shopping. I thought maybe you might need to do some, too."

Julian placed the controller on the coffee table and slid her arms around Drake's torso, burying her face in his white t-shirt. "I don't know why any of you are so nice to me."

His arms closed around her. "Well, we're all suckers, and I'm the biggest one."

She looked up to see the playful grin on his face and smiled back. His normally clean-shaven face sported a day's worth of stubble. "You know, I'm surprised our moms haven't had more to say about you staying here. I thought they might have offered to stay overnight so you wouldn't."

"They tried to convince me to leave, but I told you I'd stay with you. I try to keep my promises."

Julian felt the familiar surge of appreciation for Drake. Hardheaded, bossy, overwhelmingly attractive Drake. She leaned forward and kissed his cheek. "Thank you, boss-of-everyone."

Drake rolled his eyes, and scrubbed a hand over his face in mock exasperation. His expression softened as he looked at her again. "Think you can sleep now?"

She closed her eyes. "I don't think so."

"Let's watch a movie," he offered.

* * *

Drake woke when he heard the door open, sure it was Gale. Julian still rested in his arms on the couch. He hated to wake her, but for the first time since the incident with the stalker, he felt embarrassed for her mom to see them sleeping together. Gale walked in wordlessly and looked at them. She placed a bag from a fast food restaurant on the counter and took off her coat. "Good morning, Drake." Her tone had an edge to it, and Drake inwardly cringed.

The first night, Julian had been injured and scared, and both Mary and Gale trusted him. After that, they knew Drake and Julian had slept in separate rooms. Now Gale saw Drake laying on the couch with Julian stretched out against him, her face resting on his chest.

Julian surprised him by answering her mother without opening her eyes. "Oh, don't start, Mom. Nothing happened." She softly snored against his chest again.

Gale placed her hands on her hips and ordered, "Get up then, Smart Mouth. I brought y'all some biscuits. How late were y'all up? It's already nine o'clock."

Drake and Julian sat up, her stretching and him rubbing his eyes. He fought the urge to remind Gale they were both adults, who didn't need chastised like teenagers.

Julian's shoulders drooped. "I had trouble sleeping so we watched a movie."

Gale walked by the couch and kissed each of them on the top of their heads on her way to open the blinds. Drake's indignation disappeared. Julian met his gaze, and they grinned at each other.

"Here. Eat you two." Gale handed Julian the bag, and she opened it.

"Bacon or ham?" Julian asked him. He gave her a look. She snorted. "Why did I even ask?" She handed him the bacon, egg, and cheese biscuit. Drake leaned back on the couch and folded the paper wrapper back.

Gale sat in the armchair and looked at them. "Hannah offered to come stay with Julian this morning, if you want, Drake."

Drake chewed his bite of biscuit then said, "It's okay. Julian and I were gonna go Christmas shopping." He turned to Julian. "Unless you've changed your mind."

"Nope. I still want to do some Christmas shopping. I'll call Hannah to let her know." Julian left the room to retrieve her phone from her bedroom. She returned to the room with a pale, perplexed look. "My publisher called to tell me he's been getting weird calls about my books."

Unfazed, Gale said, "I'm sure people ask about your books all the time."

"They don't normally ask what happens to the rights if I die."

Drake and Gale exchanged glances.

Julian sighed and sat on the couch next to Drake. Wearily, she handed her phone to Drake and said, "You call Detective Reynolds this time."

His phone rang as if on cue. "I don't have to. This is him calling." After a brief conversation with Detective Reynolds, Drake whispered to Julian and Gale, "They found my truck. They're running prints and DNA."

Detective Reynolds went on to tell him that they would need to keep the truck as evidence. Once he finished explaining the process, Drake told him about the calls to Julian's publisher. He put Julian on the phone for the details and turned to Gale. "Guess I'm stuck with the rental for a while."

"Just keep using Julian's car. She shouldn't be going anywhere on her own right now anyway."

"I don't want to inconvenience her."

Julian handed the phone back to Drake after the call. "He's going to contact my publisher and see what he can find out. The emails are still a dead end. They're being routed through multiple IP addresses. So your truck is being held indefinitely?"

"Guess so."

"That sucks, but don't pay for another rental. Just use my car. I'm practically under house arrest anyway."

Gale put a hand over her mouth to cover her laugh and gave Drake an "I told you so" look. He sheepishly agreed.

Julian sighed. "Good. Settled. I'm gonna take a shower so we can go Christmas shopping, and I can pretend my life is perfectly normal."

Once she disappeared to her room, Gale said, "Thank you,

Drake. She's got to get out of here." Gale sat next to him on the couch and put a hand on his arm and smiled. "She's not helpless. You were there to scoop her up, but she got out of that truck on her own."

Drake smiled. "Yeah, she did."

Gale put an arm around his shoulders. "Still, thank God you were there. She got out on her own, but who knows what would have happened after that." The older woman shuddered. "I try not to think about it."

Drake wished he could stop thinking about it, too.

* * *

Julian looked at the wound at her temple in the mirror as she stood, wrapped in a towel, in the bathroom. At least the cut had been smaller, and in another two days, the stitches would be gone. She debated on what would be more appalling in public—the bandage or the stitches. She decided to use smaller adhesive strips she could cover with her hair. After putting on makeup and blowing her hair dry, Julian dressed in jeans, flat boots, and a red knit shirt. She frowned in the mirror as she put in her earrings and a thin silver chain with a simple pendant. Drake had to be getting tired of her by now, but she felt safe with him in the house and couldn't make herself suggest he leave.

When Julian emerged from her room, Drake had already showered and dressed. He stood in the kitchen with a cup of coffee, looking handsome in his jeans, t-shirt, and flannel shirt. She looked around quizzically.

Drake grinned. "Your mom left while you were in the shower, but she said she'd be back later tonight."

Julian gave him a once over and drawled, "I like your lumberjack look."

He glanced down with alarm. "I look like a lumberjack?"

She approached him with a smirk. "You look rugged." She ran a hand over his flannel-clad stomach, and her face fell. "I owe you a shirt. You used yours on my head the other day."

Drake placed his coffee mug on the counter and hugged her to him, his chin resting on top of her head. "I have more. Don't worry about it."

Julian took a deep breath. "You smell really good." She instantly wished her verbal filter did a better job, but he did, and it muddled her brain.

She heard him chuckle, her ear still against his chest. "So do you. Your shampoo smells like flowers."

She smiled. "Thanks."

"C'mon. Let's go buy some gifts." He pulled her back to look at her. "I have a favor to ask of you, though."

Julian blinked her surprise. "Of course."

"You'll help me wrap the gifts, right? I'm really bad at it, and every year I'm harassed around the Christmas tree."

She burst into laughter. "I'm not the greatest at wrapping presents, but I haven't been mocked for it yet. I'll help you."

Drake gave her a quick kiss as they grabbed their coats. Julian blinked in surprise at the simple action. He kissed her as if it was the natural thing to do. Like a real couple. Julian bit her lip. Were they a real couple? She looked at Drake as he sat in the driver's seat of her car and couldn't imagine dating anyone else. Who could live up to that standard?

He caught her staring. "You okay?"

"Yeah. Just thinking about stuff."

He raised an eyebrow but kept his eyes on the road. "Stuff? Care to elaborate?"

"Not at this time."

Drake chortled. "Okay."

They decided on a couple of stores. Drake groaned at the amount of people crowding the first store. Julian grinned at him. "Oh, suck it up. Besides, it kinda puts me in the holiday spirit." She hummed along with the Christmas carol playing over the speakers and grabbed a cart. "Do you have your list?" she asked.

"People really make lists?"

Julian placed her purse in the seat of the cart, dug in a pocket, and produced a handwritten list. "Voila."

He playfully grabbed the list and perused it. "What're you getting me?" She tried to get the list back, laughing as she reached for it, but he turned away. "There's nothing by my name," Drake said as he let her snatch the list back.

Indignantly, she placed the list on top of her purse. "I haven't decided yet. Besides, if you had seen it on the list, I'd have gotten you something different. Christmas gifts are supposed to be a surprise." She sashayed away with the cart. Drake followed along behind her with a chuckle.

Julian continued to hum as they walked through the store as she checked names off her list with each item placed in the cart. After Drake offered to give her money toward several gifts if she would put his name on the card with hers, Julian stopped the cart and gave him a pointed look. "I don't mind sharing credit for gifts, but… Well… Couples put their names on the same gifts. I don't want you to feel uncomfortable when we start handing them out, and everyone assumes something."

They stood amongst rows of kitchen accessories staring at each other. He tilted his head back to regard her, and Julian shuffled her weight from one foot to the other. "I hope you know I don't mean to sound like I'm…"

Drake gave her a smirk. "We're a couple. I mean, what more does a guy have to do to prove he's serious about a woman?" Julian smiled at his mischievous grin. He continued, "I taught you how to shoot. I chased a guy down with a gun. I even took up residence at your house to take care of you."

Julian blinked rapidly, still smiling. "Okay. I'm not arguing." She took one of his hands and squeezed it before she said, "So what had you thought about getting your mom?" They resumed shopping as if nothing had happened, but Julian's heart thudded in her chest. The middle of a department store seemed like an odd place to have that discussion, but there it was. They were a couple. She had a hard time concentrating on her list but forced herself to seem nonchalant. After they finally left the store together and put the bags in the trunk, they sat together in silence. Drake looked at Julian, and she looked at him. They both grinned like idiots.

Drake leaned forward and fervently kissed her. She enthusiastically returned the kiss, leaning toward him and wrapping her arms around his neck. He pulled her onto his lap, the awkward angle making Julian laugh. "Drake!"

He just murmured against her mouth, refusing to release her, but she could feel his lips curling in a smile. When Julian's bruised shoulder bumped into the steering wheel, she hissed at the pain. Drake loosened his hold. "Are you okay?"

She nodded as she rubbed her shoulder. "Just still banged up." She reluctantly crawled back to her seat. "I'll survive."

Drake frowned as he touched her shoulder then started the car. They went to an outdoor mall and ended up at an international specialty store looking at rugs, knickknacks, food, and wines. Julian tried on hats, making a different face for each. Drake eventually plucked the last one off her head with amusement. "Keep moving, woman." They made a few decisions, some imported food for Anthony in particular. As they stood in the wine section, Julian glanced over the racks and racks of different wines separated by color and taste. From the corner of her eye, she saw Drake watching her intently.

After a few moments, he picked up a bottle with a casual head tilt. "Interested in learning the wine-making business?"

Julian kept her focus on the bottled of red wine in front of her. "It was interesting to hear you talk about it Thanksgiving Day. Most people don't think about how much work goes into it. I know I hadn't known."

Drake came beside her and tucked a stray lock of her hair behind one of her ears. "I'm not supposed to mention this, but I thought you might like the heads up."

"Okay…"

"Mom and Pop want to offer you a job at the vineyard."

Julian turned to him, blinking in surprise. "What? I don't have any experience with wine-making."

"I know. But if you're interested, you can learn. I think they're hoping you'll help with more of the administrative stuff. Plus, it looks like we'll be starting tours, and we'll need someone to help with that. You're really personable." He watched her face carefully. "It'd be full-time pay, but they'd make sure you have a lot of time to write and be free to go do publicity for your books, if you want."

Julian frowned. "I don't know. It feels like I'd be taking advantage of your family."

He smiled. "I told them you wouldn't be crazy about the idea. I knew you'd feel like you were ripping them off, but it would actually be a lot of help. Just think about it."

"Drake…"

"Like I said. Just think about it."

Drake suggested a lunch break as they left, and Julian gratefully accepted. They walked from the last store to the Asian bistro nearby. After their meal, Drake asked, "Tired?"

"Yeah," she sighed.

"Let's get you home."

CHAPTER FOURTEEN

Drake put his arm around Julian as he led her back to the car parked in the overflow parking behind the restaurant and store. He didn't like her pale face and tired eyes. She needed rest. He knew when Julian saw Arnold because he felt her entire body tense. Julian's ex-husband leaned casually against her car with his arms folded. Drake checked the urge to growl at the man. What did this joker want?

Arnold held his arms out as if to hug Julian. "There you are. I thought this looked like your car."

Julian narrowed her eyes at him. "Really? You just happened to notice my car? You live on the other side of town, Arnold. Why are you really here?"

He dropped his arms and gave them a cocky smile. "I was feeling nostalgic. It's almost Christmas. I know how much you love Christmas. I thought I'd come say hello."

"Hello. Goodbye." Julian moved to walk around him.

Arnold grabbed her arm to stop her, and she winced. Drake struggled to maintain control as he snatched the man's hand away and sandwiched himself between them. "You cannot be this stupid."

The idiot actually smiled at Drake. "So you decided to hang around for awhile?"

From behind Drake's shoulder, Julian said, "After the divorce, when I said I never wanted to see you again, that's what I meant."

He shrugged. "We don't always get what we want." He narrowed his eyes and noticed Julian's bandaged temple. "Wow. That looks pretty nasty." Arnold turned his amused gaze to Drake. "I understand. Sometimes she makes you just want to hit her."

Drake glanced around the parking lot. Seeing almost no one nearby, he reached back and slammed his fist into Arnold's face. Drake grimaced at the pain in his knuckles but enjoyed the satisfaction of the moment as the man went down, moaning.

Julian yelped in shock. Ignoring the sound, Drake stepped around Arnold's prone form and opened the door for Julian. She closed her gaping mouth and slid into the car. He closed her door and turned to round the car. As Drake passed by Arnold's moaning form, he grabbed the man's shirt to pull him out of the path of the car and growled between clenched teeth, "I've never thought of hitting Julian, but I've fantasized about pummeling you into the ground. Take my advice and stay away."

He forced himself to walk slowly to the driver's side of the car and got in. Once inside, Drake flexed his hand and looked at the blood. Julian hissed in concern and started to reach for his hand, but Drake stopped her. She silently sat back, folded her arms, and looked out the window. He had reached the main road to her house before he heard her. Regret washed over him as her shoulders heaved, and he worried he'd scared her. The last thing he wanted was for Julian to be afraid of him the way she'd been of her ex-husband.

Then he realized she was laughing. She shook her head. "It's not the Christian thing to laugh, but I can't help it. The look on his face before he fell…"

Drake smiled with relief even though he chastised himself for acting like some young, hotheaded kid. But knowing that Arnold had ever hurt Julian made his blood boil. And now someone else had hurt her. Someone he couldn't make pay. Yet.

They pulled into the driveway and carried the bags into the house. Then he stopped in the kitchen to wash his bloodied hand. Julian appeared beside him with a first aid kit. She took his hand in hers and dried it with a towel. Gently, she rubbed some antibiotic ointment over the cuts. "I'm sorry, Julian," he said.

She looked at him then back down at his hand. "Why?" Julian carefully used a paper towel to mop up the excess ointment.

"I don't want you to think I just go around hitting people or be scared I would ever lose my temper with you." He swallowed hard. The last time he had punched someone over a verbal confrontation he had been twenty and drinking. He had used his fists since then but only when he had no other recourse. "I'm embarrassed."

Julian placed bandages over the small cuts and met his eyes. "Drake, I'm not afraid of you. I'm not young and dumb anymore. Well, I'm still dumb. But I've learned something about people and judging their character." She still held his hand as she continued. "We're all stressed beyond reason, and, frankly, Arnold deserved it. I won't act like I'm sorry you hit him." Julian placed his hand on her waist and reached for his other hand, bringing it to the other side of her waist. "Just a word of warning, though. I have a neighbor up the street who looks at me kinda funny. Don't beat him up, okay? I think he's just a lonely old man." She cupped his face with an amused expression.

He rolled his eyes with a grin. "I'll try to control myself."

She laughed at him then pulled his head down toward hers. Her kiss was soft, tender. She threaded her fingers into his hair.

Drake groaned and pulled her close against him, the kiss quickly escalating. His hands moved over her back as hers slipped between his flannel shirt and the cotton t-shirt. When one of her hands brushed his gun holster, Julian froze. She leaned back to look at him. "You're wearing a gun."

"Yes." Her sudden expression of horror caught him off-guard. When she tried to pull away from him, he held her fast. "What is it? Why do you look like that?"

Julian's eyes glistened. "It's so dangerous to be with me, we can't even go Christmas shopping without a gun."

Drake touched her cheek, his chest tight at the look on her face. "It won't always be like this."

The doorbell rang. Julian smiled and took a calming breath. "I'm glad you're brave enough to live on the edge and stick with me." Drake leaned against the counter as Julian left him to answer the door and escort Hannah to the kitchen.

Hannah hugged Drake, then said "I hope you guys don't mind me interrupting. I'm keeping your mom at bay by coming over."

Drake smiled at Julian who smiled back. "Actually, I'm glad you're here. I need to do some Christmas shopping without Julian so I'm gonna abandon you ladies for a bit." He put his arm around Julian's shoulders and asked, "Are you sure about me using your car?"

She nodded and kissed his cheek. "Go."

* * *

"You are never gonna believe what happened," Julian said after

Drake left then told Hannah about seeing Arnold. "And then Drake decked him. I mean, really drew back and hit him. Arnold went down like a rag doll. I know I should've been mad or scandalized, but I just had to fight the urge to kick Arnold while he was on the ground."

Hannah chortled. "Arnold's had that coming for a long time."

They chuckled together for a few minutes. When the laughter did down, Julian asked, "Why do you think Arnold's really hanging around all of a sudden?"

Hannah scowled. "I wish I knew, but maybe Drake's warning will work." She grinned. "I wish I could've seen it."

They dissolved into giggles together. Hannah waved a hand. "Anyway, let's get to the really good stuff. You guys were Christmas shopping together? That's a very couple-ish thing to do."

"I thought so, too, so I asked Drake what he thought."

"And?"

"And he said we are a couple."

"Thank God," Hannah breathed and flopped over on the couch, her arms flailing. "So obvious."

"Evidently," Julian drawled, rolling her eyes at her friend's antics.

Hannah shot up to ask, "Does he know about 'the oath'?"

Julian gave her a murderous look. "Good grief, Hannah. How many times have I asked you not to call it that?"

Hannah ignored her. "Does he?"

"Yes," Julian replied. Drake hadn't brought it up again. He hadn't pressured her even though she knew he was frustrated. She was frustrated.

"He's too good to be true," Hannah told her.

"No one's perfect. And he can be so authoritative. I wouldn't say he's controlling or possessive. Just when it comes to trying to keep me safe, he gets fanatical. And don't even get me started on that ex-wife."

Hannah leaned forward, practically drooling. "Oh, do tell. You haven't mentioned her before."

"The former model ex-wife? Probably because I'm trying to hard to forget about her."

"A former model? What's her name?"

"Mariella Cortez."

Hannah gasped and grabbed Julian's arm. "Are you kidding? I know that name. She was an 'It Girl' in her twenties. She's still known in the industry for recognizing the next big thing."

Julian frowned. That would have been about the time Mariella and Drake had been married.

"Oh, yeah. And her sexual escapades were not hidden," Hannah continued.

Julian's frown melted into a pucker of sympathy for Drake. To have the whole world know about a spouse's infidelity? "That's awful," she whispered.

"It's like they pretended she wasn't even married. It was ridiculous. I feel really bad for Drake."

"Don't mention knowing about her unless he brings it up," Julian said then told Hannah about the way she plastered herself on Drake in front of Mariella. "I felt bad about it that day, but I feel a little less guilty now."

Hannah laughed at her again. "Woman, you're supposed to be above that kind of stuff."

Julian put her head in her hands. "I know, I know, but Drake looked so annoyed to see her. I knew something bad had happened with them and just wanted to give him some justice."

Hannah's eyes widened as she grinned. "You're even more smitten with Drake than I realized."

Julian's face burned. "I guess I am. I mean, how do you resist that?"

"Why would you try?"

They wrapped Christmas presents until Julian leaned her

head back on the couch and closed her eyes, vaguely aware Hannah was asking her a question. When Julian woke, she found a throw blanket draped over her and Mary sitting in the armchair next to the couch. Mary's hands worked furiously with the knitting needles at a scarf. Julian rose to give Mary a hug. The older woman smiled happily at her. "You look better than the last time I saw you. How do you feel?"

"Better. Just still tired all the time."

Mary nodded. "Yeah. I read that online about concussions. Be careful not to overdo it."

Julian smiled and kissed Mary on the cheek. "Have I told you how much I appreciate you?"

Drake's mother simply smiled at the scarf she knitted as Julian made her way to the kitchen and found a plate of leftovers to microwave. As the food warmed, Mary cleared her throat.

"Anthony and I have been doing some talking. We know your severance package only contained a month's worth of pay for you, and you haven't had a chance to look for a job." Julian braced herself and came to sit on the couch with her plate. Mary described the idea of Julian working at the vineyard with diplomacy. She concluded with, "If you don't like it or your writing takes off or you just get a better job offer, there'd be no hard feelings. We'd just need some notice to replace you." The older woman smiled. "We truly have to hire someone to help us with these things. It's not a made up job just to be nice to you."

Julian chuckled, her worries slightly assuaged. "You're prepared for any of my arguments, huh?"

Mary shrugged. "I know you don't like feeling you're taking advantage of people. I want to make sure you understand this offer clearly. We need help. Drake retiring came none too soon. He's good with the nuts and bolts of the growing and harvesting, but it's not enough." She gave a sly grin. "You do come to the top of our short list for some non-professional reasons, but mainly because you're smart. Your name was the first one out of Anthony's mouth."

Julian stopped eating mid-bite to ask, "Really?"

Mary laughed. "I promise."

Julian finished her bite and stabbed another helping of potatoes. "How soon do you need to know?"

"Within the next week. We need someone working before Christmas so we can hit the ground running with our expansion plans in January."

She took a deep breath. "I'll think about it, Mary."

"Oh, I forgot to mention salary." Mary threw out a figure, and Julian nearly choked on her food. Mary's eyebrows snapped together. "Too low?"

Julian shook her head, still coughing. "Too high, Mary. I can't take advantage of you like that. If I accept your offer, we'll renegotiate the salary."

Mary patted Julian's back. "You're a good girl, Julian."

The front door opened, and Drake strolled in using the key on Julian's key, whistling a Christmas carol as he placed the plastic hardware store bags on the kitchen counter. Julian narrowed her eyes in curiosity. "Christmas shopping?" she asked.

"A little," he replied. "But since they didn't find my keys with the truck, there's a key to your house floating around. I bought new locks for you." He pulled hardware and tools from the bags and returned to the front door.

Julian gave Mary an impressed look. "You and Anthony raised good men, Mary."

Beaming, she replied, "We sure did." As Drake worked on the front door, Mary gathered her things and stood. "Since Drake's here, I'm gonna scoot. Think about the offer, okay?"

"I will, Mary." She hugged the older woman, her eyes watery. "Thank you."

* * *

Drake finished changing the locks on the front and back doors. Julian watched him from her couch, her arms wrapped around her legs. She had the deep-thought expression that worried him—the one that told him she was thinking too hard.

"Tada," he said with a flourish when he finished. He closed and locked the doors, put his gun in her closet, and joined her on the couch.

"Thank you," she said, with a light smile.

"You're welcome." He handed her a key. "I'll have a couple more sets made for you to give your mom and Hannah." At her continued dark look, Drake put a hand on her shoulder. "It won't always be like this, Jules."

She nodded then placed her chin on her knees. Her expression lightened. "Your mom made the offer tonight."

Drake watched her face carefully. "And?"

"I haven't decided. What do you think?"

He laughed. "Oh no. I'm not getting sucked into that. You have to make that decision on your own." He reached out and tugged at a lock of her dark hair.

Julian playfully slapped at his arm, grinning. "Cut that out."

Drake laughed again. "C'mon. You know I have selfish reasons for wanting you to take the job. I'm the wrong person to ask for an opinion."

She shoved his shoulder, her eyes alight with mirth. Drake gently caught her wrist and tugged her to him for a kiss, letting his lips linger on hers before he sobered.

"I bought something else for you. I'll be right back." He walked out to the car and came back with a black case. "I didn't want to give this to you with Mom here." He opened the case to reveal a handgun. He pointed out some of the features as she paid close attention. "Would you feel comfortable keeping this here for when I'm not around? I'll take you to the range again tomorrow to practice with it, if you want."

"Yes. Thank you."

He brushed his fingers over her cheek, and his chest constricted at the worry in her eyes. "I'll do whatever it takes to keep you safe, Jules."

She took his hand in hers and lightly kissed his bandaged knuckles.

"Drake…" She hesitated then took a deep breath. "You explained yourself to me not too long ago, but I never explained myself. I appreciate you for being protective, but I want you to know it's only a small part of why I care about you."

He pulled her into his arms with a grin. "Good to know."

She looked up at him with her big doe eyes, and he felt the now-familiar pang of frustration. He appreciated that she'd been upfront with him about her decision to wait, and he wasn't a kid anymore who let hormones control him. Still, he was human, too. He had no shortage of imaginative desires for Julian.

Martin, the only person Drake felt able to share Julian's decision with, had surprised Drake with his response. "She'll know you're a good guy, and she won't have to question your motives," he'd told Drake. Drake had conceded the point.

Julian ran her fingers through the hair at his temple. "You're deep in thought."

I'm deep in lust, he thought, but said, "I'm glad you agreed to go out with me and dump Rob."

She chortled at him. "Ugh. Men and their egos. I technically didn't dump Rob. We only went on one date and never even kissed. Besides, I felt guilty even on that one date."

Drake gave her a smug look. "Good."

Julian pushed him away with a grunt, though the corners of her mouth turned up. "You're bad. Don't be mean. Rob's a good guy. I'm glad he asked Hannah out."

Drake grinned. "Me, too."

She closed her eyes and leaned against him. "I forgot. I can't go to the range in the morning. I've got church."

He had forgotten that she'd told him earlier she planned to try to go in the morning, having missed a lot already. He offered, "I'll go with you. Then we can have lunch and go to the range."

Julian smiled. "Okay. If you don't mind going to church with me."

"I wasn't lying when I told you I'd just gotten slack. I'll go with you." He paused before clarifying, "Unless there are snakes involved. It's not that kind of church, is it?"

"No!" She laughed.

"That's a relief," Drake teased and stood, putting the gun high in a closet, the case locked. Afterward, they watched a movie. Julian went to bed before he did, and he sat on the couch reading one of her books for a long time before going to the guest room himself.

In the parking lot of the church the next morning, they stepped out of the car, and Drake took in the building with simple stained-glass windows and a plain steeple. People in the parking lot greeted Julian warmly, eyeing him with interest and smiles. He recognized a couple of them who had brought food—Lillie and Jarred Taylor, the siblings Julian had gone to school with, Kassandra Davis, the music teacher, and even Didi Blakely, who ran a small bakery downtown. Julian introduced him to several other people as they walked through the foyer into the sanctuary. They were all friendly and genuine, if curious. He understood why she liked this church. Julian spotted her mother in the sanctuary, and they sat with her. He saw her approving smile and forced himself not to roll his eyes. Instead, he hugged her.

After the simple service, Gale invited them to lunch with

her and some church members. Julian looked at him, knowing those around him would assume she wanted to know if he wanted to go to lunch. But he knew her question was whether he thought it was safe. Her trust in him did something funny to his heart he'd think about later.

"Lunch sounds good. I'm starving," he said.

The group met at a small local Mexican restaurant, taking up almost half of one room. Most of the meal was eaten with small talk. As the waiter brought out their checks, one of the church members asked the question Drake figured was on everyone's mind.

"Do the police have any leads?"

Julian shook her head with a frown. "Not yet. We're kinda in a holding pattern. There's not much to go on."

A man at the other end of the table offered, "You should consider getting the local news stations to do a story on it and see if the police get any tips. I'm sure they'd do it to follow up on the story about the accident."

Drake had noticed the man earlier, a little older than most of Julian's friends, with a very observant expression. Someone had introduced him as Didi's uncle, Randall Johnson, but no one mentioned what he did for a living. Drake would put money on ex-military.

Julian asked Drake, "What do you think?"

He nodded to Randall then turned to Julian. "That's probably a good idea, if you don't mind being on the news again."

After lunch, Drake drove them back out to the firing range for more practice. Julian once again impressed him with her accuracy for such little training. Despite the gravity of why they practiced, Drake found himself laughing more than he would have expected at a firing range, enjoying Julian's quick wit and good-natured teasing.

Once done with practice, they stopped at Drake's house, and

he ushered her into the living room. "I'm just grabbing some clothes and weights to take back to your place so I can work out later."

Julian shrugged. "Why don't you just work out now?"

"That's okay. I don't want you to be bored. I can wait."

She made a face. "I'm bored at home. I can read as easily here as there." She held up her phone. "Downloaded a new book this morning." With a flourish, Julian dropped onto his couch and kicked off her heels. She leaned back against the arm, stretching her legs out on the cushions. He stared at her in her black pencil skirt and pink sweater, relaxed on his couch as if she lived there and reading away already. She waved a hand. "I'm fine. Really. Do whatever you gotta do."

* * *

Julian watched Drake from the corner of her eyes as he headed upstairs, her heart aching with gratitude. Drake never bullied her, always watched out for her, laughed with her. He made her feel beautiful and smart. Hanging around in his living room so he could get a workout in felt like small potatoes in return.

After almost an hour, Julian's phone rang, interrupting her novel just as it was getting good. She glared at the caller ID. Blocked. Her throat constricted. She told herself it could be a telemarketer as she let it go to voicemail. But within seconds, the phone rang again, Julian ignoring it again. When the blocked number called a third time, Julian answered the phone with a tentative, "Hello?"

A digitally altered voice replied, "You don't need to be afraid of me. I just want us to be together."

She shot to her feet. "Who are you?"

"The man who was intended for you. I'm Hank Jefferson. I'm Roger Stansfield. I'm Thomas Shepherd."

All three names were names of characters in her novels.

Julian opened her mouth, but no sound came out.

He continued, "I'll be seeing you soon."

Julian's heart thudded as the call disconnected. She tried to speak again, but only managed Drake's name in a strangled cry. She heard the footsteps on the stairs as he hurried to her.

"What's wrong? You're white as a sheet," he said, his stance tense.

She held her phone toward him, her hands trembling so badly it slipped from her grasp and clattered to the floor. Her eyes filled with tears as she looked at the phone as if it could bite her.

Drake cupped her face. "Was it him on the phone?"

"He said he'd be seeing me soon."

Drake's lips thinned as he dug his phone out of his pocket, dialing Detective Reynolds. Julian listened mutely until Drake handed her the phone. "Tell him every word."

In a quavering voice, she complied as the detective took the information. By the time she finished, her voice had dimmed to a whisper. She handed the phone back to Drake, who talked to Reynolds for another few seconds, agreeing to bring Julian to the station to fill out a report. He ended the call, and Julian remained fixed where she stood.

"If I ever get my hands on this guy…" Drake muttered and placed the phone on the coffee table then met her eyes. He let out a long breath and put his hands on her shoulders. "Are you okay?"

Julian dropped back onto the couch. Drake sat next to her. "I don't know," she said. "He scares me."

Drake turned to face her, his hands on her shoulders again. "Jules, I will do everything in my power to make sure you're safe."

"I know," she said. "But I don't want you to get hurt either." She touched his cheek. "I couldn't stand it if something happened to you while trying to protect me." Her vision blurred, and hot tears stung her eyes. "I couldn't stand it," she repeated before she broke down into sobs, annoyed with herself for it.

Drake dragged her onto his lap, wrapping his arms tightly around her and murmuring reassurances in her ear. He stroked her hair as she cried and let her cling to his neck.

As the crying slowed, Julian made no move to leave his embrace. Instead, she tightened her own hold on him. "You're all sweaty," she said in a husky voice.

She felt his chuckle. "I was on the treadmill," he said.

Julian leaned back to look at him in his sweats and t-shirt, and her mouth went dry. "You were wearing something like this at the hospital that day," she muttered, unable to think of anything else. The man looked like he'd been sculpted from clay by a Renaissance artist, every exposed part of him beautifully male.

"Yeah. My dad grabbed my gym bag that day," he explained, his own voice low.

She could feel the coiled tension in him, but he didn't move. Julian met his dark eyes and something in her snapped. She pressed her lips to his in a greedy kiss. He kissed her with the same fervor, his hands on her back pressing her closer. She clung to his shoulders, as Drake kissed her jaw line then her throat. Her hands slid under his t-shirt to stroke the smooth skin of his back. He shifted them so that they lie on the couch, her beneath him. She cupped his neck to bring his mouth back to hers.

He kissed her then went still. "Julian." He pulled his head back and tilted it toward her phone on the floor. "Do you think this might be a knee-jerk reaction to getting that phone call?" She struggled to slow her breathing as she met his eyes. He struggled for breath as well, but continued, "Don't get me wrong. I'm a man. I'm not above being persuaded, but I'm afraid you'll resent me later and feel bad yourself. I don't want it to be like that between us." He made a face. "And I feel like an idiot for pointing that out."

Julian sighed with resignation. She knew he was right. She would feel like he took advantage of her fear and desperation, and she would struggle with her own guilt for throwing herself at him. Julian ran her fingers over his cheek and jaw with a soft smile. "I'm sorry. I never meant to be a tease. I'm so embarrassed." She could feel her cheeks burning.

Drake smiled at her as they sat up. "You're not a tease." He kissed her chin. "You're human." He laughed. "Just don't ever tell anyone about this, or I'll be forced to turn in my man card."

"No one could ever make you turn in your man card." Julian gave him another quick kiss.

He grinned. "That's my girl."

* * *

Julian passed another restless night thinking of the phone call and the incident with Drake. Despite her exhaustion, her mind refused to shut down for the evening. By the time the sun finally began to filter through her window, she had gotten only a couple of hours of sleep at best. Still, Julian rolled out of bed and took a shower. Once dressed, she staggered into the kitchen. Drake sat on the couch drinking coffee, obviously lost in thought. When he heard her shuffling into the kitchen, he turned to her with the smile that normally warmed her. After a practically sleepless night, she said gruffly, "Stop looking so happy." He laughed as she placed a mug under the single cup coffee brewer and muttered.

He asked, "Rough night?"

She gave him an evil look and waited for her coffee. He stood and made his way to her. He cupped her face and grinned. "Today is a new day, Julian. New possibilities." He gave her a quick kiss.

Julian smiled despite herself. "Not that I'm not glad you're in an exceptionally good mood, but why?"

He shrugged and kissed her forehead before returning to the living room. Julian found herself still grinning at him as she added sweetener and creamer to her coffee.

Drake announced, "So I need to get out to the vineyard today. Care to join me? Maybe you can see what you could help with if you take the job out there."

Julian sipped her coffee in thought. "That's a good idea. I still need to contact the news station, though."

"I've already called. They want to interview us together. I set up a time tomorrow. I hope you don't mind. I can call back and change it."

She shook her head with her mouth clamped shut, happy not to have to call the station, but she had the feeling Drake was up to something. "Well, since you're managing my life this morning, where's my breakfast?" she asked as she looked in the refrigerator.

"Top shelf," he said from behind his newspaper.

Sure enough, a covered plate awaited her. Julian looked at Drake with incredulity. She pulled the plate out and placed it in the microwave while eyeing Drake suspiciously. "Okay. What's this about? What do you want from me?" He smiled again. As the microwave hummed, Julian fixed him with a look. "You're trying to convince me to take the job your mom offered me, aren't you? Trying to get me in a good mood to prime me for your parents to seal the deal?"

His smirk revealed the answer. She considered him. This was his plan of attack when he wanted something? No badgering. No fussing. Just trying to pamper her into being open to an idea. Not bad. Certainly not what she had come to expect from Arnold.

After breakfast, Drake drove them to the vineyard. At the house, Drake and Julian found Amerigo hobbling around on crutches in the kitchen. Julian rushed over to help him get a mug from the cabinet. He thanked her and accepted her help with making coffee. She brewed a pot as he sat at the table in the breakfast nook. Drake sat with him. "Where's Mom and Pop?"

Amerigo grunted as he struggled with his bulky cast. Drake gently reached down to help him prop his leg on the seat of another chair. As the coffee brewed, Julian sat with them at the table. "They're in the barn looking for the rest of the Christmas lights. They've got big plans for you, Drake." Amerigo's amused smile tickled Julian. She cast a glance at Drake who rolled his eyes.

"Let's go see what they have in store for me." Drake stood.

Julian shook her head. "I'll catch up. I know where the barn is."

He shrugged his shoulders. "Sure." He raised an eyebrow at the pair as he left. Julian waved with a devious grin then turned to Amerigo.

Amerigo's eyes twinkled with amusement. They waited until Drake descended the stairs from the patio to the yard which led to the vineyard grounds. "What are you up to?" Amerigo asked.

"I've got a Christmas present for you. I've got something for your parents. But I have no idea what to get your brother for Christmas. You've gotta help me." The younger man laughed. Julian rose to her feet and poured a cup of coffee for him. "How do you take your coffee?"

"Just some cream. Thanks."

She handed him the steaming mug, and he took a sip. "Thanks," he said.

"Sure," she replied with a chipper tone. Then she dropped her voice. "Now spill."

CHAPTER FIFTEEN

Leaving Julian with Amerigo seemed like trouble, but Drake smiled as he made his way to the barn in the cold December morning air. The doors of the barn were open as far as they could swing, and his parents stood on the second level of the large wooden structure. They dug through trunks and laughed together. Mary caught sight of Drake and waved him to the ladder. "Good morning! Where's Julian?"

"She's inside with Amerigo." Drake climbed the ladder to meet Mary and Anthony. Mary kissed his cheek, and Anthony slapped his shoulder. Drake explained, "Amerigo was limping around like an invalid so she made him a pot of coffee."

Anthony nodded. "Good. This gives us a minute. Do you think she'll take the offer?"

Drake grinned. "Well, if she doesn't, it won't be my fault. I even made her breakfast." His grin faded a little when he added, "She had a rough night last night, though." He explained the phone call, and his parents both scowled.

Anthony's fingers balled into fists. "I wish I could get my

hands on this person."

Drake said, "That makes two of us." He dug into one of the trunks to pull out a string of lights balled into a knot and placed it on a table next to others. "Don't bring it up, okay? It makes her really self-conscious, and I want her to enjoy today."

Mary took one of the strings and fought to untangle the mess. "Of course, dear. We want her to feel comfortable here." She focused on the bundle of lights as she said, "The church wants to bring people out here for hayrides, and we could really use some help coordinating that."

"You know she doesn't have any experience with any of this, right?" Drake asked.

Anthony snorted. "I know people. That girl can do anything she puts her mind to."

"Of that, I have no doubt," Drake replied with a proud smile. He caught his mother's knowing look and cleared his throat.

"I appreciate everyone's confidence in me," Julian said as she topped the ladder, her eyes meeting Drake's with a warm expression. She kissed both Mary and Anthony on the cheek in greeting and joined in with the untangling process.

Anthony explained their plan to decorate the outside of the house and some of the grounds to prepare for hayrides. Julian's eyes lit up. "Hayrides? That sounds like fun!" They gathered the decorations and used a pulley system to lower them to the first level and place them on Anthony's truck. Once the decorations were loaded, Drake and Julian climbed in the back. They drove to driveway lined with trees that led from the road to the actual vineyard.

After parking, they took ladders off the truck and worked at stringing lights through the trees limbs and around the trunks. Normally, Drake dreaded the process, though he enjoyed the end results of their work, but Julian's enthusiasm coupled with his mother's infected the men by the time they finished and headed back to the house for lunch.

At the house, they found Gale bustling around the kitchen with Amerigo at the table. The pair giggled together like teenagers over juicy gossip before they greeted Drake and Julian. Julian rolled her eyes with a grin as she gave them a quick hello and passed them to use the restroom. Mary joined Gale in lunch preparations while Anthony started another pot of coffee.

Drake marveled at the effect that Julian and Gale had on people. They laughed easily. They seemed to always try to do the right thing. And their loyalty… He had only seen that kind of loyalty in two other places—within his own family and with his brothers-in-arms. Drake offered to set the table in the dining room. Julian joined him shortly, following along with silverware at each place setting. They worked in comfortable silence, Drake finding an opportunity to tug at a lock of her hair. She predictably elbowed his ribs, and he laughed.

They ate a simple lunch of pan-fried chicken cutlets with homemade mashed potatoes, green beans, and rolls.

Still at the table talking over empty plates, Julian gasped. "I'm supposed to go to my family doctor and have my stitches taken out." She grimaced, pointing to her temple. She dug her phone out of her purse and frowned. "I turned off my phone last night and forgot to turn it back on so I didn't get my reminder."

Anthony asked, "When is the appointment?"

"In an hour."

"I'll go with her," Gale offered. "We'll take my car."

Drake opened his mouth to protest but stopped at Julian's warning look.

Julian and Gale stood and retrieved their coats. "We'd better hurry," Gale warned. "Your doctor's on the other side of town from here."

Drake walked with them to the car. Gale handed Julian her

keys and dropped into the passenger seat. Drake whispered, "Be careful. Do you want to take my pistol?"

Julian smiled and squeezed his hand. "You know how to turn on the charm."

He frowned as he squeezed her hand back. "I'm serious, Jules."

"No, but thanks. I'll be careful." Julian kissed him on the cheek.

* * *

They had barely left the driveway when Gale launched into her interrogation. "So. Arnold paid you another visit, huh?"

Julian cringed. "For the love of Pete, I'm gonna stop telling Hannah anything."

Gale folded her arms over her chest and glared. "Well, it's the only way I know what's going on. Don't be mad at her."

Julian bit her lip. "What exactly did Hannah tell you?"

"She said Arnold was waiting for you at your car in the parking lot the other day."

"Yeah, but Drake was with me."

Gale's glare turned into an amused look. She asked, "Did Drake really hit him?"

Julian's expression mirrored her mother's. "Oh, yeah."

Gale squeezed her arm. "This is the kind of man you deserve. Someone who cares enough to look out for you. His momma raised him right."

Julian smile faded. "Did Mary tell you about his ex-wife?"

Her mother replied, "Yes, and she told me you're the first person he's shown sincere interest in since the divorce."

"Really?" Julian thought about that as they drove.

Gale clucked. "Please. Did you see his face when I said I'd go with you to the doctor? He looked so worried." She twined her fingers together, a grin on her lips. "He's protective."

A pang of guilt shot through her. Was she putting her mother in danger by going with her instead of Drake? "Mom, I got another call last night."

"What?"

"Yeah. That's why my phone was turned off."

"Jules," Gale breathed.

"I know." She bit her lip again and focused on the road before she continued. "That's why he looked so worried."

Gale ran a hand over her forehead. "When is this ever going to end?" She didn't wait for Julian to answer. "Well, at least I brought my gun today. It's in the glove compartment. I've got my concealed carry permit with me."

Julian's jaw dropped open. "Since when do you have a concealed carry permit? Or even a gun?"

"Since that lunatic grabbed you." Gale's eyes burned. "I made Drake's friend, Martin, teach me. He's an instructor with a private company. He did it for free."

"I didn't know," Julian said, her mind buzzing with the image of her sixty-something mother at a firing range with Martin. She choked out a laugh.

Gale said, "Drake can't be with you twenty-four seven, honey, and I'm not going to let something else happen if I can help it."

Julian sniffed. "I can't drive and cry at the same time, Mom. I won't be able to see the road."

They laughed together, but Julian's eyes watered despite her effort to remain poised until they got to the doctor's office. After she parked, she turned to her mother. Gale gave her a knowing smile. "Everything's gonna be okay, Julian."

She nodded her reply, afraid to open her mouth. Gale accompanied Julian inside. They talked about Hannah and Rob while they waited. Gale approved of the match as if she had any say over it. Julian supposed she had a little. Gale had been a surrogate mother to Hannah when they were kids. They talked on a regular basis even without Julian.

Gale abruptly shifted gears on Julian as they watched the nurse take another patient back. "So are you going to take the job from Mary and Anthony?"

Julian made a face. "I don't know. What if something happens, and Drake and I break up? How awkward would it be to keep working there?"

Gale shrugged. "Mary and Anthony don't just like you because you're dating Drake. Besides, you won't be under threat of death to stay there. You could give a notice and leave."

The nurse called Julian back, and Gale stayed behind. Dr. Jones removed Julian's stitches and inspected the wound. She nodded approvingly. "It looks good." She removed her latex gloves and threw them in the biohazard trash. "Have they caught the guy?"

"Not even any real leads right now."

The doctor scowled. "I hope something turns up soon to help, and I hope he goes to prison for a long time."

Julian sighed. "Me too, Dr. Jones."

In the car, Gale told her Mary had suggested Julian go home after the doctor's appointment. On the ride back to Julian's house, her publisher called.

Hanging up the phone, Julian tapped the steering wheel.

"What's wrong?"

Julian said, "I forgot I have a table at the convention downtown this Saturday."

"What kind of convention?"

"It's a comic convention. My fantasy novel is doing well, and my publisher set this up months ago. I forgot."

Gale asked, "Do people come dressed up as characters from movies and TV shows?"

"Yes, ma'am."

The older woman shook her head. "I don't understand people sometimes."

By the time Drake arrived at Julian's house, Julian and Gale sat tensely on the couch, bickering in hushed tones. Both women clammed up when Drake entered the room. Julian saw his look of concern, but she met his eyes with a warning to stay out of it. He raised his eyebrows but went to the kitchen with the takeout he carried. "I brought something for us all to eat."

Gale rose. "Thanks, Drake, but I need to be getting home."

"Are you sure? There's enough food."

Julian shot Drake a look, and he shrugged sheepishly.

Gale shook her head. "Thank you, but I'm gonna go."

As her mother headed for the door, Julian stood and followed her, her chest tight with a question. Would she want this to be their last conversation should something happen with her stalker?

Julian put a hand on her mother's shoulder. "I love you, Mom." Julian hugged Gale, who patted her back as she returned the embrace.

"I love you, too, Jules."

After Gale left, Julian met Drake in the kitchen to help put the food on the plates for them. Drake looked at her quizzically. "What was that all about?"

Julian frowned. "Nothing. It's stupid."

Drake gently turned her to face him. "Doesn't look like nothing."

"It's nothing," she said again and took their plates to the table.

Halfway through their meal, Julian took a deep breath. "So my publisher called today and reminded me I'm supposed to man a table at the comic convention downtown Saturday to promote my latest book."

"No."

Julian blinked. "Pardon me?"

"It's too dangerous."

"Drake—"

"Lots of people. Little security. No weapons allowed, I'm sure."

Julian stopped eating to stare at him. "When I said 'pardon me,' it was so I could clarify that what I said wasn't a question but a statement." She saw a muscle in his jaw work. Undeterred, she continued, "I don't need permission. I was letting you know."

"I know you don't need my permission, but—"

"If I can't live my life, what's the point?" She took his empty plate with hers to the kitchen, rinsed them, and put them in the dishwasher. Drake remained silent as she put the leftovers in the refrigerator. When she turned around, Julian bumped into the wall of Drake's chest.

Drake caught her when she would have stumbled. He met her eyes, and she saw his concern. Some of her anger subsided. "Don't you get tired of escorting me around everywhere?"

"I just want you safe." Realization lit in his eyes. "This is what you were arguing with your mom about?"

Julian pulled away from him and folded her arms. "She started thinking about it once we got home and started freaking out."

"Well, yeah," he said. "Because this is a bad idea."

She gritted her teeth. "Drake, this has been in the works for months, and the comic convention put my appearance on the website and everything. It's a big deal for a local writer's book to do as well as mine is. I can't cancel now."

"Yes, you can, Julian," Drake countered. "Your safety is more important than this event."

Julian placed her hands on her hips and squared her shoulders. "I don't think I'm making myself clear. I'm going Saturday. I procured a ticket for you should you care to accompany me."

Drake stared at her, his face unreadable. She waited, her heart in her throat. He ran a hand through his hair and gave a grunt of frustration. "I'll go with you." After a moment of staring at each other, he muttered, "Thanks for getting a ticket for me," and hooked his thumbs in the back pockets of his jeans.

Julian released the breath she'd been holding, and her bunched shoulders relaxed. "Thanks for going. I'm not sure this will be your kinda crowd."

Drake surprised her by grinning. "Don't worry about that. Amerigo and I are closet geeks." She chuckled at him, and he took one of her hands. "And for the record, no. I'm not tired of escorting you around. I'll do whatever I can to keep you safe."

She looped her arms around his neck. "You know, you're always talking about keeping me safe. I worry about you, too. What if you get hurt trying to protect me?"

His arms closed around her. "We're in this together, Jules."

* * *

Morning came too quickly for Julian. She dreaded talking to the local newscaster about her stalker. Drake seemed just as unhappy, but he feigned a smile and took her hand as they walked into the building together. The whole process went fairly smoothly and didn't take as long as expected. Drake told her the reporter had offered to come to them, but he thought she would prefer not to have a crew at her house or his. After answering copious questions and recounting their story together, they left. Both heaved a sigh of relief. "Since we're downtown, want to see if Hannah can meet us for lunch?"

Julian called Hannah, who told them she was meeting Rob in an hour and said they'd be willing to meet up with Julian and Drake. To kill some time, Drake suggested they walk around the capitol building downtown and look at the

Christmas tree. Julian squeezed Drake's hand as they walked. "You know I'm gonna work for your parents, right?"

He stopped walking to look at her. "Are you sure it's what you want? I know it seems like a lot of nothing right now, but it can get really busy and really tough."

"I'm sure."

Drake beamed at her. "They'll be so happy when you tell them."

She scrunched her nose and asked, "Are you sure you're okay with this?"

He put an arm around her shoulders and smirked, "Yes."

By the time they reached the restaurant, Hannah and Rob waited by the hostess' podium. Julian gave them both hugs with a bright smile. Drake shook Rob's hand and accepted Hannah's hug. The hostess led them to a booth by a window and gave them menus.

After they all ordered, Hannah asked, "How was the interview?"

Julian shrugged. "It's done. The reporter seemed kinda in love with Drake."

He scoffed. "I don't think so."

"You guys should have seen her," she insisted. "She looked like this." Julian gazed at Drake with wonderment and batted her eyelashes.

Hannah and Rob laughed. Drake squirmed in his seat, but he grinned. "You're exaggerating."

Julian hooked her hand in the crook of his arm and smiled. "Not much. Besides, you're pretty amazing so it's only appropriate." She turned back to Hannah and Rob. "Did you guys know he was awarded a Silver Star?"

All eyes turned to Drake, who fidgeted with his napkin.

Rob spoke first. "Drake, that's impressive."

"I don't really talk about it, but thanks," Drake said.

Julian laced her fingers with his and gave him an

encouraging smile. He smiled in return.

Their food came then, and conversation slowed. When it resumed, Hannah talked about latest gossip in her office. Julian listened with interest. Occasionally, she chimed in with a "No!" or "You're kidding me!" Julian grinned at Rob and Drake. "Her office is better than a soap opera."

The men laughed at them. Hannah swatted at Julian's arm on the table. "Hey, did you get me a ticket to the comic convention Saturday? I forgot to check with you. You promised way back when it was set up." Hannah wagged a finger at her.

Julian rolled her eyes. "Of course." Ignoring the way Drake tensed, she continued, "My publisher confirmed some details this week, and I wiggled a ticket for Rob and Drake, too."

Rob raised his eyebrows. "That's kind of you, but do you think it's a good idea?"

Drake held his tongue admirably, in Julian's opinion, though she caught the look he gave her.

She told Rob, "Drake's not crazy about the idea, but I've been looking forward to this. I can't live in a bubble."

She saw something pass between the men as Rob said, "I'd love to go. Never hurts to have a couple more sets of eyes to be on the lookout for trouble." He grinned, "And we get to go to the comic convention." He winked at Hannah.

She smiled in reply then said, "I forgot to ask when the interview airs."

"Tonight," Drake told her.

Hannah tilted her head. "You guys wanna come over for dinner, and we'll watch it together?"

Julian shook her head. "Thanks, but I'd rather be home hiding from the embarrassment."

Once back at her house, Julian paced. She sat at her laptop in an effort to work on a new manuscript. Then she tried playing a video game. After that, she attempted to read a book.

All the while, Drake had watched her from behind his laptop on her couch.

When Drake stood and took Julian by the shoulders, she expected him to be annoyed. Instead, he gave her a sympathetic look. "I'm nervous, too," he admitted.

She leaned against him. "I really, really want this to work."

Drake ran his hands through her hair and took a breath. "Me, too."

After picking at her dinner and more pacing, Julian finally sat on the couch with Drake to watch the interview. She could feel him practically holding his breath with her. They watched a couple of local stories before their featured story began. Julian cringed at seeing her face on the screen. Drake cringed at his own, but they agreed the news anchor did a good job of laying out the series of events and the need for community help. At the end of the story, the news show displayed the tip hotline number and advised it would be available from their website as well.

Julian and Drake looked at each other and breathed.

Drake rubbed the back of his neck. "Now we wait."

They didn't wait long before phone calls from friends and family came rolling in. Julian thought everyone they knew must have watched the news. They answered call after call to answer questions about their relationship and Julian's abduction.

After the flood of phone calls died down, Drake and Julian sat quietly next to each other. Julian rubbed her hands over her face and admitted defeat. "I gotta get some sleep." She dropped a kiss on Drake's forehead then headed for her bedroom.

Julian skipped her normal nightly rituals and headed straight for bed where she fell asleep almost as soon as her eyes closed.

She found herself in Drake's truck again, blood staining the seat and cowboy boots in her vision. She struggled to sit up and look out the windshield. Drake stood down the road in front of the truck as it barreled forward, gaining speed. He raised a pistol. The man in the Santa Claus mask slammed his foot down on the accelerator. Julian gasped and fought to grab the steering wheel. With one arm, her captor held her at bay as he continued to accelerate. "Stop the truck!" Julian screamed. Drake stood still holding his handgun, aiming at the driver, who released the wheel to grab Julian's arms. The truck stayed on course for Drake. Julian screamed again as the truck would have hit Drake, the impact jerking her awake.

Then Drake faced her in the darkened bedroom with his hands holding her arms. "You're okay," he assured her, his voice steady as he met her eyes.

Julian gasped as reality sunk in to her dream-addled brain. Drake stood over her bed wearing a t-shirt and flannel pajama pants. Julian blinked, and her throat burned. "Drake." Julian ran her hands over his arms and chest to reassure herself he was truly unharmed. "You're okay." She closed her eyes. "He wouldn't stop the truck. He was going to run you over with your own truck, and I couldn't stop him."

"I'm okay, Jules. It was just a nightmare."

Even in the dark, she could see he was pale, but he was safe and whole and standing next to the bed. The relief of it overwhelmed her. Julian covered her face with her hands and sobbed. Drake sat next to her and clutched her to him. Julian let herself cry as Drake held her. He stroked her hair and rocked her. She won the battle for control in increments, but eventually, Julian's sobbing turned into ragged breathing. She sniffled against him. She felt his weight shift and a tissue appeared before her from the box on her nightstand. Julian ventured a look up at his face.

"Thank you," she croaked.

His eyes held compassion. "You're welcome."

Julian mopped her face as Drake grabbed more tissue and handed it to her. She used those as well and drew in a long, deep breath. "Drake, it was… You were…" She shook her head, unable to continue.

He placed a finger on her lips. "You don't have to talk about it." She could hear his frantic heartbeat in his chest. After a quiet moment, he admitted, "You scared me to death."

"I'm sorry." She ran her hand across his flat stomach and sighed. "It was so real. He was going to hurt you." Julian closed her eyes in frustration. "This is not fair."

"I know. You're right." He kissed her cheek. Julian turned her face toward him and tried to smile. Drake leaned down and tenderly kissed her lips. All thoughts fluttered from Julian's mind except how much she had wanted his mouth against hers. When he raised his head to meet her eyes, he brushed his thumb over her lower lip. "It's the middle of the night, Julian. You should try to go back to sleep. Want me to leave?" She shook her head and let Drake rearrange them so that they were laying instead of sitting. He pulled the covers over them and instructed, "Close your eyes. Nothing will hurt us tonight."

* * *

Drake woke with Julian curled up next to him. He sucked in a deep breath of air and rubbed his eyes. Her screaming had woken him from a dead sleep, expecting to find her injured or fighting an intruder. He glanced over at the pistol on the nightstand where he had left it to try to wake her. Julian's strength had surprised and pleased him. He hoped if it ever came to it, she unleashed everything she had. Then he shuddered at the thought and prayed she never faced that possibility. He rolled to his side to look at her, brushing his fingertips over her cheek. He was going to hurt you, she had said. The terror had been for him and not herself, and it overwhelmed him.

Julian murmured and snuggled closer to him. Drake put an

arm around her and watched her sleeping face. He gently lifted the hair near the cut at her temple and looked at the angry red line with a frown. After a few minutes of watching her, her eyes slowly opened. She looked up and gave him a sleepy grin. He grinned back at her.

"What time is it?"

Drake reached across her to look at her cell phone. "Almost eight." He dropped the phone back onto the nightstand and pulled the covers back over them. He nuzzled his nose in the crook of her neck. "Go back to sleep." He closed his eyes and kissed the base of her throat.

She placed one arm around him and the other against his chest. "Don't you need to get to the vineyard?"

Drake sighed and reached across her again. He used her phone to text Mary telling her he would be coming to the vineyard after lunch. "There. I have a reprieve until after lunch."

Julian laughed at him. "Drake!"

He didn't answer, enjoying the feel of her fingers through his hair with a murmur of approval. Drake kissed the base of her throat again and then across her collarbone. She sighed. He smiled against her skin. "I'm gonna tell the folks I'm staying here today," he said.

She clucked disapprovingly, but he heard the smile in her tone. "You're a terrible son."

He raised up on one elbow to look at her. Her eyes were soft with emotion, and he faltered as the warm feeling in his chest expanded. At his expression, she asked, "What's wrong?"

Drake swallowed hard. "Your nightmare. You said he was going to hurt me."

Her eyes clouded. "I was in the truck with the guy who snatched me, and he was going to run over you with the truck." Julian shuddered. "I was trying to stop him."

He shook his head. "I don't deserve to have you in my life."

"Of course not," she teased. "But you have me anyway."

Drake shifted so he could cup her face. The words he wanted to say hung on his lips, but he hesitated. The only woman with whom he'd ever used those words had tossed him aside like a bad habit. Looking at Julian, some of the sting of the old wound smoothed away. She watched him, her curiosity obvious. "Jules, I—"

Her phone rang. She gave him an apologetic look as she reached for it. Drake rolled on his back and listened to her confirm details of her appearance at the comic convention with one of the organizers. Afterward, she placed the phone back on the nightstand. "Sorry about that. What were you going to say?"

He sat up, worrying creasing his forehead. "I still don't like this idea. I'm sure everyone would understand if you cancel this event."

Her previously soft expression tightened. She sat up next to him and drew her knees up to her chest, wrapping her arms around them. "Drake—"

He slid his arm around her shoulders, pulling her into his side. "I'm just worried."

She turned so she could meet his eyes. "Do you have any idea how scared I am?" His chest squeezed as her eyes glistened. "But I can't let this guy dictate my life." Her eyes narrowed. "I won't let anyone dictate my life."

"I'm not trying to—"

"I dealt with enough of that before."

Drake's jaw tightened. "Don't compare me to your ex-husband."

Julian held his gaze. "I'm going to the comic convention. Join me or don't." She swung her legs off the bed and rose, leaving him alone as she disappeared into her bathroom.

He scrubbed a hand over his face. How had he gone from nearly admitting he loved her to this? He took a deep breath.

He loved her. Had been going to tell her. And she'd compared him to that piece of crap Arnold? He stood, fully intent on going back to the guest room, but he stared at the bathroom door. When it opened, Julian blinked at him, her eyes red-rimmed. She bit her lower lip. "I'm sorry. I'm just a wreck."

Drake felt his shoulders drop. "Come here," he said, reaching for her. She practically fell into his embrace, sniffling against his t-shirt.

"I know you're not trying to dictate my life. I know you're not like Arnold," she said.

"It's all right, Julian."

"It's not."

He held her back to look at her. "When I first came home from a tour in Afghanistan, I was a bear to live with. This is mild."

She gave him a watery smile. "Thanks for being so understanding, Drake."

He cupped her face again and kissed her. Say it, his heart ordered, but Julian melted against him, and his mind emptied of rational thought. He held her tightly as she wound her arms around his neck.

When they came up for air, he struggled to regain his composure and chuckled, his forehead against hers. "I both admire and hate 'the vow.'"

Julian gasped. "You've been talking to Hannah. Only she calls it that."

He released her and winked. "Your mom does too," he told her. "And on that note, I need a shower," he said and made his escape.

CHAPTER SIXTEEN

Drake dreaded the comic convention. His gut told him Julian's appearance there put her in danger, but he loved her spunk and refusal to be cowed. Julian had a point. She couldn't live in a bubble. His best option was to be by her side every minute of the event. Drake braced himself over the next two days spent at the vineyard so he could help his parents, and Julian could learn the basics of how things worked. She listened attentively and asked smart questions. Drake had seen the look of approval from both of his parents when Julian couldn't see them. By Thursday afternoon, she had already begun working on promotional materials for their hayrides and Christmas lights tours.

Friday morning, they left for the convention. Julian wore a black skirt, black knee high boots, and a t-shirt bearing the name of a geeky sci-fi television show they both liked under a black leather jacket. Drake felt that familiar surge of desire when he saw her. In the car, she kissed him hard, and he realized she trembled. "You don't have to do this," he reminded her, rubbing her arms as he met her gaze.

"I don't want to be scared forever. Besides, it might even draw him out. I'd almost rather just get it over with."

Drake felt his blood chill with the idea. He pulled her into his arms and held her tightly. "No. You stay close to me, and tell me if you see anything suspicious. Don't take any chances today." He felt her head bob up and down against his shoulder then held her back to look at her. "Let's try to have fun, though. You've earned it."

They met Hannah and Rob outside of the convention center and entered together. They checked in and received passes. Julian found her table set up, and her eyes widened with amazement. Drake scanned the line of tables and noticed a voluptuous, dark-haired woman giving him a once over. He looked at Julian who grinned. "That's Jodi," she whispered. Julian called her over. The woman came when beckoned and told them, "I got us set up next to each other."

Julian hugged her and introduced everyone. Jodi shook hands with each of them and smirked at Drake in particular. "You need to work on your descriptive skills, Julian. You didn't do this man justice in your emails."

He raised his eyebrows at Julian, whose cheeks pinkened. "Jodi and I write a lot of emails." Julian held Drake's hand and pulled him a little closer than usual, her actions sending a possessive signal to her friend which amused him. As if after all they had been through, he would look at this woman over her. But he liked seeing Julian showing this side of herself. "Jodi wrote the book you read that was on my coffee table."

His eyebrows rose even higher. "That was some book."

"Did you read all of it?" Jodi asked, eyes sparkling.

"Only a small section, but it was intriguing."

Hannah stepped between them, reaching out to shake Jodi's hand. "I read the entire book. Actually, I'm a fan. I've read a lot of your books."

Jodi smiled in genuine appreciation as she accepted the handshake. "Thanks. I'm always happy to talk to someone who likes my work whether they've read an entire novel or just a small section." She winked at Drake, and Julian squeezed his hand.

"Okay, Jodi. Enough ogling my boyfriend."

Drake suppressed his laughter, but Jodi chuckled. "Message received. Sorry." She hugged Julian.

Rob took Hannah's hand. "We're abandoning you guys for a while to see everything. This con isn't as big as the one they have in Atlanta, but it's still pretty extensive."

Julian shooed them off. She looked at Drake. "Why don't you check everything out with them?"

He shook his head. "I'm good. I'll wait till you can go."

Before long, fans began to stop by the table, purchasing books and asking for autographs. As Drake stood near the table or sat close by, one young woman asked, "Who's that?" When Julian looked at him with that grin he found irresistible, he said, "I'm her bodyguard."

Julian rolled her eyes the first time. But when the queries continued, she used the answer herself.

Drake watched Jodi enjoy the same adoration as Julian but from an almost exclusively female set of fans. Curiously, despite the romance label, men seemed to appreciate Julian's latest book as much as women. Hannah and Rob returned after some time. Hannah gushed to Julian about the booths and different celebrities. Rob stood next to Drake and spoke low enough the women wouldn't hear. "Any sign of trouble?"

"Not yet."

Rob heaved a sigh of relief. "Let's hope that continues." Then he watched the next group of fans approach and ask for autographs. "How steady has that been?"

"Pretty steady. I didn't realize Julian had such a following." Drake scanned the room again.

"There's definitely a cult following that's gaining momentum. If she writes a sequel, they'll eat it up. We heard people talking about it as we walked around."

Drake glanced at Julian talking animatedly to a group of young men. He allowed himself the swell of pride. He would have to tell his parents to be prepared to replace her. "I haven't read the book everyone's going on about."

Rob sighed. "It's labeled a romance novel, but it's not. It's got a wider appeal."

Julian turned to catch his eye with a broad smile. He returned the smile and realized why she felt it so important to come. Julian might not like being recognized in the coffee shop, but here she was in her element. She liked talking to fans about her book. She paid attention to what they liked and didn't like, digesting each critique whether good or bad. He overheard a couple of teenage girls talking about the news interview. "It's so romantic the way you two met," one of the gushed. She deflected their questions and deftly changed the topic to featured events at the convention.

Drake looked at Rob. "She's good at this."

"Yeah," Rob laughed.

Hannah joined them. "You guys need to have some lunch and look around." When Rob joined Julian to chat about the steady stream of fans, Hannah took advantage of the opportunity to lean close to Drake. "I've never seen her act as goofy about someone as she does you. Who's said the L-word?"

He cleared his throat. "Neither of us yet."

Hannah blinked in disbelief. "Are you kidding me?"

Drake shook his head. "I'm working on it, but I just haven't yet."

Hannah narrowed her eyes at him and put her hands on her hips. "Disappointing."

He had let his mouth drop open as he struggled with how to

respond. Before he could, Julian interrupted him. "Lunch? I'm starving." Her gaze darted between him and Hannah. "What's wrong?"

"Nothing," they responded in unison.

As he walked away with Julian, Drake looked back at Hannah who mouthed the words, "Tell her."

They ate quickly. Julian too excited to sit still for long. They looked at every booth she could squeeze into the time she had before she had promised to be back. She spoke to authors she indicated she knew from writers' conferences. Then she stopped dead in her tracks. Every muscle in Drake's body tensed. He steeled himself for danger and stood closer to her. Julian turned to him. "I have to get a picture with him." He followed her eyes to Nelson Fabian, an actor from the television show featured on Julian's t-shirt. The man gleefully took pictures with fans, even accommodating silly requests. Drake had to smile. Julian practically sprinted toward the man and fell in line.

"Um, should I be jealous now?"

"Absolutely," Julian teased.

"Don't you have to sign up in advance to get your picture taken with celebrities at these things?" Drake asked.

"Yeah, but since this convention is small enough, the website said after the prepaid customers were done, people could wait in line," she explained.

The actor noticed Julian and beckoned her to the front of the line. Drake watched her look around to make sure he meant her. She pointed to herself, and he nodded. She took Drake's hand and dragged him forward. He greeted them both with a handshake as he introduced himself. Julian chuckled, "We know who you are."

He grinned. "I know you're here for your book and probably need to get back, but I wanted to get a picture together. I love your book."

Julian turned scarlet. "Really?"

"Yeah. I mentioned it to the director of my last movie." Drake took Julian's phone and prepared to take a picture. The actor moved her into a traditional pose with him then frowned. Then he whispered to Julian who laughed. She nodded, and he grinned. She put her arms around him and pretended to dip him backwards as he put a hand to his forehead and pretended to swoon. The waiting crowd laughed and applauded. Drake took several quick pictures as others in the crowd did as well. Afterward, he stood back up, and Drake watched as they exchanged cell phone numbers. "Send me some of those. Mind if I post the pictures online?"

"Knock yourself out," she responded and hugged him. Julian looked at the time on her phone. "Uh-oh. We better run." She surprised Drake by breaking into a slow run as she asked, "Did that just happen?"

"It did," he assured her, his grin as wide as hers.

She giggled as they jogged through the people. Hannah and Rob were chatting with Jodi when Drake and Julian returned. Julian's eyes widened at the people waiting for her at her table. "Wow," she breathed. With enthusiasm, she relayed the events with the actor to her friends. Hannah and Rob looked stunned but excited. She turned to Drake. "Do you mind texting the pictures from my phone to Nelson?" she asked him.

He agreed and set to work saving the actor's number in her phone and forwarding the pictures. When he finished, Hannah and Rob chose to go to a television show panel together. Julian once again urged Drake to join them and once again, he declined. "I'm here to look out for you. I'm your bodyguard, remember?"

Julian kissed his cheek. She turned back to the gathering crowd. Within half an hour, the actor had posted the pictures on Twitter and Instagram, and many of the fans at the convention had seen it. Julian's book flew off the tables. Within an hour, the books had sold out. The publicist practically melted with joy. He produced glossy pictures of Julian to be signed in place of the book. A website address adorned the back of the pictures. "These are five dollars for the fans. Make sure to tell them the books are available at the website on the back."

Drake saw Julian balk. "Five dollars? Are you kidding? I'm not going to have people paying for an autographed picture of me."

He frowned. "The going rate here is fifty."

"I don't care if the going rate is five hundred bucks, I'm not doing that. My books just sold out. You guys can pay for some promotional swag."

Jodi slyly smiled; her own books also almost gone. When the publicist capitulated, Jodi patted Julian on the back. "Good girl."

The pace continued to increase. When fans heard the pictures were free, the pictures flew off the table as well. Countless people asked about her picture with the actor. Julian gave Drake an overwhelmed smile. "Good grief. A simple picture…"

Jodi warned, "Get used to it, honey. I think you just earned your own geekdom fan base. Once they read that book, it'll grow. Brace yourself."

As the convention wrapped up, Julian sent a text to Rob and Hannah to locate them. She awkwardly danced around behind the table. "I have really got to go to the bathroom. I got so excited I forgot."

Drake asked, "Can you wait for Hannah and Rob?"

Jodi offered, "I'll go with you. You shouldn't go anywhere alone with your creeper still on the loose." Drake gave her a grateful look. He watched them leave and sent his own text to Rob, unsettled by the lack of response. Rob and Hannah had been gone for hours. The longer Julian remained away from the table, the more Drake paced. Finally, he sent Julian a text to check on her as well with no response.

His heart dropped when he saw Jodi running to him alone, her pale face panicked. "She's gone. I can't find her."

Drake dialed Detective Reynolds as he interrogated Jodi for details which he relayed to the detective.

She told him, "We went in the stalls at the same time. When I came out, she wasn't in the bathroom anymore. I checked every stall. Outside, I saw this." She held up Julian's cell phone.

CHAPTER SEVENTEEN

Julian chided herself for waiting so long to go to the restroom. She washed her hands as she waited for Jodi and felt her phone vibrate in the pocket of her jacket. She dried her hands and looked at the text. Attached to it was a picture of Rob and Hannah sitting back to back on a floor, bound together with silver duct tape. Rob's head slumped forward and his eyes were closed, but Hannah's expression relayed her terror. Julian felt her body go cold at the text with the picture

Come outside by the rear entrance alone. I have a ride waiting for you. Leave your phone on the way out of the bathroom.

A second text buzzed immediately. I'll see if you don't, and your friends will pay.

Julian swallowed the lump of fear and frustration and tiptoed from the bathroom. Once outside, she placed her phone on the top of the trashcan by the restroom door. She took a deep breath and followed instructions. Heart pounding and chest tight, Julian thought of Hannah and Rob as she opened a back door of the convention center. An arm swept around her torso as her captor jabbed a needle into her thigh. She thought of Drake even as the world blackened and disappeared.

When she next opened her eyes, Julian's head felt fuzzy and her mouth dry. She fought to shake off the fog in her brain. A familiar face came into view. John Hatcher?

"You're awake. Good. The sedative should wear off quickly."

Julian tried to speak, but duct tape covered her mouth and held her hands together. She had been placed on a long, wood table in a conference room. She turned to look through the glass wall to her right to see the center of the downtown library with its large open concept. All floors surrounded a gaping center with escalators between each level. She could see shelves of books and the glass banister that lined the opening. Tears pricked her eyes as she thought of the hours and hours she had spent in this library growing up, reading and listening to guest speakers. Then she heard Arnold's voice.

"We had a deal. I get a few minutes alone with her, you give me my money, and she's all yours."

Bile rose in Julian's throat. As fear crept over her, adrenaline quickly reversed the effects of the remnants of the sedative. She craned her neck to look at Arnold standing by the door and saw the pistol in John's hand. "No one will ever touch Julian again except me," he assured Arnold then raised the gun and shot Arnold in the head.

Julian jerked at the shot. Blood sprayed the wall behind Arnold as he slumped to the floor. She cowered from John as he turned back to her. "Don't worry, baby. He won't ever bother you again. You'll stay with me from now on." With his free hand, he stroked her hair. "If I take the tape off, promise not to scream?"

Julian just stared at him through her violent trembling. He removed the tape without waiting for her reply. Though she feared the answer, she asked, "Where are Hannah and Rob?"

John continued to smooth her hair. "They're in the room across the hall. I'll take care of them later." John brushed his fingers over her cheek. "Don't be scared. As long as you stay with me, I won't hurt you. Someday, you can learn to love me."

She tried to make herself think. Drake had told her to be calm in a dangerous situation. Just be calm and think. Think. She glanced around the room. John seemed to have the only gun. The only other objects in the room were the dry erase board, the table, and chairs. The florescent light bothered her eyes. She licked her dry lips. "John, why don't you let Hannah and Rob go? It'll be okay."

He grinned as he shook his head. "Your loyalty to your friends is one of your best qualities. So noble. And the way you help people, even if you don't know them… It's one of the reasons I was behind you on the road that day. You were so kind to me at the conference. I took the video to watch when I was alone, but then I thought, everyone should know how brave you are. So I sent a copy to the news stations."

John looked at her with such tenderness that Julian wouldn't have been able to guess he was capable of murder if she hadn't just seen him kill Arnold. He sighed with regret. "I wish I could let them go for you, sweetheart, but they saw my face, and they'll tell the police. You'll get over losing them once you better appreciate me. You'll understand what I did. Now, just relax here while I go get rid of your boyfriend."

Fresh panic gripped Julian. "Drake hasn't seen your face. Leave him alone. I'll go with you."

John chuckled. "Julian, you know he'll never stop coming for you. He won't stop until he's dead. Just like me. So I'll just have to make sure he's dead."

She shook her head. "I'll do whatever you want. Just don't hurt him or my friends. I'll sneak out of here with you. We can run away together where no one will find us."

John gave her a look of pity. "I'm sure you've been told you're a bad liar. Now, let's get you situated." John slid her off the table, still holding the gun in one hand. He hauled her into a chair and taped her hands to the arm of the chair, covering even the tips of her fingers. Then he placed another strip of tape over her mouth. Patting her cheek, John assured her, "This will all be over soon. Just wait here." He leaned down and met her eyes, his expression almost joyful. He sucked a deep breath through his nose and whispered, "You smell so good." Then he was gone.

From the chair, Julian could see Arnold's dead body, and on his feet, she saw the cowboy boots she'd remembered from the abduction. Julian cringed before looking around the room. John had thwarted her ability to gnaw at the tape with her teeth or grasp at it with her nails, but her feet remained free and the chair had wheels.

Julian awkwardly stood, dragging the chair as she made her way to the door. She placed her foot by the bottom of the door as she used her chin to push the handle down and pull the door open just enough that she could shove her foot between the door and its frame. Julian avoided looking at Arnold as she moved onto the tiled floor of the hall. She made her way to the conference room door across the hall and used her chin to open the door with less effort as it swung inward.

She used her head to flip the light switch and made a noise against the tape as she saw Hannah and Rob, just as she had seen them in the text. They had been taped together around their torsos and their arms were trapped by their sides. Julian dropped to the floor and scooted until her face lined up with Hannah's fingers. She could see the question in Hannah's eyes until Julian pushed her taped mouth against her fingers. Hannah fumbled until she caught a corner of the tape and pulled it back, tears streaming.

Julian whispered, "Hold still." She used her teeth to rip at the tape holding their hands. When she ripped the tape enough, Rob twisted until he could tear the rest of the tape and free them. He stood and helped Hannah to her feet before turning to Julian. She tilted her head toward the door. "Just get out of here. He wants me to go with him so I have some time, but he plans to kill you two."

Rob ignored her, righted her chair and set to work on the tape around her hands. Hannah tore at Julian's other hand as she sobbed, "We thought he shot you when we heard the gun."

"He shot Arnold. Rob, get her out of here," Julian said again, wheeling the chair from them with her back to the door. "Go!"

Rob glanced out the door as Hannah frantically continued working on freeing Julian. He said, "He's headed to the escalator. Looks like he's going downstairs."

Julian swallowed hard as one hand came free at Hannah's ministrations. "He's setting some kind of trap for Drake," Julian said. "You guys have to get out and warn him to stay away."

Hannah and Rob looked up at the door at the same time, fear washing the color from their already white faces. Julian reacted before she could even digest what she did, placing her feet on the floor and kicking herself toward the door with all her strength. Julian felt the chair connect with John's body, and they tumbled back onto the floor. The last of the tape on Julian's hands ripped. "Run!" she screamed to Rob and Hannah as she scrambled off the chair. She turned toward John, who aimed the gun at Rob. Julian took advantage of their positions on the cold floor and shoved John. The arm holding the gun went awry, and the shot hit the ceiling instead of her friend. Hannah screamed, but from the corner of her eye, Julian saw Rob grab Hannah's hand and drag her away. John struggled to free himself from Julian's hold, but she refused to relent. She drew her knee up between his legs.

Air whooshed from his lungs, but he kept his grip on the gun she tried to wrestle from his hands. He groaned in pain and grabbed Julian's hair. With amazing speed despite his discomfort, John rolled them over and righted himself. He dragged Julian by her hair as she howled in pain and clawed at his hands. Unable to gain purchase on the smooth floor from her position, Julian slid along the floor at John's mercy. He dragged her toward the escalators in an attempt to catch up to Rob and Hannah. When John stopped at the top of the unmoving escalators, he grabbed Julian's arm, hauled her to her feet, and held her by her waist as he looked around the large open library. Julian realized when he caught a glimpse of Rob pulling Hannah toward the back door. John aimed at Hannah, but Julian tossed her head back against his face and felt a flower of pain in the back of her head as she connected. His shot missed again.

CHAPTER EIGHTEEN

From outside, Drake saw Rob and Hannah running toward the back door and heard the shot. The bullet ricocheted above the pair running toward the door. As Drake reached for the door, Rob and Hannah waved for him to stop. Rob dropped to his knees and slid to the door. Drake then saw the wiring to a small, makeshift device. Explosives. He yelled through the glass, "I've seen something like this in the war! You need to disarm it."

Rob ordered, "Hannah, get back." Drake carefully led him through the process and within seconds, the door opened. "Get far away from the doors," Drake told the couple. "I've called the police. Call them back, and tell them about the explosives." He shoved his cell phone into Rob's hand.

They obeyed, and Drake hurried into the building, weapon drawn. A shot rang out near him but missed. He traced its origin and saw Julian struggling with the man from the movie theater—John Hatcher. Blood poured from the man's nose. Rage swept over him. Julian's cheek bled and another trickle of blood ran from one side of her own nose. "Get out of here!" she yelled at him, writhing in John's grip and holding his arm with both hands.

Drake yelled at John, "Let her go, and you can come out of this alive!"

John's snort came with a sneer. "You're not good enough for her. You can't have her."

Drake kept his gun trained on John, but Julian's body obstructed his shot. "I'm warning you one more time." He looked at Julian, whose jaw set in determination at something John whispered to her. He could see the wild fury in her eyes. She used his grip to hold her as she jumped and put her feet against the railing of the glass barrier around the open upper level. She pushed with her legs, and Drake saw the pair tumble backward. He raced toward the escalator.

As he ran the stairs two at a time, he heard Julian cry out in pain again. Then John emitted a strangled sound as well. He could hear the scuffling and saw Julian desperately scrambling for the upper hand. With a well-placed elbow, she broke free and twisted to her feet. Drake darted behind a corner as she disappeared into shelves of books. He aimed at John, who threw himself around a column before Drake could fire.

Drake stood with his back to the wall and peered carefully around the corner. A bullet hit the wall near his head, chunks of white plaster spraying by him. He gritted his teeth. Did the man have some training? Another bullet hit the same spot in the wall, and Drake bit back a curse. That was too accurate to be a fluke. He glanced around looking for Julian. Not seeing her, he peeked around the corner. When he didn't hear another shot, he crouched and hurried to the column John had used for cover. He caught a glimpse of John creeping in between the shelves of books. Drake considered shooting but without knowing Julian's location, a shot could go through John and hit her.

Drake padded silently onto the carpet around the shelves,

hoping to better muffle his foot falls. A blur of movement through the shelves to his left caught his attention. He turned toward it but saw nothing. A shot rang out over his head. He ducked further down and darted to another row of books for cover. He had the tactical disadvantage at this point and knew it.

Drake grasped at any ideas for changing his disadvantage when he heard a slight rustle above. He glanced up and saw Julian sprawled on top of one of the bookshelves. She held her head just over the edge of the bookshelf closest to the walkway around the second level escalator and pointed a finger toward a row of shelves to indicate John's location. Drake nodded. As Drake inched in the direction, he heard her clothes rustling again and glanced up at her again. She shook her head and gestured that he should go the other way. When he ignored her, Julian inched forward with him.

He saw the wire before he reached it. Booby traps. Great. He wondered how many had been laid. A quick check toward Julian revealed she had kept up with him from her vantage point on the shelves. She frantically pointed at John through the shelves, now aiming at Drake. At her warning, he ducked as a bullet ripped through the books where his head had just been. Drake leveled his gun through the books and returned fire. John screamed in pain as Drake's shot caught him in the left shoulder. He went down, and Julian shrieked, "Get back!"

Drake jumped back, but the blast from another booby trap caught them both with its concussion, tossing him backwards and knocking Julian from her perch. He shook his head to reorient himself and attempted to dispel the ringing in his ears as he realized Julian's warning had saved his life. Drake could smell smoke and see fire burning some of the books. The sprinkler system kicked on, and stagnant water drenched everything.

He looked around for Julian then heard her screaming. He

stumbled to his feet, still holding his pistol when John tackled him. John no longer held a gun, but grappled for Drake's. They wrestled with each other until they rolled out onto the tiled floor of the walkway. Drake's heart almost stopped when he saw Julian. She dangled on the outside of the railing, having been thrown over it by the blast. She curled one arm around the top but couldn't get a foothold to pull herself over.

John took advantage of Drake's momentary distraction to punch him in the jaw. He then clawed at Drake's hand with the gun. As Drake rolled them over, their flailing against each other finally resulted in the gun skidding across the tile floor. He again recognized John had combat training but had no time to wonder about it. After a few moments of fighting, Drake struck John in the face with enough force that the man went limp. Drake scooped up his gun and shoved it in his waistband as he rushed to the railing to help Julian back over.

Blue lights flashed through the walls of windows, and officers drew their weapons while waiting outside for the bomb squad. Julian clung to Drake's arms as he dragged her back over the railing. They fell to the floor together then stood slowly. He wrapped his arms around Julian and crushed her against him. "Drake!" she exclaimed. He followed her eyes to where she looked. John, having regained consciousness, dug a gun from a hidden holster. Shoving Julian behind him, Drake beat John to the draw with the pistol in his waistband and fired. John's body convulsed as Drake pulled the trigger two more times. Julian's fingers clutched at the back of Drake's shirt as he backed them toward the frozen escalator with his pistol still trained on John. The man's vacant eyes faced the ceiling, and blood pooled around him. Once they were just out of eyesight or the body, Drake turned to face her.

"Drake—" Her voice broke, and he hugged her to him. She shivered against him, her teeth chattering. He struggled to maintain his composure as feet mounted the stairs and approached.

Detective Reynolds instructed, "Give me the gun, Mr. Salvatore." To the other officers flanking him, he instructed, "Approach the suspect with caution."

Drake allowed the detective to take his weapon while maintaining his hold on Julian. "Shouldn't you be waiting for the bomb squad?" Drake asked.

Reynolds shrugged. "Since you and Mr. Overton disarmed the back door, we took our chances to come help you."

One of the other officers called, "He's dead."

Julian kept her face buried in Drake's shirt as she told Detective Reynolds, "He shot Arnold in the first conference room. He's dead, too." Her expression told Drake she'd seen it, and his heart convulsed. More sirens wailed, and he watched ambulances pulling in front of the library. Detective Reynolds nodded his head toward the escalators.

"You two should go downstairs, and let the paramedics check you out. There's some ambulances out back, too." Drake nodded and led Julian toward the escalators. She shook so violently that she teetered on the first stair.

Drake said, "Hold on to my neck, Jules."

She complied, and he lifted her in his arms, descending the escalator and heading for the back door. The bomb squad rushed past them. Paramedics steered the pair to a waiting ambulance where Rob and Hannah waited swaddled in blankets. Drake placed Julian on a stretcher and clutched her hand as paramedics tucked blankets around each of their drenched shoulders. One looked at Julian's cheek and nose. Julian would probably have a black eye. Another paramedic urged Drake to sit next to her, pointing to his jaw. John's blow had cut him, and the spot stung.

The paramedics patched them up as they gave their statements to the police. By the time they finished, Drake wanted nothing more than a hot shower and to sleep for a week. He looked at Julian's tired, pale face and decided she needed two weeks.

CHAPTER NINETEEN

Julian listened as Drake made several calls when they returned to her house. She sat on the couch with a throw blanket and a hot cup of tea while he called her mom, his mom, and Jodi, who had been sick with worry since Drake left the convention center. They had both changed into dry clothes, and Julian sat curled up waiting for Drake to finish making the calls. When finished, he sat next to her and met her eyes. She placed her mug on the coffee table and reached out to take one of his hands. "It's not lost on me that you came for me knowing John had set a trap. I don't know how to thank you."

Drake leaned toward her, pulling her close to him. "You would have done the same thing."

Julian sighed as he put both arms around her waist. She wrapped her arms around his neck and kissed him ardently. She could feel the desperation in his response, and he murmured, "I didn't know if either of us would come out of there." She shuddered as he continued to kiss her. His warm lips chased away thoughts of the evening, and nothing existed in that moment but Drake. He whispered to her, "I have to tell you something."

"Okay," she said.

"I love you, Jules."

She kissed him again and smiled against his mouth. "I love you too, Drake. I have for a while."

He drew his head back, eyebrows raised. "Why didn't you say something before?"

She snuggled into his side and tucked her face into the crook of his neck. "Just felt like you needed to go first."

He chuckled and tightened his hold on her, sprawling them on the couch. "Liar. You were too scared."

She kissed his stubbly jaw then placed her cheek against his chest. "Don't you feel better for having said it first?"

She grinned as Drake's laugh rumbled against her ear. "Yes, actually. I do."

* * *

Drake let Detective Reynolds into Julian's house, which was now filled with family and church members. Everyone wanted to see for themselves that the couple had survived, and everyone brought food. Drake wouldn't turn homemade macaroni and cheese down for anything short of the Apocalypse.

"Wow," the detective said, staring at the milling people crammed into the small living area.

"Yeah," Drake replied. "But they come bearing genuine, homemade Southern food, so who am I to turn them away?"

The man chuckled. "Thought I'd give you and Ms. Fursey an update on the case in person."

Drake found Julian surrounded by Martin and Jill, all three chatting about more baby name suggestions. "I need to steal her," he said and took her hand.

Julian gave the couple a shrug and allowed Drake to lead her down the hall to Reynolds. She motioned for them to use her bedroom to talk. Drake and Julian sat on the bed while Reynolds sat in the reading chair in the corner. He pulled out a small notepad and put on a pair of glasses from his pocket.

"So I just wanted to give you two an update on what we've learned."

Drake took Julian's hand in his and squeezed. She squeezed back, her shoulders stiff and her mouth tight.

Detective Reynolds said, "John Hatcher was dishonorably discharged from the Army Rangers for misconduct. Accused of stalking a woman. Surprise, surprise. She mysteriously disappeared after his discharge."

Drake felt Julian's fingers grip his hand like a vise and released his hold to place an arm around her shoulders instead, pulling her into his side. Her voice was nearly a whisper as she asked, "Did they ever find her?"

"No," Reynolds said, his face grim. "Law enforcement in North Carolina is searching the property he owns there as we speak." Julian shuddered.

Drake nodded. "His Army background explains his training. What about Arnold Woodley?"

The detective explained, "He'd been helping Hatcher all along. Convinced some girl at the cellphone carrier that Ms. Fursey had his kids and was a bad mother and that the kids were in danger." He looked at Julian. "Every time you changed your number, Woodley used this girl to track you down." He patted her arm. "But it's over now."

Julian nodded mutely before swallowing hard. "Thank you," she croaked.

"I'll leave you alone now. I hope you're able to get back to your normal life," Reynolds said and stood. Drake walked him out then returned to Julian. She hadn't moved.

He sat next to her again. "How ya doin'?" he asked.

She met his gaze with shimmering eyes. "Better, but I feel like a terrible person for being glad they're both…" She looked away as a tear slid down her cheek.

Drake wiped her cheek with his thumb and made a reassuring sound. "You're not a bad person for being glad you're safe."

She threw her arms around his neck and sobbed. He held her tightly, one hand cupping the back of her head as she cried. When the gut-wrenching sobs slowed, she sniffled against his knit shirt. "Thank you, Drake."

"For what?"

"For everything. For coming for me. For letting me get snot all over your shirt. For loving me."

He smiled and threaded his fingers in her hair to tug her head back. "No, Jules. Thank you for loving me," he said and kissed her.

CHAPTER TWENTY

Having decided to celebrate their own Christmas at Drake's before the family get-together, Julian arrived early with egg nog and spiced cider.

Drake chuckled at her excitement. "You're not kidding when you say you love Christmas."

"Nope." She jumped up and down, clapping. "I want you to open what I got you." After tossing the egg nog and cider in the refrigerator, Julian grabbed his hand and led him to the tree. They opened their gifts, leaving the wrapping paper littered around like Christmas snow. Their gifts for each other made them smile and laugh. Julian and Drake sat on the couch with cups of cider, deciding against the egg nog until after dinner with the family.

"Oh, look," Julian said, giving him a mischievous grin. "I forgot one." She put her cider on the coffee table and produced a small box neatly wrapped with red paper and a gold bow.

He gave her a broad smile. "What's this?" he asked as he took the box and tore the paper away.

"Amerigo suggested it. He said, 'Once a Marine, always a Marine.'"

Drake opened the box and blinked at the watch inside, the face featuring the eagle, globe, and anchor emblem. Julian held her breath. She'd researched the quality of the watch—from its water resistance and durability as well as the detail of the emblem. She'd been determined to put thought into Drake's gift. When he met her eyes, she released the pent up breath. "You like it," she sighed happily.

"Yes, I really do," he told her, hugging her close before kissing her soundly. He replaced his watch with the new one and looked at it on his wrist. "Not bad, Jules." Then he gave her his own mischievous grin. "I forgot one of your gifts, too," he said and stood. He reached into the branches of the tree and produced a small, black, velvet box.

Julian's heart thudded wildly in her chest. "This isn't what I think it is?"

Drake cleared his throat as he turned the box in his hands. "Nothing in this courtship has been traditional, but I wanted something to be old-fashioned." Julian covered her mouth with her hands as he knelt before her and opened the box.

"Will you marry me?" he asked.

Julian blinked at the emerald cut diamond set in a platinum ring. It sparkled with the lights from the Christmas tree. "I wasn't prepared for this."

"Answer before it gets awkward," he said on a laugh.

"Yes!"

Drake stood and pulled her to her feet. He gripped her tightly to him, the box still in one hand. His kiss seared Julian from the tip of her head to the tip of her toes and was so thorough she almost forgot he still held the ring until he released her. He smiled and said, "Let's make sure it fits."

He slid the ring onto her finger. Julian looked at the diamond and then at Drake's happy face as he sighed in relief.

"Good. It was a pain trying to get your ring size. I finally made your mom steal one of your rings so we could figure it out." She laughed and kissed him again, matching the passion of his earlier kiss. "See, I have to marry you so I can travel with you when you go on your book tour after the holidays and not upset our parents."

Julian giggled and swatted at him. "Gee, thanks. You know how to make a girl feel special." He grinned at her. Julian's shaking knees gave out, and she sat on the couch looking at the ring on her finger. Drake sat next to her. "Are you sure, Drake? We haven't known each other all that long."

He brushed his thumb over her cheek and gave her a contemplative look. "Sometimes in life, the answers are obvious. If you're lucky enough to have something so obvious right in front of you, why wait? I love you. I want you to be the first thing I see in the morning and the last thing I see at night. Seems simple enough to me."

Tears flooded Julian's eyes. "I never used to cry this much." She leaned against his shoulder. "How am I supposed to go to your parents' house and show them this ring and not cry all day?"

Drake shrugged. "More importantly, before our moms take control, what kind of wedding do you think we should have? I know it's a rushed question, but if you don't decide now, they'll railroad you into what they want."

She tilted her head at him. "Do you want a big wedding?"

He shrugged again. "I want whatever you want. Mom and Pop knew I was going to ask, and they already offered to pay for everything, and they suggested a big wedding, but it's not about the groom. My only request is to get married before you leave for your first trip."

Julian bit her lip. That only gave them a couple of weeks to plan. She supposed most women would already have an idea planned out for their wedding, but Julian hadn't given a second wedding much thought. "I had a big church wedding with Arnold. It was nice, but now, it doesn't seem as important. But if it's what you want, I'll happily jump into a wedding dress again." She smirked at him.

"We could run off someplace like Vegas and get married."

She thought about that for a moment. "I'm not sure I want that extreme, either. Maybe we could just do something small at either your church or mine. Our families could be there, and we could have a small reception."

Drake chuckled. "With your mom and my mom, be prepared to have this small church wedding turn into more."

When they reached the vineyard, Mary, Anthony, Gale and Amerigo waited with expectant faces. Julian held up her hand with the ring. "I know you busybodies all knew so don't act surprised," she said with a laugh. Julian and Drake accepted congratulations and hugs from everyone. Mary and Gale gave them teary-eyed smiles.

Mary held her hands together in front of her lips before saying, "I'm so happy I could cry."

"Please don't cry," Julian said then chuckled. "Then I'll cry and Mom'll cry and then Drake'll cry. There will just be a lot of snot."

Gale swatted her shoulder as she handed Julian a glass of eggnog. "Stop that," she hissed, but her face wreathed into another smile.

When they opened presents, Julian struggled to maintain her composure with each wedding-related gift. She caught Drake's amused expression and narrowed her eyes at him. During a lull, she leaned close to him as they sat on the floor by the tree and whispered, "What if I'd said no? Could you even imagine their broken hearts?" She tipped her head toward the rest of their families gushing over their gifts to each other.

Drake's mouth dropped open. "Their broken hearts? What about mine?"

Julian's eyes welled, and she leaned into his side as he put an arm around her shoulders. "You know. I think you're a keeper," she said.

As predicted, their mothers took the wedding torch and ran. Drake and Julian set a date a week before she needed to leave for her first convention trip. They planned a honeymoon in historic downtown Savannah. Once they settled on those details, Julian gave up and turned the rest of the event over to the older women. She told Drake, "As long as we end up married at the end of the ceremony, they can plan whatever they want." The only other detail Julian took charge of was the dress. As the "small wedding" blossomed into something more elaborate, Julian decided to choose the dress herself. Gale, Mary, and Hannah went with her, and they made a day of it.

While everyone bustled around them, Drake and Julian focused on other things. With her publisher, they planned her schedule for the next couple of months. Drake determined which conventions and publicity events he could make, and they solidified decisions and details. They decided to live in Drake's house and put Julian's on the market. Julian took Amerigo to most of his physical therapy visits so the Salvatores could stay at the vineyard to work. She also spent as much time as possible working on the sequel to her last novel.

When the day arrived, Julian finally felt the pinch of wedding nerves as her mother and Hannah fawned over her. Gale sat with her in the Sunday School classroom as Hannah held her dress. Julian had already had her hair and makeup done by the professional they had hired. Her fingernails and toenails were perfectly manicured. She'd never spent this much money or even time on her appearance.

Hannah helped the wedding planner slide the dress over Julian's head to avoid mussing her hair and makeup. Julian sighed once Hannah finished zipping it, and looked in the mirror. Gale approached with the carefully selected jewelry, all pearls. Julian took the items and adorned herself with them. The wedding planner helped Julian with her tiara and veil. She slipped into her low satin heels and faced them. All three women looked misty-eyed. Julian took a deep breath and ordered, "No. None of that. I'll start blubbering with you and mess up my makeup." She sat in a chair and wrung her hands together. The photographer took pictures at every turn. Julian made faces from time to time just to be difficult. Gale chastised her on a regular basis. She just smiled at her mother and told her, "Shouldn't I be in a good mood?"

"Behave, or I'll pop you."

Mary slipped into the room. She saw Julian, and tears welled. Julian held up a hand, "This room has a no tears rule." Mary laughed and hugged Julian.

"I've prayed for this from the moment we met you. I know that sounds weird, but we just knew." Mary held Julian's hands as she looked at Gale.

Gale nodded. "We talked about it that first night we went to the hotel from the hospital."

Julian and Hannah looked at each other with gaping mouths. Then they looked back at the older women. "You schemers!" Julian said with disbelief then gave an evil grin. "That's all right. Turnabout's fair play. Mary, you might already be married, but Mom isn't. I'll start the matchmaking as soon as possible."

Hannah tapped a finger on her chin thoughtfully. "Actually, I saw a distinguished man in a uniform on Drake's side of the church. He looks close to your age, and he's very handsome." Gale turned pink, and Julian doubled over with laughter.

"I'm on it at the reception," she teased.

"Don't you dare," Gale warned.

When Julian met Anthony near the church entrance, she had to give him the no tears lecture as well. He swiped at his eyes and smiled. "You look so beautiful. We are so lucky you are joining our family today."

Julian hugged Anthony. "I'm the lucky one."

When the doors opened, Anthony held out his elbow, and Julian slipped her hand into the crook of his arm. She took in the sight of their friends and family turning to look at her. As her eyes locked onto Drake, her breath caught in her throat. He wore his Marine dress blues and looked impossibly handsome. Amerigo stood next to him, leaning on crutches. Hannah stood on Julian's side. Once Julian reached the altar, she smiled at Drake with appreciation. After Anthony placed their hands together before the pastor, Drake whispered, "You look beautiful."

She whispered back, "You look fantastic, yourself." Unfortunately, the pastor's microphone switched on at that very moment, and her words echoed throughout the sanctuary. Laughter erupted as Julian rolled her eyes heavenward and turned pink. Drake thanked her with a grin.

The ceremony went quickly as they used traditional vows. Once announced as husband and wife, they kissed, turned, and exited the sanctuary. In the room set aside for them, they held hands and laughed about the microphone and their parents and their frantic separate mornings. Once the sanctuary had emptied, they returned for the obligatory pictures before heading to the fellowship hall for the reception. As they walked outside and waited to be announced, Julian admitted, "I'm glad the old ladies did this for us after all."

Drake kissed her and agreed. "We're lucky."

"Yeah, we are."

Hand in hand, they entered the fellowship hall when announced to a room of standing loved ones applauding. Julian blinked in surprise when she recognized Nelson Fabian. She asked Drake under her breath, "Did you add him to the guest list?"

Drake smirked. "I surely did."

The actor smiled at them with his beautiful date and applauded.

They waved to him, and Julian shoved her elbow in Drake's ribs the minute no one would notice, but she laughed. "Nice touch."

"Hey. He's a fan. I thought I should be nice to him."

Their first dance together allowed them one more moment to chat before they would be overrun by well-wishers and family. Julian placed her cheek against his and whispered to him, "One day, I was just driving along the road without knowing it was the day my entire life would change for the better."

She could feel his smile against her ear. "If I had known it would take a car accident to meet you, I would have driven off the road a long time ago."

ABOUT THE AUTHOR

Kassie Ward resides in South Carolina surrounded by three cats and two dogs. A lifelong reader, Kassie discovered she wanted to tell her own stories after attempting to write fan fiction episodes for The A-Team and The Monkees. She started writing during third grade and never stopped.

When not writing fiction, Kassie spends her time daydreaming about Henry Cavill and helping further the cause to convince Chris Hemsworth to wear a kilt.

Keep up with Kassie Ward online -

Facebook: facebook.com/authorkassieward

Blog: kassieward.blogspot.com

ABOUT THE PUBLISHER

Daisy Rose Publishing is the dream of two cousins who love romance and mystery and want to share that love with others. From our earliest experiences as kids reading books and writing our own stories, we learned what makes a novel memorable.